Bitter Herbs

Bitter Herbs

NATASHA COOPER

Crown Publishers, Inc.

New York

Originally published by Crown Publishers, Inc. 201 East 50th Street, New York, New York 10022.
Member of the Crown Publishing Group.

Random House, Inc. New York, Toronto, London, Sydney, Auckland

Published in Great Britain by Simon & Schuster, Ltd. in 1993

Crown is a trademark of Crown Publishers, Inc.

Manufactured in the United States of America

Library of Congress Cataloging-in-Publication Data

Cooper, Natasha.

Bitter Herbs / Natasha Cooper.

1. King, Willow (Fictitious character—Fiction.) 2. Government investigators—England—Fiction.
3. Women detectives—England—Fiction. 4. Women novelists. English—Fiction. I. Title.
PR6073.R47B57 1993
823'.914—dc20
93–32546 CIP

ISBN 0-517-59023-9

10 9 8 7 6 5 4 3 2 1

First American Edition

For

Dione Johnson,

who was there when it mattered.

Acknowledgements

I should like to thank the following, who have all provided me with facts, suggestions and details for this novel: Ib Bellew, Mary Carter, David Elliott, Lucy Ferguson, Sheila Green, Gerald Johnson, Jennifer Kavanagh, George Lewinski, Jane Meara, Dr Charles Pumphrey, Alison Pitts-Bland (Senior Press Officer, Special Operations, New Scotland Yard), Camden Pratt, Bob Rhodes of Ashton Funeral Services, James Turner, and Maureen Waller.

'Better a dinner of herbs where love is,
than a stalled ox and hatred therewith.'
Proverbs 17

1

'SHE'D BEEN NAGING ME AND so I hit her and she wouldnt' stop moneing and so I hit her till she dide I did'nt want to kil her but I no I did.'

Willow King looked up from the pathetically unformed scrawl and faced the new Home Secretary.

'I understand exactly why you want to make education in prisons compulsory. I didn't need to see this,' said Willow, handing the botched plea for parole back across the desk. 'I sympathise with what you're trying to do, and I hope you succeed, but it'll have to be done without me.'

'Why? Are you one of those people who think that forcing literacy on prison inmates infringes their civil right to ignorance?'

'I could make out a case for it,' said Willow slowly. 'After all, I'm a civil servant: I could make out a case for anything. But my reluctance is more selfish. I want my own freedom. Before I took the sabbatical last summer, I had done eighteen years' hard labour in the civil service – longer than your illiterate murderers spend in prison – and I want out. I really do.'

'I know,' said Elsie Trouville, accepting the smudged paper. 'You wouldn't have worn those clothes if you hadn't already left in spirit.'

Willow looked down at her Yves Saint Laurent suit and Ferragamo shoes and then back at the Home Secretary, unable to conceal the first, reluctant, smile of the morning.

'You're right, of course,' she admitted. 'I hadn't thought it through, but I see that I have presented myself as the successful novelist rather than the spinster civil servant.'

She glanced around the big, light room in the fortress-like building by St James's Park, and smiled more easily.

'It feels most uncomfortable to tell you the truth.'

'What? Wearing expensive clothes in the Home Office?'

Willow, who had spent so long concealing her emotions from everyone around her that she often found it hard not to hide them from herself as well, screwed her courage to the sticking place and said:

'No: trying to combine my two lives. It was hard enough even before your intervention.'

Mrs Trouville stared down at her very short, very clean fingernails and seemed to make a decision.

'I need you,' she said as she looked up again. 'I need your stringent intelligence, your determination, your refusal to take any nonsense from anyone, your . . . '

'You're flattering me,' said Willow severely.

'Yes,' answered the Home Secretary with all the amused frankness that had so appealed to Willow when they had first met at the Department of Old Age Pensions. 'It usually works, even with people as acute as you.'

Willow had to laugh.

'I hate being managed into things,' she said and noticed that there was a gleam in the Home Secretary's eyes that made her look almost malicious.

'All right, then I'll put it more honestly. I want you on this committee and I know that you could fit it into your life if you tried. Writing those novels of yours can't possibly take up all your time. I've been reading them, you know.'

'Home Secretary,' said Willow, taking advantage of what was beginning to feel like her last moment of freedom, 'you are a monster.'

'No doubt. But even monsters need feeding. Won't you

postpone your resignation for a year or so and take on this last – very important – job?'

As Willow still hesitated the Home Secretary added one more goad:

'Think what good copy the committee could give you. It might even add some realism to your books.'

'That would probably be the kiss of death,' said Willow, still fighting her doomed battle. 'They're bestsellers, you know, as they are.'

Mrs Trouville stood up and held out both her hands.

'Come on, admit defeat and let me get on with the day's work.'

Willow stayed in her chair, scowling. The Home Secretary said nothing, merely picking up a discussion paper from her desk and starting to read the first page.

'Oh, all right,' Willow said eventually.

'Excellent.' The Home Secretary took a grey folder out of the middle drawer of her desk. 'These are the people who have been invited to serve on the committee. Oh, and there's a list of the civil servants you'll have in the secretariat as well. I'll see you first thing on Monday. Good morning.'

Willow grimaced, silently apostrophised herself as a fool, accepted the file, and shook hands with her brisk conqueror.

'Cheer up,' said Mrs Trouville, 'you've hardly ever had to surrender to anyone in your entire career.'

'I'm sure it's bad for me,' answered Willow from half-way across the threshhold. 'But it's an interesting sensation.'

She took the lift down to the ground floor and walked out of the building to stand, shivering, on the steps as she looked down the street for a taxi. The damp coldness of the air seemed to eat into her, making her bones ache in a way that only happened in London. She had just returned from a small mill house she had recently bought in Berkshire, where the weather had been just as cold but somehow less insidiously revolting.

The mill house was far less comfortable than her London flat, but already she missed it. The views across the mill pool to the river and the frost-hardened fields beyond were bleakly satisfying in a way that even the most beautiful of London houses could never be. Day after day in the country the winter sun had hung like a huge orange in the clean white sky and for much of the time the scrubby grass had been white, too, so that the only dark things in the landscape were the spiky black hedges and the looming trees at the edge of the road. Nothing had moved except for a few questing birds. Even the river seemed to have slowed down to an imperceptible trickle. Looking at it all, Willow had felt blissfully alone and nearly at peace again.

Trying to mock herself out of her sudden longing to be back in Berkshire, alone and untroubled, she silently noted that there was nothing moving in Queen Anne's Gate either, not even a taxi.

Hunching her shoulders against the wind, she set off across St James's Park to walk to her publishers' offices on the far side of Trafalgar Square. She tried not to think too much about the mill house and failed.

Its interior echoed the satisfying bleakness of the winter landscape. The walls were whitewashed, the furniture was old and countrified, mostly made of dark oak, and the stone floor was covered with simple matting. Only the orange flames in the cavernous fireplace and the red rep curtains provided any colour.

Willow had spent her days there enjoying the silence and the solitude, thinking and occasionally pulling up the extraordinarily resilient nettles in what would one day be the garden. The stings she had suffered from what ought to have been only dead stalks provided a nasty parallel with the mental stings that her London life seemed to be delivering every day.

The first specific blow had come just before Christmas when her agent, Evangeline Greville, had telephoned one morning to announce that Willow's publishers did not like the plans for her new book. Having had a big success eight years earlier with a wholly frivolous novel written in time taken away from her civil service job, Willow had followed it with equally saleable sequels every year since then and never again contemplated failure.

The books had brought her not only a lavishly appointed flat in Belgravia but also the power to have two quite separate lives, which she had enjoyed. For half the week she had inhabited her original small, damp flat in Clapham, walking daily to her job as a part-time Assistant Secretary in the Department of Old Age Pensions. Every Thursday evening, she had moved to Chesham Place, a wardrobe full of designer clothes, a supremely efficient housekeeper, a growing band of friends, and a life of pleasant self-indulgence.

Becoming accustomed to Belgravia luxury, Willow had found herself increasingly at odds with the other half of her life and had taken a six-month sabbatical to see whether she could do without it altogether. Discovering that she could, she had written a formal letter of resignation to the civil service and instructed builders to make the damp and depressing Clapham flat saleable. Two days later Eve had telephoned and Willow had had difficulty in not seeing her publishers' rejection as a judgement.

Willow was still struggling with the sense of outrage – and ferociously suppressed alarm – that her agent's news had roused in her.

Almost worse than that had been the continually draining effect of Tom Worth's moroseness. Willow had never expected to be given happiness by another person and it was hard not to feel cheated by the fact that Tom had virtually tricked her into being happy with him, only to turn round and start making her miserable.

Willow crossed the iron bridge over the lake in the middle of St James's Park without even glancing towards the pretty view of Whitehall's roofs to her right or the pale solidity of Buckingham Palace to her left. A fat pigeon crash landed in an icy puddle just by her feet, startling her into a sharp curse. She looked up to see a pin-striped professional man staring at her in disdain and felt her cup running over with irritation.

Glaring at him, she struck off up a diagonal path to the

right, planning to emerge from the park just across the Mall from Admiralty Arch.

'Oh, Tom,' she said aloud, having established that there was no one else within earshot.

They had met over a murder, when he was the investigating officer and she a suspect, and had become lovers a little later. Part of his tremendous charm for her had always been his detachment, his refusal to invade her private boundaries, and his lack of fear of either her brains or her success. Like her, he had enjoyed the luxurious Belgravia flat and the ministrations of the magnificent Mrs Rusham, but he had been amused by them, too, and had never let the trappings of her life as a bestselling author affect his own habits. Neither of them had been at all dependent on the other, and Willow had liked that.

But for the past three or four months he had been changing. Where he had once been relaxed he now seemed tense. His amusement at the way she had earned most of her living and all her luxuries had given way to something that seemed horribly like contempt, and the relationship that had once been easy and equal and free was beginning to become a burden.

Tom had recently started a new job within the Metropolitan Police and was clearly finding it stressful, but Willow could not believe that it was enough to explain his silent anger. She had tried to ask him about it on several occasions, but her attempts to help seemed only to have exacerbated whatever was wrong with him.

If he disliked her company so much, she had often said to herself before fleeing to the mill on Boxing Day, then why did he keep coming to her flat?

One horrible possibility was that he felt himself in some way bound to her and came out of a sense of obligation. As Willow thought about that she came to a standstill, staring at the corpse of a cat that was lying under a dense evergreen shrub in the flowerbed at the edge of the path.

The cold eating into her flesh brought her back to the present and reminded her of the necessity of getting to the offices of Weston & Brown in time for her meeting with the managing director. She hurried on, trying not to choke on exhaust fumes as she walked through the arch and out into the noisier bustle of Trafalgar Square.

The traffic lights changed and she crossed into the square itself with a chattering horde of foreign schoolchildren. They surged ahead while Willow picked her way through the litter and pigeon droppings, past Landseer's lions and Nelson's phallic column, between the fountains that had been refilled after their New Year's Eve emptying, past the soaring Christmas tree to the further edge of the square in front of the National Gallery, and up the steps.

Concentrating on the subject of the forthcoming meeting so that she could ignore the even more difficult ones, Willow crossed the road in front of St Martin's-in-the-Fields and, resisting the temptation to buy a bag of hot chestnuts from an old man tending a brazier, made her way into the narrow street that housed her publishers' offices.

'I have a meeting with Ann Slinter,' she said to the young receptionist who greeted her there. 'My name's Willow King.'

'Would you just like to take a seat, please? She's on the telephone at the moment,' said the young woman, showing no sign of ever having heard of Willow.

Obediently, she walked into the small waiting room, where she found her agent sitting with a cigarette in one hand and a bound proof in the other.

'Hello, Eve.'

Eve Greville looked up, blowing out a cloud of smoke, and got to her feet. She was a short, noticeably thin woman with sharply cut grey hair and pale grey eyes. As always her dark clothes were both unobtrusive and impeccable.

'Willow,' she said, smiling. 'You know, I still can't get used to that. Addressing you as Cressida Woodruffe for ten years makes it almost impossible to switch. How was the country? Inspiring, I hope.'

'Well it was certainly quiet. I'm not so sure about the inspiration. Perhaps it was too cold. I've got a few ideas, but

I don't know whether . . . Oh, I like that!' She half-turned and pointed to a large, glossy poster for her latest book. 'I didn't know they were going to have a new poster. Good quotes!'

'Yes, they're taking a reasonable amount of trouble to keep the book in the shops for more than the usual month or so. But . . . '

'Ann's free now, if you'd just like to go up,' called the receptionist from her desk at the door to the waiting room. 'D'you know the way?'

'Yes, thank you,' said Eve, stubbing out her cigarette. She left the room first, looking extraordinarily small in her black suit. Only her sharp eyes and her strong, smoke-filled voice gave any indication of the power she wielded with what her client considered to be almost indecent glee. 'Come on, Willow.'

Ann Slinter greeted them at the door of her chaotic second-floor office. In contrast to the room, which was lined with crammed bookshelves against which leaned danger-ous looking towers of dusty manuscripts and proofs, jacket artwork, paste-ups, ozalids and photographs, she looked both attractive and in control.

Her plain dark-green skirt was topped with a loose navy sweater decorated with green suede patches, green-and-blue stitching and a single streak of gold. Her blonde hair was cut to hang an inch or two above her shoulders and her subtle make-up emphasised her large blue eyes. She was two years older than Willow and, having bought her first novel, had always been her editor. It was partly the success of Willow's books that had given Ann the chance to rise so fast within the firm. Nine weeks earlier she had been promoted from editorial to managing director.

She had a tray of coffee waiting for them in front of a pink-and-grey sofa that was loaded with papers.

'Push that lot on to the floor,' she said, pulling forward a grey-seated chair for herself. 'Now, help yourselves to coffee. Isn't it a foul time of year? Like a hangover, an emotional and spiritual hangover. Where shall we start?'

'I rather like it,' said Willow, wanting to gain control of the meeting. 'Quite apart from the lovely boost of one's Public Lending Right statement flopping on to the doormat just after Christmas, it's a chance to begin again. New Year's resolutions and all that. On which subject, Ann, perhaps you could explain why you think I ought to change tack. My books seem to sell considerably better than most of the other authors I talked to at your Christmas party.'

Ann laughed, tossing back her smooth hair to reveal her youthfully unlined neck.

'That is perfectly true, but there has been a worrying fall-off in the sales of the paperbacks, subscriptions for the new book were much lower than they should have been and the Christmas sales did not pick up as much as the reps had expected.'

'Isn't that simply the recession?' suggested Willow, unnecessarily irritated by the booktrade jargon. No book had actually been offered 'on subscription' since the nineteenth century and it would have made more sense for Ann to refer to 'pre-publication orders'.

'No, I don't think so,' she said. 'The market seems to have become saturated with what I might call romance-and-revenge novels like yours. They are good of their kind, but, as I said to Eve, the genre itself is becoming much less popular than it was when you started. There's less interest in business success for romantic heroines these days, and the whole feeling of the big books coming out now is different. I think it's important that you should change before the booksellers have decided that it's your name that is a turn-off rather than the genre.'

'And what do you think, Eve?'

'That it may be more a question of poor marketing than a diminution of interest in the books themselves. After all your Public Lending Right is holding up well,' said the agent, automatically defending her author as she lit herself another cigarette.

Willow knew that Ann Slinter loathed smoking and that it was a tribute to Eve's power that she was allowed to indulge her addiction anywhere in the building, let alone in Ann's own office.

'But I agree with Ann that a new direction would not come amiss,' said Eve through a cloud of smoke. 'You don't want to get stuck in a rut. You said you'd had some ideas.'

'Yes,' said Willow, opening the slim, black-leather brief-case at her feet. The thought of Tom's unspoken contempt, the Home Secretary's specific mockery of her books, Ann's criticism and now Eve's implied disapproval was making her feel like a fox running only just ahead of a pack of hounds. Wishing that she could go to earth, Willow pulled out two sets of papers just as the telephone began to ring.

'Damn them,' said Ann, getting out of her chair. 'I told them not to put any calls through. Excuse me a moment.'

She strode over to her desk, seized the telephone and administered a sharp reprimand. Half-way through it, she stopped, gasped and said:

'You're joking! Really? What amazing news!' She talked for a little longer before putting down the telephone and turning to her two visitors to explain. They were both try-ing to pretend that they were not at all interested in the one-sided conversation they had overheard. 'Gloria Grainger's dead.'

'Good heavens!' said Eve, her mouth twisting into something that could have been a grimace but looked to Willow surprisingly like a smile. 'Apoplexy, I take it. Or did someone finally whack her on the head in desperation? I was often tempted to do that in the days when I represented her.'

'I'm afraid not,' said Ann, laughing guiltily. 'No, they say she had a heart attack.'

'How dull!' said Eve as Ann turned to Willow, who was staring at the pair of them with obvious disapproval on her thin face. In normal circumstances she would have felt little sympathy for an outmoded novelist she had never met, but, after the criticism she herself had endured, she was ready to feel solidarity with anyone who wrote almost anything at all.

'I'm sorry, Willow. I shouldn't have laughed. Eve always

has that effect on me. Of course it's sad that Gloria's dead. We'll have to do something to mark the occasion. Even though she was never quite a household name, her books really kept the entire firm afloat from the war to the early sixties.'

'But you still publish them, don't you?' said Willow repressively. 'I'm sure I saw one in the autumn list you sent me last year.'

'Unfortunately yes, we do. We couldn't really get out of it, although . . . Look: she's a real case of what I've been trying to explain to you. Her books outsold the rest of the list for nearly twenty years, but the recent ones have done very poorly. Readers of romantic fiction are more sophisticated these days. Her hero – and there really was only one – is horribly *passé* in the nineties. Popular novelists have to move with the times.'

'Indeed,' said Willow, half-amused and half-appalled to find herself feeling so sorry for Gloria Grainger, whose books she had always despised even though she had never read any of them.

'Ouf, it will be a relief to . . . to be able to plan the next autumn list without having to cost in Gloria's latest effusion,' said Ann, pouring herself a second cup of coffee.

Willow wondered what Ann had really meant to say. There was a smile on her lips that seemed to express supreme satisfaction. She looked up and, catching her author watching her, altered her expression to one of apparently synthetic sadness.

'There are a lot of people who'll find this news a relief,' said Eve, both her honesty and her directness providing a welcome distraction from Ann's theatricals.

'You're telling me!' said Ann, once more losing her grip on the proper expression of regret at an author's death.

'I've had a thought,' said Eve. Her eyes were half shut and seemed to be squinting out beyond the book-lined walls.

'Yes?'

'You said you'd have to make a gesture towards Gloria's memory and I quite see that you should.' Eve's eyes resumed their normal shape and focused on Ann's face. 'Why not commission Willow to write a short memorial to her – a mixture of biography and critical analysis of Gloria's success and its sequel – which you could rush out in a few months' time as your gesture?'

'Well I suppose we could,' said Ann, frowning. 'Would you be interested in doing something like that, Willow?'

'Perhaps.' At the thought that she might be able to distract herself from all the difficulties of her own life by immersing herself in someone else's, Willow began to smile. 'I've never thought about biography before, but it could be interesting.'

'It wouldn't exactly be a biography,' said Eve, stubbing out her cigarette, 'more a memoir, or an appreciation. A sort of hugely extended obituary, really. About, what? Ninety-six pages, Ann?'

'Probably. Sixty-four is just possible, if pretty slim, and it's certainly never worth printing anything shorter than that. I do see what you mean, Eve,' said Ann, 'but I rather hate those rush jobs: instant books about an event that seemed dramatic at the time but six weeks later interests no one but the participants and their relatives.'

'This is hardly like a siege or a political disaster,' said Eve drily. 'It would give Willow a breathing space in which to let her mind roam around finding her own new direction, and it would also help you to generate a little interest in the Grainger backlist and shift some of the stock out of the warehouse before everyone completely forgets who she was.'

'And no doubt it will serve as a dire warning of what will happen if I don't change,' said Willow lightly enough to wring smiles of acknowledgment from both Eve and Ann. 'Perhaps I should take it on. Yesterday's popular novelist assessing the merits of the day-before-yesterday's.'

'You're not yesterday's yet,' said Ann energetically. 'I simply want to ensure that you don't become it. Eve, it's definitely a possibility, but I'd have to put it to the next editorial meeting.'

'Nonsense. You're the managing director now. Tell the

meeting what you've decided.'

'As you very well know, things are not that simple. We have systems. But it is an idea, although it's unlikely to have a huge market and we couldn't pay a big advance.'

Willow realised that Ann was automatically protecting her own position, just as Eve had been a little earlier when she had put the blame for Willow's falling sales on to the publishers' marketing department.

'We can discuss money later,' said Eve firmly. 'Why don't we agree simply that Willow does a certain amount of research for a fixed fee in order to produce a synopsis. When we know how the memoir is likely to turn out, and how long it will be, we'll have a better idea of its probable sale and be able to fix the advance more sensibly.'

'All right. I can have a word with Bill then and we can settle it one way or the other.'

'Good,' said Eve, tucking her photostat of Willow's ideas into her handbag and thrusting the second copy back at her client. Willow raised her eyebrows, but Eve glared at her and so she replaced it in her briefcase.

'Ann, we'd better leave you to deal with the Gloria repercussions. There are sure to be plenty. I'll give you a ring later on to discuss the fee. Come along, Willow.'

As soon as they were outside the building, Willow said:

'Why on earth did you do that? We'd hardly got anywhere with the real purpose of the meeting.'

'No, I know, but I looked at these while she was telephoning and they're not right. They're simply tinkering with the old formula. You've got to do something radically different before we talk to Ann again. This memoir of Gloria Grainger will give you time.'

'Perhaps,' said Willow, surprised by how troubled she felt at Eve's businesslike rejection of her plans. Her sympathy for the dead – and clearly much disliked – Gloria Grainger grew.

'Let's have some lunch and talk about it.' Eve was looking at her client with beady intensity. 'It's far too cold to hang about here.' She stamped her tiny booted feet on the icy pavement and pulled on her fur-lined gloves.

'All right. It's still early so we'd get into any of those places in Covent Garden. There's quite a nice winebar,' said Willow.

When they were sitting on either side of a table with a bottle of good burgundy between them, Willow made herself smile despite her feelings of angry rebellion.

'All right, Eve, tell me: what kind of book is it that you think I should write? The fat sort to do with fearfully glamorous people earning fortunes and having extraordinary sex all over the world or the thinner kind full of vicars and entrancing children and wonderful dogs and interesting emotions in pretty English villages?'

'Steak for me, rare, please and a green salad with no dressing.'

Willow, who had not noticed the silent approach of a waitress, looked slightly self-conscious at the memory of her mockery of some of the current bestsellers. Without thinking she ordered herself a plate of cheese and some salad and then changed her order, as she considered the temperature outside, to Toulouse sausages and potato gratin.

'No.' said Eve, frowning at her author as the waitress left, 'I don't think either would suit your peculiar talents. I was thinking on the lines of something a bit more challenging. It seems absurd with your brains and experience that you should be writing stuff that could just as well be produced by a frustrated housewife in Purley.'

'Aha,' said Willow, who was fast regaining her usual critical confidence in spite of having had to make what felt like a series of abject surrenders that morning, 'then do you mean jewelled prose describing the gross, the violent or the obscene? Or perhaps minute dissections of a troubled modern marriage descending into the bitter realms of unreason written in stark, minimalist language? I thought you always told me not to wallow in pretension.'

'Not those either.' Eve's stern expression was beginning to break up into laughter at last. 'I know precisely what you mean, just as you know perfectly well what I mean.'

'I suppose I do, Eve, but the whole delight of the books so

far is that they've been entirely fantastical . . . I haven't had to put any effort into them.'

'Yes, but you've been putting effort into the civil service – and all the lies you've had to tell to keep that life secret from us and your novels from them. That's all ended now. You'll have far more energy and imagination for the books and you should make good use of them and move up at least one step – possibly two.'

'It's not entirely ended,' said Willow, feeling almost as guilty as Ann Slinter had looked when she realised how much pleasure she was displaying in her author's death. 'I've just agreed to stay on for another year or so as secretary to a committee looking into the possibilities of increasing education in prisons.'

'Is that the influence of your wretched policeman?' Eve lit yet another cigarette just before the waitress brought their food.

Willow fanned away the puff of smoke and glared at her agent until she stubbed out the cigarette and picked up her knife and fork.

'No,' said Willow when the waitress had gone. 'In fact he knows nothing about it yet and will probably disapprove.' She was surprised to find that a part of herself found the idea of Tom's disapproval quite welcome.

2

'YOU'VE WHAT?' TOM SOUNDED THOROUGHLY disapproving, but Willow found that she did not enjoy it as much
as she had expected.

He was looking extraordinarily tired, she thought as she
tried to be charitable, and even more full of suppressed fury
than he had been before she went away. She was not certain
whether his rage was caused by her week's absence or his
work or by whatever it was that had been making him so
morose before Christmas. Irritated with herself for even
thinking that he could be possessive enough to object to her
absence, she tried to amuse him with a description of just
how Elsie Trouville had managed to persuade her to stay in
the civil service.

Tom smiled a little as he listened and looked slightly
better.

'Is there any whisky?' he asked when Willow had finished
her self-mocking story.

'Plenty. Help yourself.'

He heaved himself out of the deep, down-filled chair and
went to pour out a stiff drink from the tray on the pretty
satinwood table to the right of the fireplace.

'What for you?' he asked over his shoulder, looking at

Willow as she lay along one of the two matching sofas. Her short red hair was tousled against the copper silk cushion she had put behind her head. The light from the pale salmon-pink lamps gleamed over the clashing colours.

'I shared a bottle with Eve at lunchtime to console myself for my surrender to Mrs Trouville,' she said, straightening the skirt of her suit. I think I'll just have fizzy water if there is any there.'

'You know perfectly well that the efficient Mrs Rusham would never leave your drinks tray short of anything.' Tom laughed, but he sounded neither happy nor amused. 'Oh, for a life that ran on wheels like yours. What other news have you got for me?'

Willow tried to decide whether he was doing his best to show concern he did not actually feel about her life or whether he was seeking distraction from his own much harder job. Deciding that what he wanted was distraction, she described her meeting with Eve and the struggles they were both having as they tried to invent a wholly new kind of commercial book. Willow saw that Tom's attention was slipping half-way through her description and so she changed tack.

'Oh, and I heard that Gloria Grainger has just died.'

'Who the hell's she?'

'Tom, what on earth is the matter?' Willow asked before she could stop herself. She knew she sounded like an irritable school matron and detested it.

'Nothing,' he said, staring down at his drink as Willow sighed.

'All right,' she said, deliberately making her voice pleasanter. 'To take your question at face value: she was a romantic novelist of an old-fashioned type. She was published by Weston & Brown. Everyone there seems to have disliked her. I don't know much about her yet, but I shall be finding out more because I've half promised to write a memoir of her for them.'

'I can't see that doing much for your falling sales.'

Willow stared at him, astonished by the contempt in his

17

irritable comment. She searched his face for clues to his unreasonable antagonism.

Physically he seemed much the same as usual as he sat in her yellow chair, his dark hair a bit unruly, the broken nose and broad shoulders making him look a rugby player. He had changed out of his suit into a pair of baggy dark-green corduroy trousers and an old Guernsey he kept at her flat, but he had not relaxed at all. His restless dissatisfaction ruined the peace of her elegant drawing room and she resented it, longing to be back at the mill. There were no comfortable, silk-covered cushions there, or lovely furniture or beautiful paintings, but it was miraculously lonely.

'Tom, I don't know what it is that is making you so aggressive, but I wish you'd tell me about it,' Willow said seriously and with unusual directness. 'We can't start snapping at each other every time either of us says anything. That would be absurd.'

He glared at her and then drank some whisky. After a while he shrugged.

'There's nothing the matter with me except that I'm having a tough time at work. I didn't mean to snap.'

Willow smiled with difficulty.

'I always told myself that you and I were too intelligent to play games with each other. You're obviously troubled about something more than work. I can feel it, for heaven's sake. Why pretend?'

He shook his head and blew, as though he had surfaced after a long swim underwater.

'It's probably just that I've a hellish and upsetting murder case – nothing to do with you and me,' he said coldly, 'but its nature makes one think about all sort of things. I really can't discuss it. You know better than to expect me to.'

Willow stood up and went into the bathroom to stare at her reflection in the large mirror over the basin. Apart from the shorter hairstyle, she was exactly the same as she had been when he had first wanted her. She had not changed and there was no reason she could find for him to have done so. It seemed unfair of him to have invaded her life and then started to behave as though she were causing him trouble.

'Perhaps it is just the case,' she said aloud. But she knew it could not have been. There had been other difficult cases before and they had not made him nearly so bad tempered. He had often discussed them with her, too. This time there was something different the matter with him, something more.

In an effort to distract herself, she looked admiringly around at her cherished possessions. Of all the rooms in the large and elegant flat, the bathroom best expressed the comfort of her Belgravia life. Quite as big as an ordinary bedroom, it had been decorated as though the bath were incidental, with paintings and bookshelves, an open fireplace and bowls of flowers. There was yet another superbly comfortable, down-filled armchair beside the bath and a table carrying not only the latest novels she was still waiting to read but also a pyramid of black grapes, tangerines and brazil nuts arranged on an antique pewter plate.

The room did not have its usual soothing effect. She walked round it four times, wishing that she had never invited Tom to dinner that night and for a moment that she had never even met him. There seemed to be no way of dealing with him that would not escalate their shared dissatisfaction. After all she could hardly ask him about his troubles for a third time.

She flushed the lavatory and went back to the basin to repair her makeup and wash her hands again, and at last returned to the drawing room to ask Tom whether he would like to eat whatever Mrs Rusham had left for them in the Aga. He stood up at once.

'Thanks. As I was saying, it's an upsetting case – one of those messy murders of a young woman. Clearly a lot of hate and anger behind it. It's making me irritable.'

'I had noticed,' said Willow nearly as coldly as he had spoken earlier. It seemed a pretty poor apology to her. 'It's also corrupting your judgement of other things.'

'Perhaps.' He followed her into the dining room and sat at

the perfectly set table. When he looked up at her he managed to smile slightly. 'Tell me stories, Will. Please.'

'So that you don't have to think about the dead woman – or about things I've said to you?'

'The murder.'

As he produced those abrupt syllables, Tom held out a hand and smiled. Willow tried to ignore the other, unpleasant, emotions she had seen in his face and to remember her affection for him. Part of her mind told her that Tom had just given her the perfect excuse to lose her temper with him and smash the remains of their pleasure in each other. Unfortunately she still liked him far too much to do that.

Playing for time, she fetched the *boeuf bourginon* and baked potatoes from the kitchen and then spun stories out of her uneventful solitary days at the mill as urgently as though she were Scheherazade talking for her life. So long as she talked she would not have to think about his feelings or her own.

Later he took the dishes out to the kitchen for Mrs Rusham to wash up in the morning and made a pot of coffee, and later still they went to bed. Willow continued to do everything she could to prevent herself thinking and was mostly successful.

The next morning she woke to discover that Tom had already left. She lay surrounded by all the luxury her books had brought her, asking herself why she had ever allowed someone else's state of mind and criticism to matter so much to her. One of the most exasperating aspects of Tom's moods was that it appeared that there was nothing whatever she could do to change them.

Willow turned over on to her side, telling herself that since she could not change his state of mind, the only thing to do was to ignore it and concentrate hard on something else. The obvious thing was the memoir of Gloria Grainger. Finding out what had made her tick might become enormously interesting. Distracted and therefore feeling better, Willow got out of bed and went to run herself a bath.

Having put a match to the remains of the previous day's fire, she turned on the taps and took from the mahogany cupboard a clean, yellow towelling dressing gown, which she draped over the hot pipes. Lying back in the hot, scented water, eating a tangerine, she started to think of questions she would need to ask the dead woman's friends and family. The questions would have to be carefully framed to establish what kind of woman she had been and why she had written the novels Ann Slinter disliked so much.

When the water had cooled uncomfortably, Willow took the plug out of the bath and sat in front of the fire, wrapped in her warm towel, until the scent of frying bacon called her to breakfast. She went to dress and start the day properly.

Mrs Rusham had grilled mushrooms to go with the bacon. Willow ate them as she read the letters piled beside her plate. She was half glad to be back in the warmth and luxury of Belgravia and yet something in her yearned for the breakfasts of strong tea and hunks of bread she had made herself at the mill and eaten huddled over the fragrant wood fire. The beds at the mill were hard, but she had slept better there than ever she did in London.

There was nothing particularly interesting in her post except for a derisive review of her latest book in a quarterly magazine published mainly for writers, publishers and booksellers. The critic had taken exception to Willow's characters, their assumptions, their habits, tastes and dialogue. Only at the end of the review did she add any comment on the novel itself, which she had found:

> sentimental and full of the worst kind of fantasy. One wonders at the motives of an author who can base an entire novel around the notion that extravagant spending and arousing admiration are in themselves desirable points of aspiration. Only the satisfaction taken by the astonishingly selfish heroine in her revenge on the woman who had once ruined her is more unpleasant. It is regrettable that this kind of trivia is so remunerative for its authors.

'Hell!' said Willow aloud, looking at the reviewer's by-line. 'Posy Hacket. Never heard of her.'

Coming right on top of the previous day's vicissitudes, the journalist's contempt seemed too much to bear. Depressed, Willow contemplated her future as a gradually less and less popular commercial novelist, becoming despised by the very journalists who had once sought interviews she had refused to grant in the days when the real identity of 'Cressida Woodruffe' had been a secret shared by very few people.

'I bloody well won't,' she said loudly as she thought of ways to throw the contempt back in the faces of her detractors.

The memory of the Home Secretary's stated admiration of her brains and her refusal to take any nonsense – and even the prospect of going back to work in the civil service – cheered Willow up a little, which seemed ironic. But at least it made her laugh.

'Did you call?' asked Mrs Rusham from the door leading to the kitchen. Willow shook her head.

'I was just talking to myself, Mrs Rusham, a foolish habit.'

'Indeed.' The housekeeper's severe mouth relaxed just enough to show that she was making what passed with her for a joke. Before Willow could retaliate, the telephone rang. Mrs Rusham answered it, pressed the silence button and then turned to say:

'It's Evangeline Greville. Shall I tell her you're here?'

'Yes, please. Thank you.' Willow took the receiver. 'Eve? It's Saturday. Surely you're not working a six-day week now.'

'Good morning to you too, Willow. How are you?' Eve sounded sharply sarcastic.

'I'm fine,' she said, wondering why everyone had suddenly started to attack her. 'I hope you are.'

'That's better. Actually, I'm getting extremely bored with this weather and the fact that most people I want to talk to are taking extended holidays. I agreed with Ann late yesterday afternoon that she'll pay you a non-returnable thousand pounds to produce a synopsis of a memoir of Gloria Grainger. If they don't like it or don't think it'll suit their purposes, you keep the money and forget about writing the full text.'

'You're a brilliant agent. I'm not sure I'd have had the bottle to ask for that.'

'You know it is nice sometimes to have authors who don't have overblown ideas about their own importance.'

Willow was amused to think that the first compliment she had received from Eve for weeks should have been for her meekness. Perhaps Tom would soon be congratulating her on her domestic skills. That would be just as incongruous. Her self-mockery dissolved a little of her resentment at his behaviour and she managed to concentrate on what Eve was saying to her.

'I thought you'd better know straight away. A thousand pounds is not much considering that some journalists get that per thousand words, but the work need take you only a day or two. I have asked Ann to send you a complete set of Gloria's paperbacks and you'll have to browse through them when they arrive on Monday. But after that you can get going on plans for your own book.'

'That sounds fine,' said Willow. 'You're right, I'd better start. I need something to get my teeth into. You obviously know a bit about Grainger; can I begin with you? Is that fair at a weekend?'

'Fine by me. We'll have to do it by telephone though. I can't leave the house and it's too wet to let you come here. I've had a flood and there's supposed to be a plumber. You know what they're like. He was due half an hour ago.'

Willow thought of her Clapham flat and quailed at the prospect of persuading the voluble but dilatory builders to do the work she wanted in a sensible sequence, within their estimates and within a reasonable time. Their idiom and habits provided excellent copy, but she would rather have been able to do without them.

'Poor you,' she said with some sympathy. 'But you're lucky all the same. All my blokes in Clapham are on holiday until Monday. What I need to know really is why you ever agreed to represent Gloria, how long it lasted and why you stopped.'

There was the sound of a lighter clicking and a deep inhalation before Eve answered.

'She approached me soon after I'd set up on my own and, not knowing all the gruesome details of her reputation, I was rather flattered.' Eve stopped, as though she were having to work hard to remember herself being as naive and easily manipulated as that. Then she laughed. 'It lasted for an unspeakable eighteen months before I told her that I was simply not big enough to handle an author as important as she.'

'Goodness, Eve, how tactful!'

'I know. I'm far more brutal these days, as you know. It saves time – and trouble – in the end.'

'I see. What exactly was it that she did to cause you to sack her?' Willow hoped that her irrational sympathy for the dead writer was not making her sound aggressive.

The agent considered for a moment.

'It's impossible to list everything but you could sum it up by saying that she behaved as though I had no other authors, that my time was entirely at her disposal, that I was a suitable receptacle for her ill-humour,' said Eve briskly. 'I won't go on or I'll lose my temper, which would be a fearful waste of energy.'

'That's clear enough,' said Willow, pulling forward the notebook that was always kept beside the telephone. 'When we were at Ann's office, you talked about some people who might have whacked her over the head and killed her, and . . . '

'That was a figure of speech,' said Eve with enough sharpness to surprise Willow and set her imagination working madly.

'You also told me that there would be lots of other people relieved to hear of her death. Whom had you in mind?' Willow hoped that the polite formality of her question would serve as a rebuke to Eve for taking so seriously what she must have known Willow had intended only as a mild joke.

'Ann herself, I suppose, whoever is agenting Gloria these

days, whoever was in her power in any way at all . . . and Posy Hacket.'

'Well, I haven't much sympathy for her,' said Willow tartly as she wrote down the short list.

'Why on earth not?'

'Haven't you read the review she's just given me in The Readers' Quarterly?'

'No. I haven't got to the current issue yet. It's never top of my list of priorities and I've still got a daunting heap of manuscripts. What did Posy say?'

'She accused me of pandering to the lowest tastes of the mob for pecuniary gain.' A little of Willow's sense of humour returned in time to make her add: 'Justifiably no doubt.'

'How brave of her!' Eve's voice contained a note of real admiration, which prompted Willow to remind the agent whose corner she was supposed to be fighting.

'I am, Willow, believe me. But Posy wrote a highly critical piece about Gloria, which led the old bat to sue her. The case wasn't due to come to trial for ages, but if Posy has had the guts to go on writing offensive pieces about popular novelists you have to admire her.'

'Perhaps I do, but I'd rather not have been her target. Thanks, Eve,' said Willow, feeling her sympathy for the dead woman increasing still further. 'You've been helpful. Oh, yes, one more thing: do you know anything about Gloria's family?'

'Not a lot. I expect you'd get far more up-to-date information on that from her current agent – or her editor.'

'Fine. I'll ring Ann. Thanks. By the way?'

'Yes?'

'Are many authors as personally hated by their publishers and agents as she clearly was?'

There was a gasping laugh from the other end of the telephone and then Eve said carefully:

'At various stages in their careers many authors become a little trying. If that coincides with an editor or agent having a difficult time with other aspects of work – or life – it can lead beyond ordinary anger to actual hot hate. But I'd have said

25

that Gloria was the only one I've met who could make even the most reasonable people feel truly murderous.'

'I see.' The iciness of Willow's voice was not apparent to her.

'Profitability always dilutes dislike and Gloria was no longer profitable enough,' Eve went on as though an explanation might melt the ice. 'The real bestsellers can behave pretty much as they choose, although quite often it is the most professional and successful who behave best.'

'I see,' said Willow again, hoping that she could still be considered part of the last category. 'Well, I'd better ring Ann and see what I can find out from her. Good luck with the plumber.'

'I'll need it. Look, you may not get Ann today, although I know she sometimes goes into the office on Saturdays.'

'I'll be in touch, Eve. Thanks for your help.'

'Good bye.'

Willow stood, her eyes unfocused and her brain running over what little she had heard about Gloria Grainger. Eve had clearly disliked her and Willow respected her agent's judgement and intuitions. On the other hand she could not forget the sight of Eve and Ann Slinter almost congratulating each other on Grainger's death. However badly she had behaved in the past that seemed a most unfair reaction to the news that she was actually dead.

At last Willow went back to her cooling breakfast and tried to clear her brain by rereading Posy Hacket's review. As she got to the end of it, she suddenly thought of something else she should have asked Eve and went back to the telephone. It was answered at the first ring.

'Me again.' said Willow, 'I . . . '

'Damn.' Eve sounded even more irritable than she had earlier. 'I thought you might be the bloody plumber. What?'

'Have you got the *Readers' Quarterly* issue that had Posy Hacket's article about Gloria in it?'

'Yes, somewhere. D'you want me to fax the piece to you?'

'Would you? That would really help. Thanks, Eve. I'll leave you to the plumber. 'Bye.'

'May I bring you some hot coffee?' asked Mrs Rusham from the door into the kitchen.

'That would be nice. Thank you,' said Willow, holding out her half-full cup.

The housekeeper took it away with all the rest of the dirty crockery, to reappear with a clean cup of well-foamed cappuccino a few minutes later. Willow drank it quickly and retreated to her writing room, where her big word processor stood shrouded in reproach and anti-static plastic covers. She ignored it and waited for her fax machine to come alive. After ten minutes, during which she imagined Eve searching piles of periodicals for the right one, Willow pulled the telephone towards her and pressed the button that automatically dialled her publishers' office.

To her relief the telephone was answered and by Ann Slinter herself. Sounding preoccupied and annoyed to be interrupted, Ann told Willow very little beyond the fact that Grainger was no longer represented by an agent and that her novels were edited by a woman called Victoria Taffle.

'She's really a line editor, but we had to promote her to the status of commissioning editor as a sop to Gloria's vanity,' said Ann.

'Oh,' said Willow, wondering whether Ann's hostility was to Gloria or to the editor. 'Isn't that rather a big step up the promotion ladder?'

'In a large house it would be, but not really for us. It's not unprecedented by any means.' Ann laughed. 'It's just been less successful this time.'

'Could I be transferred to Ms Taffle's extension?' asked Willow, disapproving of Ann's too-obvious contempt.

'She won't be there today. She never comes in at week-ends because she lives so far out. What do you want to ask her?'

'What Gloria was like to work with and which of her relations I ought to talk to first.'

A dry laugh was all that answered her until Ann said:

'I can tell you that she had an ego the size of Mount Kilimanjaro and so was hell to work with. You probably

27

ought to talk to her niece, Marilyn Posselthwate. She, poor creature, worked as Gloria's housekeeper in Kew. But look, don't get too bogged down in all this. Your own book is far more important.'

'I'm glad you think so,' said Willow truthfully. 'But I think the memoir could be interesting.'

'Yes, so do I,' said Ann quickly, 'and it'll make Gerald Plimpton very happy, which is an added bonus.'

'Who he?'

'Have you never met him at any of our parties? He was chairman here when I first came.'

'When Gloria was so successful?'

'Precisely. He's always been upset by my loathing of her books. He's away just at the moment, but I know he'll be pleased when he hears what we're doing. It was a good idea of Eve's and I think you're the ideal person to write the memoir. I look forward to reading the synopsis.'

'Before you go, have you got the telephone number in Kew?'

'Somewhere. Hang on while I twizzle my Rolodex. Yes, here it is.' Ann dictated the number and then said good bye again before putting down her receiver too quickly to allow Willow to ask her anything else.

Willow grimaced at her telephone and then rang Kew to make an appointment to visit Marilyn Posselthwate early that afternoon.

3

GLORIA GRAINGER'S HOUSE WAS ENCHANTING, and Willow stood outside it breathless with envy. Built at the end of the seventeenth century of dark red bricks, it had double-height bays on either side of the front door and was set well back from the pavement behind perfect original iron railings. A grey-branched creeper of some kind, probably wisteria, was neatly pinned to the walls, and all the paintwork was gleaming and without chips or cracks of any kind. Well-proportioned, the house looked as though it consisted of one long or two short rooms on either side of a squarish hall or landing on each of the three floors above the basement.

Willow rang the polished brass bell beside the front door and explained who she was into an intercom.

'Hang on a minute,' said a female voice, with a slight regional accent that Willow could not identify. A moment later the white-panelled door was opened. 'Hello, I'm Marilyn Posselthwate. Won't you come in?'

She was a plump woman in her early twenties, who would probably have been pretty if she had carried herself better and managed to smile. Her short brown hair was glossy and her face looked as though it could be interesting, but she slouched, with her shoulders rounded and her heavy breasts drooping towards her waist. She looked both exhausted and nervous, but not at all sad.

She let the front door shut with a bang. As Willow listened to the harsh noise echoing round the hall, it struck her that if she did not soon meet someone who could manage to feel saddened by Gloria Grainger's death she might begin to believe that one of the novelist's enemies had indeed whacked her over the head in fury.

Dismissing the thought as unsuitably frivolous, Willow looked around her and was greatly impressed. She would happily have given houseroom to any of the paintings, rugs or chests that furnished the hall, and even Mrs Rusham would have admired the polish on the parquet floor.

'What a lovely house!'

'Yes, it is pleasant, isn't it? Come into the drawing room.'

Marilyn led the way into the room to the left of the front door, which was also perfectly arranged. An enormous amount of money had obviously been expended on it, but also a surprising austerity of taste. There were no frills, no lavishness of gilding or extravagance of colour. It did not look like the background of a traditional romantic novelist. Marilyn dropped into a chair, saying:

'Sorry, I seem to have been on my feet all day. Please sit down and let's see if I can help you.'

'Thank you.' Willow chose a relatively upright wing chair and took a fat, black, leather-covered notebook from her briefcase. 'First of all, do let me say how sorry I am that your aunt is dead. I never met her, but it must have been a blow to you to lose her.'

'Thank you,' said Marilyn, blinking as she crossed her legs and folded her hands on her knee, but giving no clue to her emotions.

Willow saw that Marilyn's tights were thick and, feeling the bitter cold of the exquisite room, wished her own were as warm.

'As I explained on the telephone,' she said, 'your aunt's publishers want me to write something about her and her work that they can publish as soon as possible. Since I never knew her I thought I should hear about her from someone who did. You seemed the ideal choice, but I am sorry to bother you when you've got so much on your plate, and on a Saturday too.'

'That's all right. Saturday has always been a working day for me here and I haven't got that much more to do today. It's quite nice to sit down.'

'When my mother died there seemed to be an enormous number of things to be settled,' said Willow, unscrewing the lid of her pen. 'You must have got through them very fast if you've none left.'

'Oh no. My aunt's solicitor and her secretary will deal with all the formal things except for the funeral, which her executor will be organising.' She rolled her eyes as though in exasperation and added: 'The solicitor told me that her will just says that the executor has all the details of what she wanted, but he's away just now, so nothing can be done until next week.'

'Isn't that going to cause rather a lot of difficulty?'

'Apparently not, thank goodness. The undertakers who took away her body said that they can keep it for a week at least before it has to be buried and the executor's due back on Monday.'

Marilyn showed none of the horror that Willow immediately felt as she thought of the body slowly stiffening in some undertaker's basement freezer. It was hard for her to repress a shudder.

'Oh,' she said uselessly as she tried to galvanise her mental faculties. 'How long have you lived here?' she asked to ease herself into the interview.

'Six years; not in the house, of course. She wouldn't have had staff actually living here. But in a cottage at the bottom of the garden.'

'But they told me you're her niece,' said Willow, surprised into a protest.

'Yes,' said Marilyn, smiling.

Willow saw that between her parted lips Marilyn's teeth

were very close together and thought that she could deduce considerable anger.

'But that didn't alter the fact that I was "staff",' Marilyn went on. 'She gave me the job when I badly needed somewhere to live and some way of earning that would allow me to stay near Sarah – my daughter – and made it quite clear that I wasn't to presume on the relationship.'

'But you must have been grateful to her, even so.'

'Yes,' said Marilyn, but the bitterness in her voice made nonsense of her agreement. 'But I have paid for what she gave me, several times over.'

'I'm sorry?'

'My aunt extracted quantities of gratitude in very concrete forms. If that sounds ungenerous, then perhaps I have inherited at least that much from her.'

Willow was silent for a moment, trying to think how to conceal the point of her next question.

'You look shocked,' said Marilyn quietly, 'but if you'd known her you wouldn't be.' She paused, but then the bitterness seemed to burst out of her: 'She had an enormous amount of money, as you can see from her house, but she paid me a pittance, and the cottage that I was so grateful to be allowed to live in is furnished with chipboard and plastic and it's always cold. There's no central heating and the electric fires cost a fortune to keep on and we've had to have them for Peter's health. And I had to pay the fuel bills out of my mean wages.'

'Perhaps you'll inherit all this now,' suggested Willow, who surprisingly *had* found herself shocked. She had always believed that she put no value on family piety and was intrigued to find that she had been wrong. There was no time to examine her own feelings then, but she filed them away for some future occasion, along with a mental note to analyse her instinctive sympathy for Gloria Grainger.

'Unlikely,' said Marilyn, looking around the beautiful room with obvious resentment.

'Had your aunt many relations then?'

'No, very few. There's my father, who's her brother, but

they never got on. He was furious when I told him what it was like living here and ever since he's wanted me to take Sarah back to live with him in Reading, but there isn't enough room there and he couldn't look after her while I was out. I'd have to work. It's not as though he could keep us on his pension and I don't want you to think I think he ought. She's my child and my responsibility.'

Marilyn gasped suddenly, as though she had realised that she was babbling about her personal affairs to a complete stranger.

'It's all right,' said Willow quickly. 'I must have seemed very impertinent. It's none of my business what your family arrangements are.'

'No, of course not,' said Marilyn, pulling a paper hand-kerchief out of her sleeve and blotting her upper lip. 'It's just that my aunt used to accuse me of believing that other people owed me a living because I had a child, and so I tend to rush in with explanations whenever the subject gets close to that.' She smiled again, her teeth still gripped together.

'You asked about relations. Apart from Dad and me, there's only a collection of quite distant cousins. I don't think I've ever met any of them and I doubt if they'll be inheriting anything; Aunt Ethel was quite . . . well, anyway, she's probably left it all to a cat's home.'

'Aunt Ethel?'

'Gloria Grainger. Ethel Posselthwate was not thought to be a suitable name for a novelist when she started writing.'

'Haven't you spoken to her solicitor?' asked Willow with an apparently friendly smile as she wondered whether Marilyn's lack of expectations could possibly be genuine. There was something about her mixture of defensiveness and resentment that made Willow feel active dislike and a certain, possibly unfair, mistrust. 'I know she only died yesterday, but I think in your place I'd have done that at once.'

Marilyn flushed and looked more convincing.

'Actually I did, first thing after the doctor had got the

undertakers round yesterday. They wanted to know all sorts of stuff about the funeral, which, like I said, I didn't know. The solicitor didn't either. You'd think she'd done it like this to get the maximum number of people involved in her death. Come to think of it, she probably did: she always liked a lot of attention.'

'Didn't the lawyer tell you anything about what you might inherit?' asked Willow, hiding even more dislike. After all she was a complete stranger to Marilyn and interviewing her for a tribute to her dead aunt. It was both odd and ungenerous of Marilyn not even to have tried to say something pleasant about her, whatever their difficulties might have been.

'Well, I did ask him, you see, even though I don't think I should have done,' said Marilyn in a silly voice. She smiled like a little girl bravely admitting that she had stolen a few sweets. Willow felt slightly nauseated, but she smiled back encouragingly.

'In the end he said that I am mentioned in the will, but that he can't give me any details yet as Aunt Ethel stipulated that all the beneficiaries should be told together after the funeral.'

'She must have had quite a sense of drama then as well as all the rest,' said Willow, scribbling a note as she remembered that she was collecting material for a memoir and not interviewing a suspect in a murder enquiry. Once again she teased herself with the absurd possibility that there might in fact have been a murder that needed investigation.

'I suppose she did,' said Marilyn, talking normally again. 'Anyway, the solicitor said that I'm to go on running the house, which will be easy without her in it to cause . . . to need things all the time. He'll pay the wages but he will speak to the bank about authorising my signature on small cheques for household expenses and things. But I don't suppose any of this is what you need to know.'

'No, it isn't really, but it's giving me an indication of your aunt's character, which is what I wanted,' said Willow, smiling. 'Can you think of anything nice to say about her?'

Marilyn thought for a long time and eventually managed to find something.

'She could be charming, I suppose, although I didn't often see it once I'd begun to work here. The charm's how she got us all in the first place.'

Willow was so surprised by the statement that she wrote it down verbatim, almost missing Marilyn's explanation of what she had said.

'She could make you feel that you alone of all the people surrounding her were worth something, but then disillusion would set in all too soon.'

'Hers or yours?'

'Both. During the honeymoon you'd tell her things: nothing necessarily awful, but things you'd be unhappy about everyone knowing and somehow she always managed to use them to torment you later.'

'What sort of thing?' Willow was busily writing notes of her questions and Marilyn's replies, but her fingers were cold and moved sluggishly.

'Oh, confidences of one sort or another. For instance, I once told her that I wanted to write. Mad of me, but I actually thought she might help me. She was always throwing it back at me. If I'd done something wrong or annoyed her or failed one of her unbearably high standards, she'd use it to beat me with. "You know you'll never have a hope of writing anything if your self-discipline is so lax", or "people who want to write have to be able to sacrifice their immediate enjoyment for the greater good of their work", and "my dear, you're like any day-dreaming housemaid; you haven't a hope", and so on. And she'd always smile that sweet smile and soften her voice as she said it as though she was producing endearments.'

'It sounds horrible,' said Willow, confused by the thought of Gloria Grainger's high standards. Nothing she had heard of the books suggested either discrimination or desire for quality. On the other hand what she had seen of the house was undoubtedly the result of both.

'It was,' said Marilyn. 'There were times when I'd have

done almost anything to shut her up.' She gasped, coughed and recovered her poise. 'I know it sounds awful to say all this now she's dead, but she did get me down sometimes and there was nothing I could do about it. If she'd sacked me I'd never have found anywhere else for us all to live.'

Willow recrossed her legs and thought longingly of both heat and tea. The perfect room was beginning to feel as though it was even colder than the icy street outside had been.

'Us all?' she said to prompt Marilyn.

'Me, my daughter, who in Aunt Ethel's charming phrase "has no father", and Peter, a friend of mine who's in a wheelchair and can't work just now.'

'Perhaps I could talk to them later,' said Willow, making an unnecessary note just to see whether her fingers would still move. She thought of putting her gloves on again.

'If you think it necessary.' Marilyn sounded surprised. 'But my daughter's at school now and Peter is having physiotherapy at the local hospital at the moment.'

'I see. Who else works – worked – here?'

'There's Mrs Guy, the cleaner, who comes every day. Aunt Ethel was good to her, which is weird. I've never understood it. Then there's her secretary, Patty Smithe, but she's been away ill for a couple of weeks. A friend of hers has been standing in for her, but of course since it's Saturday, she's not here now either. It's only me she bullied into working for her on Saturdays.'

The last sentence was spoken with real venom, which made all Willow's sympathy focus on the dead woman once more.

'Did your aunt pay the others as badly as she paid you?' Willow recognised that Marilyn's pleasure in shedding her resentment was encouraging her to answer the questions without even thinking about why they had been asked.

'Not Mrs Guy. She got about fifty per cent more than the usual rate for cleaners round here. Patty was just as badly paid. Aunt Ethel said once that you get a much nicer class of girl if you pay badly. Presumably when it came to chars she didn't care about their class.'

'It does sound as though your aunt had some unattractive traits,' said Willow.

A real smile seemed to displace the unconvincing one that Marilyn had used at intervals during the interview.

'She often said far worse things than that.' The regional accent was growing stronger as Marilyn relaxed. 'Her other great phrase whenever I tried to talk about money was from the Bible proverb. You know: "better a dinner of herbs" and all that. Well, they were pretty bitter herbs, I can tell you.'

'Yes.' Willow, feeling as though her toes were about to fall off, added: 'Do you think we could have a little heat in here? It's like an ice house.'

'Is it? Yes, I suppose it is. She always kept the heating off unless she was planning to be in a room herself because of the furniture and I haven't yet got enough courage up to break her rules. Isn't that silly? Hang on a minute and I'll do something about it.'

Marilyn bent down to each of the four radiators in the room and turned their valves. She also went out for a few minutes and returned with a modern plastic blow-heater which she switched on and placed just in front of Willow's feet.

'Ah,' said Willow in relief. 'That's wonderful. Thank you. I am going to have to write something favourable about your aunt. Do you think her secretary – Patty is it? – would speak kindly of her?'

Marilyn laughed.

'I shouldn't have thought so. She's been off with "flu" for nearly two weeks, but I suspect she had just had enough of Aunt Ethel's temper. Do you know? On Patty's last day here before she went sick, Aunt Ethel actually threw a pile of books at her.'

'Good heavens!' Willow began to think that Gloria Grainger must have deliberately surrounded herself with weak people who were prepared to play victim to her tyrant. 'What had the secretary done?'

'Misread her shorthand and typed up a whole chapter that

didn't make sense because of it. And to cap it all she'd got the name of the main character wrong.'

'But that's not such a problem.' Willow was warming up. 'All she'd have to do is a search and replace and run the chapter off the printer again.'

'My aunt,' said Marilyn in a spiteful voice, 'did not approve of word processors. She said they made secretaries lazy. Patty works on an old electric typewriter – so old it doesn't even have a self-correcting ribbon. Though, to be fair, Aunt Ethel did sometimes use it herself. Susan said she'd been typing something late the day before yesterday.'

'Well, not much point talking to Patty then,' said Willow. 'Who do you think might speak well of your aunt? Whom didn't she bully?'

After a moment's thought, Marilyn said reluctantly: 'I suspect Mrs Guy would say nice things. She seemed to really like Aunt Ethel. And Peter might, oddly enough.'

'Who exactly is he?'

'Peter Farrfield. My friend in the wheelchair. She used to summon him sometimes to have dinner with her and he usually made her laugh – which I don't think I ever did in all the years I've been here. I used to have to cook for them and serve it and if I intervened in one of their conversations I'd always get it in the neck next day from my aunt. Peter was a guest, she'd say, and therefore none of my business.'

Despite her early identification with Gloria, Willow was beginning to understand why Ann and Eve had received the news of her death so outrageously. If Willow herself had been in Marilyn's position she might well have whacked Gloria over the head. Then she corrected herself: she would simply have told her employer exactly what she thought of her behaviour and left her house for ever.

What kind of person would you have to be to put up with such humiliating treatment for so long? she asked herself. How much resentment would you have to bury and what might that lead you to do? Willow's frivolous suspicion that Gloria might have been murdered returned once more and seemed rather less frivolous than it had done at first.

Wondering about Marilyn's motives for staying with her aunt for six years of bullied misery, Willow remembered what she had read in the letter Elsie Trouville had shown her, begging for parole from a life sentence. It was a phrase that had been echoed almost verbatim that afternoon when Marilyn said that there were times when she would have done almost anything to shut her aunt up.

'Was her death a surprise, or had she always had heart trouble?' Willow asked casually, hoping that the resentment was still clouding Marilyn's judgement enough to conceal the real point of the question.

'She'd had angina for years. I think she'd had a very minor stroke, too, about a year ago, but she always dismissed the idea and it hadn't incapacitated her at all. The doctor thought it was possible she had had a stroke when I described what had happened. You see I found her on the bedroom floor one day. She said she'd just tripped, but there had obviously been a real time lag she wasn't aware of.'

'Did you tell her about it?'

'She wouldn't listen to me, and the doctor thought there wasn't any point in pushing it. He was treating her for the angina and he wasn't at all surprised when she died. He really wasn't. He said nothing could have been done about it. If it was going to happen it would happen. We couldn't have prevented it.'

'Ah,' said Willow as she absorbed Marilyn's unnecessary reiteration of the doctor's calmness. Did the lady protest too much? 'Perhaps I ought to talk to him, too. He might be able to let me say something about how bravely she put up with the difficulties and pains of ill-health that I could write up.'

'He might,' said Marilyn doubtfully, but then she smiled with real brilliance, 'but I doubt it. He's a lovely man, very kind and very sensible. I don't know what I'd have done if I hadn't had him to help me when Aunt Ethel became too difficult.'

'This is going to be a tricky assignment, I can see,' said Willow. 'I think I'll have to read her books before I talk to anyone else. Do you like them?'

'I haven't read any for ages. I loved them when I was about fourteen, but I didn't know her then. Somehow knowing her made it different. Do you want to borrow some? We have file copies of every single edition of every single book, even the big print and the braille.'

'It's all right, thank you. Her publishers are sending a full set round to my flat. Could I possibly see some of the rest of the house while I'm here? Your aunt obviously had marvellous taste, and I could write about that.'

'Yes, of course.' Marilyn got up and smoothed her pleated skirt down over her thighs. 'She did do the house very well. She picked out all the furniture herself and chose all the colours and things. It is quite nice, I have to admit that.'

'It is, isn't it?' Willow thought that anyone who used so colourless and unimaginative a description of the glory around them had little future as a writer.

Marilyn escorted her around several of the other rooms, each of which was as perfect as the last. It was obviously a familiar tour, because Marilyn could describe the origins of each piece of furniture and each painting, citing its provenance and likely value. Most of it was of museum quality and yet oddly enough, despite the perfection of the rooms, their atmosphere was almost friendly. Willow's doubts about Marilyn grew. It seemed impossible that anyone with such discernment could be as frightful a person as she had made her aunt out to be.

As they stood in the main bedroom, admiring the view over the garden to the trees that bordered the river, Willow decided to risk pushing Marilyn a little further.

'How did she actually die? I mean were you there? It must have been very difficult for you.'

'No, I wasn't there,' said Marilyn so abruptly that Willow's mildly suspicious mind began to click like a geiger counter near a lump of uranium. She moved away from the window and began to fiddle with the silver boxes and a lovely little enamelled étui on the bedside table.

'I see.'

Marilyn looked up smiling apologetically, as though she

were conscious of her own rudeness but not, Willow thought, of the oddness of the question.

'It happened when she was asleep. She'd been very tired all day and a bit breathless, and she asked me to bring her supper up here on a tray. That had been happening more and more recently. I'd bring it up and wait downstairs in the kitchen until she rang for me to remove the tray. Well, the day before yesterday she never rang. I waited until half-past nine, because she hated me coming in if she hadn't rung, and then I crept in to see if she was all right and she just seemed to be asleep. It did cross my mind that she might have got ill, but she seemed all right and I didn't want to bother her.'

'Was she in bed?'

'Not really. She was lying under the eiderdown, but I could see she still had her clothes on. She used to rest like that in the afternoons, but I'd never seen her do it after dinner before.'

'Didn't you try to wake her?'

'Certainly not!' Marilyn's protest was vibrant with horror. 'She'd have hated that and been furious with me. No, I crept away, leaving the tray where it was on the table in the window so that I didn't wake her with clinking china.'

Willow looked round the room, which was large and had obviously once been two, and tried to imagine the scene. The bed was at the garden end, a vast four-poster hung with old flame-coloured brocade and flanked by plain mahogany tables carrying lamps, books, flowers, tissues, *objets de vertu* and a silver photograph frame surrounding the portrait of a remarkably handsome man with the hairstyle and pose of forty years earlier.

'Were the lights on?' she asked.

'Just the one to the right of the bed,' said Marilyn.

Willow imagined the grey-haired woman, who must have been dwarfed by the great bed, lying with her eyes shut in the pool of light.

'She must have felt ill enough to turn off the rest of the lights and get under the covers and yet not ill enough to ring for me . . . ' Marilyn looked anxious, as well she might, thought Willow, considering she had at the very least left her elderly relative to die alone and without help.

There were other possibilities, too, but Willow's experience of genuine murder enquiries suggested that Marilyn probably would not have been quite so loquacious if she had had any real guilt to hide. She would have had to be a great deal more intelligent than she seemed, and subtler too, to take that route away from discovery.

'I don't really understand it,' Marilyn went on, gabbling again, 'but the doctor said she might merely have felt very tired and then, once she was already in bed, away from the bell, felt the pain and died.'

Marilyn looked self-conscious as she rattled off her explanation, both the secret satisfaction and the bitterness gone from her eyes.

'It is really awful,' she went on. 'Whatever I thought about her, she oughtn't to have died on her own up here in pain.'

Willow watched in silence, hoping for more, as Marilyn walked the whole length of the room to stare out of the other window, overlooking Kew Green.

'I feel dreadful about it,' she said. 'And I was so impatient, too, as I sat there in the basement and then so cross when I did go back across to the cottage. And all the time she was dead.'

Willow waited again, her eyes cold and her mind analysing all the excuses, the apparent guilt, and the renewed volubility.

'The doctor says he doesn't blame me,' added Marilyn again, sighing. She rubbed her eyes like a child.

'I can't see why on earth he should,' said Willow, hoping that sympathy might lead Marilyn to say more. 'It's none of my business and completely irrelevant, but what did her supper consist of?'

Marilyn turned and Willow saw that at last there was suspicion in her reddened eyes, but she answered the question, once again with unnecessary elaboration.

'Fish. She always had fish at night. Sole colbert and Kenya beans and a few potatoes, sautéd. Oh, and half a bottle of champagne. She always had that, too. Doctor Trenor said that moderate drinking would be positively good for her heart, which pleased her. I brought it up and put it on this table, here.'

She returned to the bed end of the room and laid one ringless hand on the mellow mahogany of a square Regency breakfast table that stood a foot or so away from the window. It was quite out of period, Willow saw, but a beautiful piece with its tripod legs and golden satinwood cross-banding, and in wonderful condition.

'Had she eaten – or drunk – any of it?' she asked, willing to arouse yet more suspicion because it seemed unlikely that she would ever get another chance to ask such questions, and increasingly she felt that she needed the answers.

'Most of it. Well, only about half the fish, but everything else. She was greedy, you know, and overweight.'

'Oh. Well, it's miserable for you, and most unfair of me to make you come up here and remember it all. Let's go down.'

Willow left the house at last, perplexed, suspicious and thoroughly determined to find out exactly how her subject had died. It was a bore that she would probably not be able to explore her ideas with Tom. Almost more than anything she missed the easy friendliness of the discussions they used to have.

When she got back to Chesham Place Willow found fires burning in every room, new flowers casually arranged in her bedroom and in the drawing room in a matching pair of black Ming vases she had recently bought at Spink's. She took off her boots and overcoat and slipped her cold feet into a pair of sable-lined velvet slippers that Tom had given her.

She had always disapproved of bedroom slippers on the basis that they looked sloppy, were generally dirty and gave an impression of slovenliness that she hated. Tom had first reminded her that she suffered from poor circulation in winter and that her feet were nearly always cold and then found the most absurdly luxurious slippers available to give her for Christmas.

Willow, who had never seen anything like them in any shop, occasionally wondered whether he had had them made for her and if so how he had managed to afford them even on a chief inspector's salary. The possible reasons for his unusually lavish generosity worried her as she battled with the phantoms of her dissatisfaction.

The slippers might even have been a guilt present, she thought, a wordless apology for some infidelity. If so, she needed to know more. The whole problem would be solved at once if she knew that he wanted to call a halt to their love affair. But, since he would never answer her questions, he made it impossible for her to decide what to do. He also confused her by alternating between the unpleasant moodiness and demands, usually unspoken, for greater intimacy.

Remembering the occasionally bleak but at least simple days when she had cared for nobody, Willow decided to return to the emotional safety of her researches into Gloria's world. She went into her writing room in search of the article that Eve had promised to fax that morning.

As Willow started to read the article, she wondered why anyone should have even bothered to sue its author, but when she had finished she was no longer at all surprised. Posy Hacket's conclusion read:

> With ideas like these being thrust at the unformed and the vulnerable, it is no wonder that young women still put themselves in situations where they are at risk of violence or that some men find pleasure – or an easing of their own uncertainties – in physically tormenting the women who live with them. Gloria Grainger's sentimental, cliché-ridden and apparently innocuous books are in fact highly dangerous. Censorship is anathema to most thinking people, but books like these can be quite as dangerous as hard-core pornography and tales of sadistic violence, and they can make the idea of at least informal censorship positively attractive.

'Whew,' said Willow aloud, forgetting that she was not

still alone at the mill. 'Isn't she using an atom bomb to break a butterfly?'

When she had recovered from her immediate shock, she looked up Posy Hacket's telephone number and rang it.

'Hello, this is Willow King,' she said clearly when the telephone was answered. 'We haven't met, but . . . '

'But I've written about you,' said Posy Hacket in a harsh voice, removing Willow's faint hope that she might get away unidentified as Cressida Woodruffe. 'Are you inviting me to a duel at dawn? Or perhaps another outing in the courts?'

'Certainly not.' Willow quite liked the angrily ironic tone of the questions and warmed to the woman a little in spite of her own anger. 'This isn't about me at all. I'm writing a memoir of Gloria Grainger for our mutual publishers and I'm puzzled about her. I wondered if I could come and talk to you. You must have known her work better than most, and you could probably help me clear my brain a bit.'

There was a short pause before Posy said:

'I don't see why not, if you really want to. I can't say I knew her personally, although I did the interview, but I have some quite strong views about her work. Do you want to come tomorrow? Half-past eleven. I shan't be working then.'

'That sounds convenient,' said Willow coolly, noticing the unspoken command to take it or leave it. She was surprised that her approach had been accepted so easily. Why should a journalist who had savaged a novelist welcome the victim into her own home?

'Where do you live?'

Posy gave the address in North London and assured Willow that there would be plenty of parking spaces around the flat.

When she returned to the drawing room with her notes of the meeting with Marilyn Posselthwate, Willow found that Mrs Rusham had brought in a tea tray. There was thin, crisp toast spread with anchovy paste, a single crumpet keeping hot over a tiny, silver spirit lamp beside dishes of butter and honey, and part of a ginger cake that had gone marvellously sticky over the weeks since Mrs Rusham had baked it.

At that moment it was sheer heaven to be presented with meals once again. Willow poured the tea and began to eat the anchovy toast in a ferment of gratitude. It was only when she had finished her tea that she let herself compare her domestic arrangements with Gloria Grainger's and tried to imagine what Mrs Rusham might have said about her to an inquisitive interviewer.

Robustly comforting herself with the knowledge that Mrs Rusham was neither her relative nor underpaid, Willow got back to work, filling out her notes of what Marilyn had told her and listing questions she still wanted to have answered, the most difficult of which was:

'Could someone really have hated Gloria Grainger enough to kill her?'

The door opened and Mrs Rusham appeared. Willow hoped she had not heard the question.

'May I take the tray?' she asked, showing no sign of interest or condemnation.

'Yes, of course. It was a good tea. Thank you.'

'I'm glad. And you asked me to remind you that you're meeting Detective Chief Inspector Worth at the Partridge tonight.'

'Oh, good heavens! So I am. Seven-thirty.' Willow looked at her watch and saw she had only three-quarters of an hour. 'I'd better go and change. Thank you, Mrs R. You're very late today. You know, you really mustn't work too hard.'

Mrs Rusham looked so surprised that for a moment Willow wondered whether she normally seemed like an ogre, but then she banished the thought. Her housekeeper was quite tough enough to fight back.

4

'AND SO YOU SEE, TOM, I'm beginning to wonder whether she might not actually have been murdered,' Willow went on as they waited for their food.

Tom glared at her, looking almost as though he hated her. Angry but undaunted, Willow explained.

'The niece, who strikes me as being a rather unpleasant piece of work, has been released from what she considers to be intolerable servitude, and she probably stands to inherit a fortune.'

'Don't be so damned irresponsible.' Tom looked as though he had only just started to listen properly to what Willow had been saying.

She stiffened and made up her mind. She had tried to meet him half-way and he had balked again. If he could not be bothered even to try to be pleasant to her any longer, she was going to have to force him to come out with whatever it was that had been making him so difficult. They had to sort it out before they made each other really miserable.

Before she could say anything, a waiter brought their crab bisque. As soon as he had gone, Willow asked even less gently than she had the day before:

'What *is* the matter with you, Tom?'

He stared at her across the prettily laid table, oblivious of the eating, smoking, chattering crowd around them, his dark eyes angry and his usually wide mouth pinched and obstinate. Willow pushed him.

'It can't just be your new case. Is it something I have done? Or not done? What?'

He rubbed his hands through his hair and she noticed that there were a few white wires in the darkness.

'The case colours everything else,' he said ambiguously.

'Do you want to talk about it?'

He looked round the restaurant, no longer unaware of the other people, and then back at Willow.

'How can I?' he snapped. She shrugged.

'They all seem far too absorbed in themselves to eavesdrop,' she said, 'but it doesn't matter. Then what would you like to talk about? The ballet?'

'Don't be ridiculous.'

Willow began to seethe. She drank her soup in silence. Tom said nothing either until their empty plates were exchanged for the next course.

'I can't think why you insisted on coming to a game restaurant and then ordering crab soup and sole Colbert,' he said when they were alone again.

It sounded like deliberate provocation, which made Willow think that he must also want to move on from silent dissatisfaction into some kind of open conflict. She stopped even trying to conceal her irritation.

'I don't remember insisting,' she said just as snappishly as he had spoken. 'You asked if I'd choose a restaurant and I'd read a review of this place, which made it sound enticing. I'm not hungry enough for game tonight. But I think the place is good, don't you?'

'I suppose so,' said Tom, picking up his knife and fork to attack the grouse on his plate. He ate about half, crunched painfully on a piece of shot, cursed, and then gave up.

Willow paid no attention to him as she concentrated on her sole and the interesting idea it was suggesting to her. Having been surprised at the quantity of butter involved in the dish, she wondered whether it was possible that Marilyn had simply been feeding her aunt cholesterol-inducing food in an attempt to precipitate the expected heart attack. That might not constitute deliberate murder, but it could have explained the young woman's apparently guilty defence of herself.

Willow was distracted from her easy thoughts of death only when Tom leaned across the table to refill her wine glass. She saw the tidily positioned knife and fork on his half-full plate.

'Aren't you hungry either?'

'Not particularly. Will, I'm sorry. I . . . '

At last, she thought, as she waited for the announcement of his impending departure from her life.

'I'm a pretty poor companion tonight. When you've finished, I'd better take you home and get out of your hair.'

'Tom, is there someone else?' she asked abruptly.

He stared at her in such obvious dismay that she began to wonder if she had completely misread his moods and rudeness.

'Why? Is there for you?' he asked, sounding troubled and much less angry.

Willow shook her head, saying: 'Certainly not. Are you working again tonight?'

'No. Why?'

'I wondered if you'd like to come back to the flat and have coffee or a drink. We could talk undisturbed there. Mrs R. went ages ago and there'd be no one to overhear us.'

'Even though I've been so bloody bad-tempered?' said Tom, laying one strong hand, palm upwards, on the white tablecloth. He looked like himself again for a moment.

'Even so,' said Willow, still puzzled. She put her hand over his for a second.

Tom sighed and drained his wine glass. Willow finished as much of her deep-fried sole and parsley butter as she could manage and signalled for her bill.

'It's my turn,' she said firmly before Tom could do more than open his mouth, let alone his wallet. After some of the things he had said to her, she was not prepared to let him pay for her food.

They walked quickly back to her flat, huddling into their coats as the cold bit into their cheeks and gripped their feet. When she had unlocked the street door, she shuddered and started to hurry upstairs.

'Come on, Tom, the only hope of getting warm again is to get to the fire fast.'

He laughed for the first time that evening and easily overtook her on the stairs.

'Here,' she said from several steps below him. He turned back and she threw him her keys. He caught them easily and stood, looking first at them and then at her with a deliberation she could not understand. After a moment he shrugged, unlocked the door for her and handed back her keys.

She let him hug her as soon as they had got rid of their coats, even though she felt that there was still a great emotional distance between them. After a moment he started to stroke her short red hair and eventually he tipped her head back and kissed her.

'Was I awful?'

'Utterly frightful,' she said, wishing that she could understand him and wishing even more urgently that he would either leave her or get back to normal. 'Go and make the coffee as a penance.'

'Okay ma'am.'

Willow left him to it and went into the drawing room to switch on all the lamps and remove the fireguard. With the light of the fire flickering on the pale walls and pointing up the warm colours of the cushions and flowers and books, the room looked quite as appealing as any of Gloria Grainger's and even friendlier in its emptiness.

Tom filled it up a few minutes later as he returned with a pot of coffee and two cups.

'Thanks,' said Willow as he handed her one. 'Now tell me about it.'

'Oh, it's just a pig of a case.'

'I didn't mean the case, Tom. Tell me, please, what it is that's eating you.'

He frowned.

'Only the case,' he said, apparently lying. He started to talk very fast, piling short, staccato sentences on top of each other. 'Young, married woman messily bludgeoned to death at home. No evidence of a break-in. Husband, apparently grief stricken, begs us to find the killer.' Tom gave a short, humourless laugh.

'He even appeared on television to appeal for witnesses. Did you see him on the local news last night?'

'No, I hardly ever watch it,' said Willow. 'It always seemed to be about murders on the tube and so I gave up.' Tom shrugged and started to talk at a more normal speed.

'Despite the television tears, he can't quite hide a kind of sickening cockiness that we've all seen before. We all know he killed her, but even though he's got no alibi we can't prove he was in the house at the time of the murder. He must have washed and got rid of his bloody clothes before he called us; there wasn't any evidence on him. We've had forensics in the drains and, sure enough, they've found traces of her blood – but that only tells us someone washed, not who. There are no fingerprints that can't be explained by ordinary domestic contact except for enough gloved smudges for a defence lawyer to use to suggest there was an intruder.'

'Tricky.' Willow's voice was cold. She could see that the case might be troubling anyone involved, but it did not sound much worse than any of the others Tom had seen.

'If we don't get any evidence that he was in the house at the time – or a confession – then he's free to go and do it again. I know that he did it, but if he keeps his nerve and doesn't confess, it doesn't look as though there's anything we can do. I hate bloody domestics!'

'Aren't most murders?'

'What, domestic? Yes. But familiarity doesn't breed either contempt or acceptance, just loathing. You wonder how the poor women managed to live with men with that much violence in them and not realise their danger; and then you look at the inadequate sod of a husband and you can't imagine anyone being afraid of him, because he seems so pathetic until you catch that half-suppressed self-satisfaction. He doesn't look sinister, just pathetic and tearful until you see that private smile. You wonder why they ever married – either of them – what they thought they'd get from it and what torment they put each other through before one of them took the ultimate sanction against the other.'

Ah, thought Willow, perhaps that's it.

'Child abuse is even worse,' Tom said so quickly that she thought he must have seen something in her face and was talking to stop her putting it into words. 'Because at least a spouse has some choice in the person he or she ends up with – and the possibility of getting away. It makes you despair sometimes.'

'More than when you're faced with serial killers?' asked Willow, knowing that she was helping Tom run away from the things they needed to sort out but suddenly afraid of what she might uncover if she forced him to talk.

'They're so rare, Will, in this country, whereas domestics are hideously common to any AMIP,' he said holding out a hand. He seemed to be showing gratitude for having been given an excuse to digress, which only added to her confusion.

'I wish you wouldn't talk in initials,' she said, noticing how pettish she was sounding and hating it.

'I thought you knew it means Area Major Investigation Pool,' he said. He frowned and looked at her carefully. 'You've never been afraid of me, have you, Will?'

'Certainly not,' she said, wondering what was coming next. 'Although I was a trifle daunted by your determination to arrest me for the murder of Algy Endlesham.'

'I never planned to do that.' Tom's eyes glinted and she was relieved to see something of his old character back again. 'The only thing I was anxious to do with you was break down your idiotic pretence of being a dowdy, prematurely middle-aged, back-room civil servant.'

'The only thing?' Willow considered the passion that had exploded between them when he had been sent to investigate a murder at the department where she worked. It seemed a great pity that it should have been lost.

'It's true that there was one other thing then.' Tom paused and then added so quietly that she hardly heard him: 'Just as there is now.'

'Is there?' she asked quietly. 'Still?'

He nodded. 'What about you?'

'Sometimes,' she admitted.

Willow thought that while they could be honest with each other about sex they might still have a chance.

'Well, thank God for that at least,' said Tom. 'Shall we go to bed?'

Over the months since they had first become lovers, their lovemaking had gradually fallen into a pleasant routine, but that night it was different. There was more desperation in Tom and yet Willow found herself resistant.

The cold emptiness of the mill seemed to beckon, but she could not yield to its paradoxical welcome without running away from him with their differences unresolved and unexplained. She was not prepared to do it, even though she had stopped short of the ultimate confrontation that evening.

With her mind clear on one thing at least, Willow eventually slept, only to wake soon after nine to see Tom dressing.

'Hello,' she said. He turned at once.

'I didn't mean to wake you. You look tired.'

'I'm all right,' she said, pushing her red hair back from her face and rubbing her smarting eyes. 'You're not working today, are you?'

'I thought I'd go back to the nick and see how they're progressing with the interviews. We've held off arresting the husband while we scrape around for evidence, because we'll only be able to hold him for thirty-six hours without charging him, but it'll have to come. I need to see how the DIs are getting on.'

'Mightn't they get on better if they didn't feel overlooked by the DCI?' said Willow, using the initials she knew made him feel at home. He managed a quick smile.

'Possibly, but it's my first murder since I was transferred to Five Area and I must crack it. If I go over the little toerag's various statements again I may hit on something we can use to force him into telling the truth.'

Willow pushed herself up into a sitting position and contemplated Tom's tight, unhappy face. In normal circumstances he never used the crude argot of his colleagues.

'You once said,' she said, smiling at him and aware that she must look awful with the remains of the previous day's eye makeup all over her face, 'that you could make anyone confess. I think you told me that you hated that, but isn't it a talent you need now?'

He stood with his sweater in his hands.

'Yes,' he said, elbowing it over his head. 'But it hasn't worked so far. I need some kind of lever – mental lever – and I haven't found it yet. But I may. Is it unfair to leave you alone on a Sunday?'

She shook her head, suppressing her instant relief at the prospect of a whole day to herself, without even Mrs Rusham's smooth, self-effacing presence. 'Not at all. I've got to go and see someone this morning anyway.' Still thinking that it might be possible to get back to what they had once had, she added: 'D'you want to come back for supper? Since there's no Mrs Rusham, it'll only be scrambled eggs.'

'I'd like that,' he said, walking towards the bed. He bent down to kiss her, smelling reproachfully of toothpaste. Willow bent her head so that his lips met her forehead. He stepped back and added more coldly: 'See you later then.'

'Good luck, Tom.'

He raised a hand and left. Willow got out of bed and scrubbed her teeth hard before doing anything else. Then, since she had plenty of time before her meeting with Posy Hacket, she made herself a pot of coffee and, collecting the newspapers from the hall, took them back to bed.

*

She drove herself to Islington in twenty minutes and had to spend another fifteen reading her notes of the meeting in Kew until half-past eleven. Tucking the bulging leather notebook into her shoulder bag, she got out into the cold and locked the car.

Posy Hacket's flat seemed to occupy the top floor of a tall, stuccoed house that looked as though it needed some serious repairs. There was no sound from the intercom after Willow pressed the relevant bell, and she was about to ring it again when she heard the sound of someone coming downstairs. A moment later she found herself face to face with a woman whose appearance fitted the sharply critical things she wrote far better than the coy, little-girl name of Posy.

She must have been at least three inches shorter than Willow, but her slim figure and tight black jeans and polo-necked sweater made her seem taller than she actually was. Looking at her intense, unmade-up face and the severity of her grey-streaked, dark ponytail, Willow wondered why on earth she still called herself Posy instead of Rosemary or whatever else her real name might be.

'Come on up,' she said, unsmiling. 'It's a bloody awful day, isn't it?'

'Horrible,' said Willow, thinking that the 'bloody' was the first sign of human warmth.

Posy led the way upstairs to her flat, which was as much of a surprise as her appearance had been. The room into which she ushered her guest was immense. Light poured into it from windows on both sides. It was furnished with a mixture of the tatty and the sleekly modern and made Willow more interested than ever in the character of its owner.

It looked like the room of a single woman, but Willow, who had for years maliciously enjoyed watching other people misreading her because of her appearance, did her best not to jump to any conclusions. All the same, she could not help looking around the room for genuine clues to Posy's identity.

A long desk, supporting word processor, fax machine and photocopier, appeared to consist of an old door slung across two short filing cabinets. Another, larger, cabinet stood to one side with an overflowing wastepaper basket in front of it. A shelf ran along one wall, carrying an eclectic mixture of old hats, each one skewered to a polystyrene wig stand with an antique hatpin. Old textiles hung on the walls between modern paintings and there was a single, very odd, modern carpet at the living end of the room, which was warmed by a Scandinavian cast-iron stove.

There were two beautifully simple, supple, leather chairs opposite a big Edwardian sofa that was piled with cushions and woven throws of assorted primary colours.

'Sit down and I'll get some tea,' said Posy abruptly. 'Tea all right for you? Or a herbal or coffee?'

'Tea would be wonderful. I've drunk too much coffee already this morning.' Willow smiled. 'It's good of you to offer. I spent most of yesterday afternoon in Gloria Grainger's icy house pining for a cup of tea.'

'What did you think of it?' asked Posy, standing in the doorway and looking over her shoulder at Willow.

'Enviable.'

The journalist laughed, suddenly looking not only much more human but also more attractive, and disappeared.

She was back a little later with an immense brown teapot on a tray with a pair of hand-thrown mugs, two silver teaspoons, an open carton of milk and a glass sugar bowl. Having poured the tea, she said:

'Okay, so what do you want to know?'

'Anything you can tell me about Grainger; if it could be favourable, so much the better.'

Posy grimaced.

'You've come to the wrong person. I thought she was poison: pernicious, vengeful, gross . . . And that's based merely on her work and on her suing me. I never had anything to do with her before the interview, thank God, but what I've heard from other people makes my loathing seem quite mild.'

'That's rather my difficulty,' said Willow. 'I've got to write something complimentary, but it's looking increasingly difficult as I talk to people who were involved with her. They all seem to have disliked her, which seems unfair even though I do accept that she was a bit of a bully and surrounded herself with victims.'

'The last point may not have been entirely her fault,' said Posy reluctantly. 'Victims have a way of finding people to bully them.'

Willow was silent as she thought through that remarkably depressing idea. After a while she said:

'Can you think of anything else to explain or excuse her?'

The journalist shook her head. 'No. All I can think of is my rage at what she's been writing all these years and about what the case was going to do to me.'

'The libel case, you mean?'

'Yes.' Posy looked up and Willow saw such anger in her eyes that she wondered about the journalist's motives for criticising Gloria Grainger's books so bitterly.

'I've spent months in hell. My legal bills are already vast. A lot of the editors who commissioned stuff from me before are wary now and so my income has been cut just when I need it most, but I will never withdraw what I wrote about her. Never.'

'It sounds as though it's been vile,' said Willow frankly. 'Do you regret your article?'

Posy shook her head, her face set and angry. 'What I wrote was absolutely justified and it needed saying.'

'Even though Gloria Grainger's books are so unfashionable nowadays?'

'Absolutely. They may be unpopular with reviewers but they're still borrowed in vast numbers from the public libraries.'

'How do you know that? Oh, Public Lending Rights, I suppose.'

'Precisely. When I was researching the article, I asked

Grainger about her share of PLR and she was frank or vain enough to give me a copy of her latest statement. She earns only just less than the maximum, which means that hundreds of thousands of people are still borrowing her pernicious rubbish.'

'What is it that's so frightful about her books?' asked Willow remembering her own novels and the exaggerated criticism in Posy's article about them.

'D'you mean to tell me that you're writing about her without ever having read any?' Posy laughed and tugged at her tail of hair to push the plain rubber band further up it. Despite her intensity there was something appealing about her. 'That explains a lot.'

'The books are a treat in store for tomorrow,' Willow said, smiling in return. 'Her publishers are sending round a complete set of them.'

'Ah.' Posy picked up her heavy brown mug again and sat nursing it with both hands. Her eyes looked hard as she stared at the far wall of her room.

'Gloria's books,' prompted Willow.

Posy turned her head slightly to look at her guest and grimaced. 'They all suggest that male violence is inherently glamorous,' she said as fluently as though she had practised her answer, 'and that it masks a frightened loveless boy who can be saved by the affection of a pure and trusting woman.'

Just as Elsie Trouville believes you can cure a tendency to crime with literature, thought Willow. Perhaps both ideas are no more than sentimental optimism. Aloud, she said:

'And it's for that analysis that she was suing you? Surely not?'

'Not precisely. What I wrote about her could be construed as an accusation of incitement to real violence, which I had not meant to imply.'

'But it sounds to me as though that is exactly what you think she did,' said Willow, not averse to letting Posy think she had not actually seen the article.

'Not really.' Posy smiled again, but there was contempt mixed with her amusement. 'I can't imagine many men, particularly those with a propensity to violence, reading the works of Gloria Grainger. Can you?'

Willow laughed again and hoped she did not sound as sycophantic as she feared.

'No. My principal accusation is that her books persuade inexperienced, under-educated and naïve young women that they need not fear male violence, that on the contrary they should find it exciting and that if it becomes too much for them, their sweetness and love will dilute it to an acceptable level.'

'Horrible!' Willow's instant reaction was far more genuine than her laughter had been.

'Yes, isn't it? But it's not only Gloria who's promulgated those ideas; her books are in a direct line of descent from, oh, from *Jane Eyre* I suppose. D'you remember that bit where Jane Eyre addresses the reader? It goes something like: "I believed that his moodiness, his harshness, had their source in some cruel cross of fate." And of course, having seen through to the man he would have been had it not been for that cruel cross of fate, Jane makes him appreciate her and be gentler with her than with anyone else. Who could have seemed more violent and sinister than Mr Rochester?'

'Heathcliffe,' said Willow drily, trying terribly hard not to think of Tom and the sorrows that might lie behind his moodiness. Ms Hacket grinned.

'You could be right. But there are plenty of more recent novels that are infinitely worse. I've been making a study of them. Have you ever read *The Sheikh*?'

Willow shook her head.

'You should try it. Do you remember how cross we all got in the late sixties when men banged on about how any miserable or discontented woman simply needed "a good screw" or even "a good rape"?'

Willow nodded, her mouth lengthening in remembered distaste.

'Considering the number of women who apparently revelled in *The Sheikh* in the twenties, that was a not entirely male fantasy. The heroine who is slender and boy-like at the beginning, disdains all idea of love in favour of adventure and sport. She gets her comeuppance when she's kidnapped and raped. Later on, as her rapist's prisoner, she discerns his inner vulnerability and falls passionately in love with him. Naturally that soothes his emotional wounds and allows him to surrender to her. By the end, his voice is trembling as he gently tells her that he can bear anything but the sight of her weeping.' Posy's voice was hardening with each word as her anger got the better of her self-control.

'I've never thought about any of this,' said Willow, interested but not convinced. 'But isn't that idea merely a development of *Beauty and the Beast*?'

'Probably,' said Posy. 'So what? The fact that novels like that were inspired by a traditional folk tale does not excuse them. That's like saying that because heretics were burned in the sixteenth century we need not object to religious prejudice now.'

'Perhaps.' Willow was determined to push the conversation back to Gloria Grainger before it got completely lost in more interesting speculation, but before she could do so, Posy's bleak face broke into another smile.

'Your novels are different. I hadn't considered that aspect of them before, but they're basically *Snow White*, aren't they?'

Willow thought for a moment and then nodded in agreement.

'Probably. Younger, beautiful, talented woman is nearly destroyed by much more powerful older one, goes through a fallow time and emerges as the victor at the end of the book.'

'And revels in the thought of her tormentor dancing in red-hot sandals until she dies.' Posy obviously saw the distaste in Willow's face for she added quickly: 'You must admit that your heroines do enjoy the sufferings of their erstwhile tormentors.'

'Isn't that a natural human instinct?' asked Willow, turning ideas over in her mind again. 'After all, didn't Thomas Aquinas say that Christians in heaven would find their pleasure greatly increased by watching the sufferings of those in hell?'

'I've no idea but I wouldn't be surprised,' said Posy. 'It's no excuse, though. Most natural human instincts are pretty revolting.'

'All right, you win. Just as you have over Gloria Grainger. You must be enormously relieved that she won't be writing any more.'

Posy looked angry as she shook her head.

'Her death won't stop the books that she's already written. There'll probably be a flurry of publicity and a series of reissues of all that tripe now and the libraries will still stock it.'

'There ought to be a law against it,' said Willow in mock outrage. Posy had begun to nod before she caught the mockery and her lips tightened. Willow looked at a large clock on the wall and wondered how long Posy would be prepared to go on answering questions.

'By the way, which of Gloria's books do you recommend? I obviously won't get through them all.'

'I imagine any one would do. I suppose the one that made me most angry was *Buttercups for the Bridesmaid*.'

'I'll look out for it,' said Willow, adding kindly: 'I can imagine a bit of what you've been going through with the case. Each time one of my books comes out I do have a frisson of terror that someone will react horribly. I really sympathise with you for all that anxiety.'

Posy took a mouthful of tea and said nothing. After a while she looked at Willow consideringly, but still did not speak.

'What have I done?' Willow asked frankly. After a long pause Posy said slowly:

'You are not at all as I'd imagined you from your books.'

'Considering what you wrote about them,' said Willow with some sharpness, and some amusement too, 'I am delighted to hear it.'

Posy frowned, clearly not amused at all. Willow was surprised that she had so little sense of humour.

'You seem worried,' she said, wanting to find out exactly what Posy was thinking.

The journalist bit her upper lip and then released it. The muscles in her face clenched.

'I suppose what's bothering me is that it is just possible that Gloria Grainger might have been different, too.' She squared her shoulders and shook her head. 'If she wasn't I can't think of any way you'd be able to say something charitable in your memoir.'

'May I ask you something?'

'That's why you're here, isn't it?' The slight doubt in Posy's voice had been replaced by something surer and sharper.

'Absolutely,' said Willow. 'Why do you hate romantic novelists so much? I'm not complaining about what you wrote about me, but your dislike seems remarkably personal. Romantic novels are pretty harmless really, even if they do peddle old myths to new generations of women.'

Posy swallowed a large mouthful of tea and then laid her thin hand flat across her throat as the liquid burned her pharynx. As soon as she could speak, she put down her mug and said formally as though she were dictating a public statement:

'Suffice it to say that I think that the myths are dangerous and have caused a lot of women to suffer, to deny their real selves and sometimes to short-change the men they marry.'

Willow looked at the journalist in the way she had always looked at new administration trainees in the civil service, trying to assess their strengths and weaknesses, to see past their image of themselves to the reality behind it. Certain that Posy had some undisclosed personal scores to settle with Gloria, Willow asked what stage the libel case had reached.

'The wretched publishers tried to settle,' said Posy with disgust.

'I can understand that,' said Willow. 'After all the *Readers' Quarterly* can't have many resources, and a full jury trial would have been very expensive – and the possible damages incalculable.'

'But it's outrageous. It's a matter of principle. I have even fewer resources than they do, but I'll never settle. I'd prefer to go bankrupt.'

'Are you serious?'

'Absolutely. To give a woman like that the satisfaction of a public apology in open court? I'd never do it. Never.'

'Well, you must be safe now, given that one can't libel the dead,' said Willow, wondering if the ending of a libel case could ever be a motive for murder.

She herself always went to great lengths to invent names for her characters so that she could not accidentally use the name of some real person who might sue her. Always terrified of the possibility, like many authors of melodramas she tended to give her villains names that verged on the incredible. 'Caliban Smythy' was the worst of the twisted scoundrels in her entire *oeuvre*. The thought of libel had always frightened her, and it seemed that Posy shared some of the fear, even if in her it was overlain with anger.

'I'm not certain that I am safe yet,' said Posy distinctly.

Seeing that Willow looked doubtful, the journalist went on:

'I talked to a legal friend yesterday and he said he thought libel cases could be inherited like negligence claims, which means that it isn't necessarily over at all.'

'Surely not!' Willow could not help thinking that if the stopping of a libel case were really a motive for murder, she had just heard the clumsiest possible defence. Posy was a journalist. She must know more about libel law than she was pretending.

'Well, that's what he said.' Posy was definite. 'I'll know for certain when the solicitor rings back. I never even thought of checking until Friday evening. The solicitors had all gone home by the time I rang, and so I fell back on the only friend I have in that world. He pointed out that the so-called libel took place while she was still alive and he seemed to think that it is just possible that her heirs will be able to inherit it. But he does commercial law, not libel, so I suppose he could be wrong.'

Yet again Willow was faced with an interviewee talking far

more than was necessary to answer one of her questions. Superficially Marilyn Posselthwate and Posy were quite different and yet both had exhibited surprising similiarities under questioning.

'But there's still hope.'

'Indeed. But I shan't withdraw what I wrote even if the family pursues the action. It had to be said. And if even one woman is made to think twice by what I wrote, it will all have been worth it. All of it,' said Posy looking at her watch. Willow obediently got to her feet.

'Thank you for talking to me,' she said. 'It's been illuminating.'

'I'm glad that you're intelligent enough to take criticism so well,' said Posy, making Willow smile. She herself had used that phrase or one very like it to preface any adverse comment she had had to make on members of her civil service staff. It had always pre-empted tantrums.

'I'll confess I thought your views of my book a bit exaggerated,' she said, 'even though they didn't lead me to telephone my solicitors.'

Posy's angry face softened slightly and she held out her hand. Willow shook it and walked down the shabby stairs to her car, thinking hard about Gloria Grainger and the effect she seemed to have had on all the people who came into contact with her.

5

WILLOW ARRIVED AT THE HOME Office the next morning determined to use her work for the committee to full advantage. She would be dealing with criminologists, forensic psychiatrists, prison governors and probably ex-offenders, too. One of them, at least, might be able to throw some light on the problem that was beginning to obsess her.

Why, exactly, had Gloria Grainger died? The chance heart attack no longer seemed completely credible to Willow. It had been just too convenient for too many people.

Dressed with elegance and austerity in a dark-grey Armani suit and a stone-coloured shirt, she took the lift up to the Home Secretary's office. Since she no longer had to pretend to be either poor or dowdy, Willow was also wearing her handmade gold earrings and a string of large, perfectly matched natural pearls. She had made up her face with as much care as if she were being photographed for the jacket of one of her books.

When she reached the Home Secretary's outer office, Willow was offered a chair and asked to wait. One of the private secretaries explained that Mrs Trouville had been involved in an urgent and unexpected meeting. Willow picked up a copy of the *Independent* and settled down to read it. Twenty minutes later she was allowed into the inner office.

Mrs Trouville greeted her warmly, but with enough calculation in her brown eyes to make Willow aware of just how much she had conceded. A tray of coffee was brought in and they discussed the chairman of the committee, a Professor Misterton of Bristol University, who was due to meet the secretariat later that day.

'It all seems rather hurried,' said Willow, raising one darkened eyebrow in defensive mockery. 'What if I had refused your blandishments and the job?'

Mrs Trouville merely smiled and told Willow that she had had an understudy available. Then they discussed those members of the committee who had already agreed to serve on it.

'It's both an impressive and imaginative group,' said Willow when she had run out of questions. 'Far fewer familiar names than I'd expected, but oughtn't we to have someone with experience of adult literacy teaching as well?'

'I'd have thought you could get enough information by using an outside expert, but do take it up with Professor Misterton if you like. It's his business not mine.'

There was a knock at the door and the Home Secretary's personal assistant put her head round the door to announce the arrival of Raymond Beete, the principal who had been seconded to assist Willow. Once Mrs Trouville had introduced them to each other, she asked the young man to take Willow to the offices that had been set aside for the secretariat.

'You'll find Sandra Bannett, the HEO, there and a filing clerk, whose name I don't know.'

'John Fund, Home Secretary,' said Raymond Beete.

'Fine,' said Willow.

'Let me know if you need anything,' said Mrs Trouville, picking up some papers from one of the trays on her desk and obviously withdrawing her concentration from them both.

Willow left with the young man, met the rest of her staff and laid down several rules about the management of their work for the committee and the research they were to put in train even before the first full meeting.

'I suspect we'll also need comparable information from the rest of Europe and Scandinavia, but that can wait,' she went on, pleased with the intelligence and apparent obedience of her small staff.

'I did a short ENA course last summer,' said Raymond, impressing Willow, who knew that only the brightest and the best of British civil servants were sent to the Ecole Nationale d'Aministration in Paris. 'And I've kept up some good contacts in France. Would you like me to ask them for information?'

'That would be splendid,' said Willow, thinking that he was going to be a useful member of her team. 'We'll have to talk to the civil liberties people, too, if we're to achieve the Home Secretary's aim of making sure no one leaves prison unable to read. Forcible education is unlikely to go down well.'

At the end of the meeting, Willow felt that she had good reason to trust her staff and she even smiled at them as she said:

'I ought to go and visit a prison fairly soon and see the governor and get myself familiar with what goes on. Can one of you talk to the Directorate of Prisons and find out which one, close to or in London, would be best?'

'Certainly,' said Raymond. 'Once we've got the trainee the Home Secretary has promised, he can do that.'

'Is there somewhere we can get hold of you on the days you don't come in to the office?' asked Sandra. 'Just in case it should prove necessary.'

Reluctantly, Willow gave them her telephone number in Chesham Place and then went with Raymond to the room where the committee was to meet. The professor from Bristol had not arrived and she sat at the long, polished table, checking everything she had asked her staff to do and asking questions every so often, which Raymond usually answered decisively.

They both stood up as the door opened and a tall, loose-limbed man in his fifties came in, unwinding a yellow scarf from about his neck.

'Miss King?' he said politely.

'Yes, but do please call me Willow,' she said, shaking his hand. 'And this is Raymond Beete.'

'Excellent. I have had good reports of both of you from Elsie, so I'm sure we'll get on all right. She's told you about the people I've got to serve on the committee?'

'Yes,' said Willow, who approved of the chairman's directness and refusal to waste time.

'That tone sounds as though you don't like all of them,' said the professor, looking at Willow out of the corners of his grey eyes. He took off his overcoat and added it to the scarf he had draped over the back of a chair. Willow was amused to see that he had not bothered to put on a suit, but was wearing old corduroy trousers and a tweed jacket over a woollen waistcoat.

'Not necessarily, but I skipped through Harriet Stabe's book a while ago and I can't help thinking that her rage may make her a tricky member of the committee – possibly even uncontrollable.'

The professor grimaced and looked much younger.

'That's rather why I want her. It's easy for these commissions and committees to become too cosy together and never produce anything worth while. I expect ours will have some lively arguments, but I'm hoping that out of the irritation will . . . '

'Come a pearl?' suggested Willow as he hesitated. He bowed slightly and she could not be sure whether he had heard her sarcasm or not. Just in case he had she went on quickly to report what Raymond and the others had been asked to do and that she proposed to visit a prison as soon as her staff had selected one and made an appointment with the governor.

'That is,' she added politely, 'if you have no objection. I won't talk about the committee.'

'I don't think it would matter much if you did,' he said.

'Good. Now if Raymond can sort out some coffee, perhaps we can settle one or two fundamentals. Is that all right with you?'

The professor nodded and sat two chairs away from Willow. He put his hands on the table and looked expectant. She took him through a possible plan of work, with suggested meeting dates, designed to achieve a draft report within six months. He listened, commented and eventually nodded.

'That sounds very sensible. Of course it can't become a strait-jacket. Until we've started, we won't know how much time we'll need.'

'No,' agreed Willow, 'but without a firm timetable things tend to get very slack and committee members do sometimes let their other work get in the way.'

'I can see you're a hard woman.'

'Just used to government committees,' she said with a faint smile.

After an hour's concentrated work, she felt reasonably sanguine about Professor Misterton's chairmanship and, looking at Raymond, saw that he too was displaying qualified approval. She asked the professor whether he needed anything else and, when he shook his head, said:

'You've clearly had quite a lot of experience of the effects of prison on lifers. Do you know much about what got them into trouble in the first place? I mean what caused them to kill?'

The professor looked more interested than he had during their discussions of the hazards of committee work.

'Anger, misery, drink, testosterone, crack, greed, fear or stupidity,' he said. 'Not necessarily in that order.'

'I actually meant the more immediate cause – the motive, if you like.'

'It's sometimes hard to disentangle the motive from a motivator like alcohol, but it's usually: she slept with the other bloke; he insulted me (in some way); he was in my way; I don't get enough respect; it was the only way out; I wanted a new car and it was the only way to get the money.

That sort of thing. Mean, stupid, greedy and a hellish waste of two lives.'

'I see. Depressing.'

'It's certainly that. If Elsie's plans can do anything to make ex-inmates think long enough to stop them killing again I'm all for it.'

'Yes,' said Willow, 'I agree. Will you let Sandra know if you need me before we next meet? She'll keep us in touch.'

Professor Misterton got out of his chair, and they shook hands.

'You're right. Time to be getting on. I'm due to lunch with Elsie. I'll see you the week after next.'

The two civil servants waited until he had gone before turning towards each other.

'I think we'll be able to cope with him, don't you?' said Willow.

'I think so, although I'm not too impressed with his memory,' answered Raymond.

'I don't see how you can judge that already.'

'He was my supervisor for my thesis,' said Raymond. 'I often used to wonder whether he was paying me any attention at all. Now I know he wasn't.'

'Perhaps he was merely being tactful. If Mrs Trouville approves of him, I can't imagine him being fuzzy-minded, can you? One thing I had meant to talk to him about is whether his understanding of her agenda is the same as mine.'

'Surely it must be. She wants everyone coming out of prison to have the education they refused or were denied in childhood.'

'That's certainly what I gathered, but it's possible that there are other aspects to what she wants. Knowing her as a friend, he may have picked up more than we did. I'll take him out to lunch after the next meeting and grill him then.'

'Poor man,' said Raymond and then hastily corrected himself. 'I mean the grilling not the lunch.'

'That's quite all right.' Willow felt her face and voice growing cool.

'Well, I'd better get on,' said Raymond, clearly having

registered her withdrawal. 'I'll let you know when arrangements have been made with a suitable prison.'

'Thank you,' said Willow with a vivid memory of the few times she had crossed the threshold of a prison. She slapped her papers into order and put them away in a folder. 'I'll see you next week. I rely on you to haul me in here if anything crops up before then.'

He left her alone with her thoughts about violent crime and the people who commit it. There was obviously anger. That went without saying. But there had to be more to it. A great many people suffered ferocious rage without resorting to violence. Someone had once written about the vanity of criminals who believed that the satisfaction of their feelings was an adequate reason to kill, while Elsie Trouville believed that they lacked the imagination necessary to understand what they were actually doing to their victims.

Both could be true of the sort of men Tom had talked about on Saturday evening, but Willow thought that there must be something more, some kind of panic, perhaps, that drove them to believe the only way out of their difficulties – or fear – was to kill.

Leaving the building, Willow once more acknowledged her private gratitude for her seduction by the Home Secretary. She crossed the park and walked up Piccadilly to look in at Hatchards and buy a selection of psychoanalytic books about the formation of criminals and about the therapies that might prevent recidivism. Selecting them almost at random on the basis of their titles and blurbs, she took ten to the cash desk and paid by credit card.

Back in her flat, much later than she had expected, she discovered that Mrs Rusham had not thrown away the lunch she had cooked but merely put it in the bottom oven of the Aga. Willow ate it, hardly noticing what it was, as she flicked through each of the books in turn. As she did so, she felt renewed in her longstanding mistrust of psychology and longed for something with harder edges and more testable hypotheses.

According to the blurbs on the back of the books, each had been written by a leader in the field, and yet many of them were wholly contradictory, and others made great leaps from one fact to another unconnected by anything Willow could recognise as logic. To her the most convincing of the theses was one about cycles of deprivation and adults' compulsion to recreate the situations in which they themselves were damaged as children.

Prepared to accept the theory and at the same time depressed, Willow drank a cup of coffee. Memories of the emotional coldness that had been imposed on her own childhood danced into her mind before she could stop them.

Shutting the last of the books with a snap, Willow refused to think about herself and decided to concentrate on Gloria Grainger's life and character instead. She picked up the telephone receiver and dialled.

'Eve? It's Willow here,' she said as soon as her agent's secretary had connected them.

'Excellent. How's the synopsis going?'

'Slowly. But it's about that I want to consult you. Posy Hacket.'

'Yes?'

'You know she was being sued by Gloria.'

'Yes. It was I who told you that.' Eve's monosyllables were becoming impatient.

'So you did. How did Posy's career begin?'

'I've no idea. Why? What relevance has that got?'

'None, unless she was once employed by Gloria, say as a secretary? Gloria seems to have treated all her staff quite roughly and the article might have been a long-delayed act of revenge.'

Eve laughed and there was the familiar sound of a lighter's click.

'No. Gloria's secretaries have rarely progressed beyond that role, apart that is from Samantha Hooper.'

'No! I never knew that. Gloria must have been sick with rage as she saw Hooper climbing the bestseller lists just as she was beginning to descend.'

'I know. She stayed just long enough with Gloria to learn how not to do it, disappeared from the book trade's sight entirely for a few years and then emerged to all that glittering success.'

'Clever old her. I wonder,' said Willow, half to herself, 'whether that was why Gloria was so keen to stamp on Marilyn's ambitions.'

'Is that all?' The impatience was back in Eve's voice.

'Yes, I think so. Perhaps I ought to try to work something into the memoir about Gloria's having given Hooper her first lessons in writing.'

There was a short bark of laughter from the other end of the telephone.

'She wouldn't thank you and you might need her one day for a selling quote on one of yours.'

'Cynic,' said Willow.

'I've always thought that was a necessary qualification for a good agent. I hope the synopsis goes well. Let me know if you need anything. Good bye.' Eve put down her receiver too smartly for Willow, who said her farewells into an unresponsive telephone.

She was impatient to get to grips with Gloria's real character and found herself wishing that she could consult her subject. Willow could not forget her first, immediate identification with the dead writer and wanted to know what she herself had thought about her subordinates and why she had bullied them so badly.

Remembering reports of various police forces employing psychics, Willow had a mental picture of herself surrounded by ectoplasm and spirit voices giving her the longed-for clues, and she laughed. There were still plenty of earthly sources of information to be tapped and she decided to tackle the nearest.

Ann Slinter had invited her to look through the old files of Gloria's dealings with the firm during her heyday and so, having checked that there was still enough time that day to make the expedition worthwhile, Willow summoned a taxi to take her to Weston & Brown.

6

A GLOOMY MAN CALLED TOBY was in charge of the post room at Weston & Brown. To Willow's surprise it was he who came to fetch her from the small reception area after she had given her name to the receptionist. Toby escorted Willow into the big basement post room, where he pointed to a large heap of dusty files that had been laid out on a waist-high table.

'Shall I get a stool for you?' he asked. 'There are some.'

'That might help,' said Willow, looking at the long packing tables, the piles of books, grey woven plastic mail sacks, rolls of corrugated cardboard and heaps of used padded envelopes. The whole depressing scene was lit by horrible flickering fluorescent lights that hung from the ceiling in long, dusty tubes. 'Is this really the only place in the whole building where I can read the files?'

'They're short of space upstairs, you know, since they rented out the top floor last year. Mrs Slinter told me to give you the files here.'

'I see,' said Willow, taking off her overcoat and reluctantly hanging it on a hook on the back of the door. 'The recession must be worse than I thought.'

For the next two hours she read through the files,

discovering nothing very much except that the copies of royalty statements proved that Gloria's sales had once been truly enormous. Her letters showed that bad temper and ferocious demands had been characteristic throughout her dealings with the firm. Willow's sympathy for Ann's original reaction to the news of Gloria's death waxed with every letter she read and her identification with the dead novelist waned.

In the middle of reading a long diatribe about the abysmal quality of the proof-reading of her latest book, Willow became conscious of an altercation behind her. She swivelled on her uncomfortable stool and saw a gangly, dark-haired woman in her late thirties standing before Toby and holding out a pile of padded bags.

'But they have to go out tonight,' she said and flinched as Toby banged his fist down on the packing table. 'I've done them all up and stuck the labels on. Honestly, all they need is weighing and franking. I'll take them across to the post office myself if you haven't time.'

'I've told all you girls before,' said Toby furiously, 'that nothing gets posted that comes in here after four-thirty. You all know that. How am I expected to do everything? My life is hard enough without you lot always being late. I'm due off in half an hour. You'll have to wait till tomorrow.'

'But they must go out tonight, Toby. I was up till one this morning sorting out most of the queries. I couldn't do the last few until this afternoon and I couldn't get them to you any quicker. You . . .'

'No. I've told you I can't.' Toby seized the parcels and flung them to the far end of his bench. Willow thought that the woman was about to burst into tears. Instead she gripped her lips together and left the packing room, her shoulders rounded and her neck poking forwards like a dejected turkey's.

Willow quickly turned back to her files, reluctant to be seen as a voyeur of Toby's fury. It crossed her mind that the woman he had vanquished could have been Gloria's hapless editor. There had been something about her and the way she walked that shrieked 'victim' and reminded Willow of Posy Hacket's depressing analysis of the people who had gravitated to Gloria.

Reaching the end of the last file twenty minutes later, Willow closed it and looked at her grimy hands in disgust.

'Toby,' she called, 'I'm filthy. Is there anywhere I can wash?'

'Yes. Through that door . . . Hello, hello. What's all this then?'

Willow stood up and eased her cramped muscles, watching a pretty young woman in jeans walk up to Toby with her arms full of parcels.

'You know quite well I can't deal with those after half four,' said Toby in a voice that suggested resignation rather than the fury that had erupted over the earlier visitor.

'I know,' answered the girl with a sexy smile, 'but Ann will kill me if they don't go off. They're all for the States and they're overdue as it is. Please, darling Toby, please. Just to save my bacon? You know you like doing it really. And I absolutely depend on you.'

'You make my life impossible,' he said gruffly.

'Oh, thank you, Toby. You really are an angel. You love it really, don't you? And me.' She dumped the pile of packages on his table, patted his arm and danced away.

'There's a cloakroom through here on the left,' said Toby to Willow. He seemed to notice some surprise or perhaps criticism in her face for he added: 'Mrs Slinter's secretary is always doing that, you know. It's just bad organisation. She means no harm.'

Willow removed herself from the sound of his excuses and washed the dust off her hands. There was a mirror hanging above the basin and she saw to her horror that there was also dust mixed with the makeup on her forehead and down one cheek. Returning to the post room for her handbag, she washed off all the cosmetics, dried her face and started again. Restored to dignity, she asked Toby whether she could borrow his telephone to call Mrs Slinter.

'Hello, it's Willow here,' she said when the managing

director answered. 'I'm down in your post room, having been through the files, and I wondered whether I could have a word with you?'

'Yes, do. Come up and have a drink,' said Ann hospitably.

Willow, thinking that life in publishing seemed remarkably relaxed and comfortable compared with the real world, took the creaking lift up to the second floor and found Ann Slinter drawing the cork of a bottle of claret.

'Come on in. Glass of wine all right for you?'

'Lovely. It's jolly civilised to have a cellar in your office.'

Ann laughed.

'One of the few privileges of running the place. We had an alcoholic editor once and ever since then the staff contract has stipulated that no alcohol may be kept or consumed in the office. But the managing director is above those sorts of rules, and I intend to take full advantage of my new status.'

'I can understand that,' said Willow, thinking of the immense contrast between Ann's casually elegant clothes and the harrassed, shambolic appearance presented by the first of the parcel-carrying women, or even her pretty jeans-clad successor. That afternoon Ann was wearing another of her full skirts, this time the colour of redcurrants, and a loosely knitted silk sweater as glossy and smooth as peach flesh.

'Now what can I do for you? Your book or poor Gloria?'

'Poor Gloria,' said Willow, trying not to smile. '*Nil nisi bonum*, won't do, you know. I need real information. True information.'

'I suppose you do. She really was the most dreadful woman.'

'So everyone keeps telling me,' said Willow, thinking of the complaints she had just been reading, 'although I have yet to be completely convinced. It's making the direction of the memoir rather hard to work out.'

Ann clasped her long fingers together round her knee, showing off her well-manicured nails.

'What we really want, I suppose,' she said judiciously, 'is for you to behave like a pathologist. She's dead and you've got to find out where the health was in her life and where the disease: dissect it all, you know.'

Willow contemplated her self-consciously elegant publisher, eyebrows raised.

'That's a superficially neat analogy,' she said. 'But it doesn't mean very much and it still leaves me with the problem that the only good things I've been able to discover so far are that Gloria was generous to her charlady and that she had remarkably good taste in furniture.'

'You've been to the house then,' said Ann with a stiffness that showed how much she had disliked Willow's criticism. 'I know. I used to wonder as each book came punctually to my desk in the old days how anyone with such taste in one direction could produce such frightful novels.'

'And yet you continued to publish them. Why?'

'In those days I had very little option. I was merely the junior editor who was stuck with them. And more recently . . . ' She broke off and looked at Willow rather guiltily.

'Well?'

'You look like a judge sitting there in that dark suit,' said Ann crossly.

'I spent the morning at the Home Office. Tell me why you went on publishing her. I'm interested.'

Ann got up and opened a locked drawer in her desk. She shuffled through some papers and then returned with a letter, which she handed to Willow.

'I've kept it as a kind of "it-wasn't-my-fault-guv'nor" excuse in case I were ever to be challenged,' said Ann with a self-deprecatory smile. 'It just shows how wet even the strongest of us can be, doesn't it?'

Willow nodded, agreeing that Ann was among the strongest of women, and looked down at the letter.

My dear Gerald,
   I think you ought to know that Ann is trying to prevent my books from being published. She has some extraordinary ideas about this wicked nonsense of feminism

and is determined to use your carefully built publishing list to see them spread throughout the country, destroying the natural modesty and self-sacrifice of English girls.

Only you can influence her and I beg you to step in, not simply for my benefit but also for the good of the firm, its employees, and the young girls growing up in this dreadful world of ours.

I know that you, who have always understood me so well, will stop her from this disastrous step.

Ever yours, my dear Gerald, Gloria

'Who on earth is her dear Gerald?' asked Willow, looking up from the remarkable letter in her hand.

'I told you about him when we spoke on the telephone on Saturday.'

'Oh, so you did. I'd forgotten. Plimpton, wasn't it?'

'That's right. He was the chairman here when I started, and I owe him a lot, not least for backing me right at the beginning of my career.'

'And so he made you go on publishing her,' said Willow vaguely as she thought of Posy's anger. In the light of Gloria's letter it seemed somehow more reasonable, as though the two women had been waging a real battle of principle. If Gloria's books had been written to promulgate a particular point of view, then Posy's critcism seemed more justified, as did her passionate anger.

'He could hardly *make* me do it,' said Ann stiffly. 'He persuaded me by reminding me that the books don't cost much to produce because they're so short and we use such cheap paper and "perfect binding"; that they still sell just about enough – if you count subsidiary rights income as well as sales – to cover their share of the overhead; and that whatever I think of them I ought to remember that they once paid my wages and kept the firm going.'

'But you loathe them, don't you?'

'Oh, yes; and they've begun to get quite childish. But Vicky Taffle manages to reduce them to something approximating correct English, and makes sure that the plots are not too obviously repeats of earlier books, that the characters have different names and so on.'

'And then, presumably,' said Willow with a guilty memory of her own furious response to some crass editing, 'she has to persuade Gloria that the changes were necessary and make her agree to them.'

'Exactly.' Ann laughed with enough sharpness to remind Willow that she, too, had once been a junior editor squashed between intransigent superiors and demanding authors. 'Drink up. We ought to finish the bottle now it's open.'

Willow finished her glassful.

'Why did you bestow Gloria on Ms Taffle? From what you said the other day she doesn't sound tough enough to cope with anyone as difficult.'

Ann busied herself finding a packet of nuts and decanting them into a small glass bowl. As she offered it to her guest, she said:

'You're right, of course, but I thought it might toughen her up. She's competent enough but she has no confidence and she won't get any further without that. I thought discovering she could cope with Gloria might give it to her.'

'But it hasn't?'

'No. She's dealt with the old bag for four years now and it hasn't made any difference. It's thoroughly depressing and I'd like to get rid of her, but it wouldn't really be fair to sack her just because she gives me the shivers. She's had one of those burdened, virtuous lives: looked after an elderly parent and all that sort of thing. And she is jolly useful in some ways.'

Willow remembered Eve's remarks about the habits of bullies and said nothing. For the first time it occurred to her that Ann, too, might have the makings of a bully in her.

'I wish we'd never had to give her the title of commissioning editor,' Ann went on with a sigh. 'Her judgement is all right most of the time, oddly enough, but she can't ever defend it or promote the books she works on. She was a good solid line editor, but she really is a walking disaster as far as strength of personality goes and that matters once you start acquiring books. We still use her for line editing, but it makes her restive and she tries to behave like the other commissioning editors with embarrassing results.'

'Poor child,' said Willow, recognising the ruthlessness that must have helped Ann rise so effortlessly above the other editors of her age.

'She's hardly that. I shouldn't think she's much more than five years younger than you or me. She's been here nearly as long as I have.'

Willow looked at Ann. Silently she said, ah, yes, but you are attractive, confident, glamorous and admired, which is why you despise her so much. Remembering her own days as a dowdy object of contempt, Willow thought she might give Victoria Taffle a hand in her battle with the managing director.

'Right,' said Willow aloud, 'I probably oughtn't to say any of this to you without clearing it with Eve first, but I honestly don't think I'm going to be able to stretch my meagre material over a full ninety-six pages. With a little help from Gloria's relations I hope I can say something about her generosity, and then give a résumé of her career, and perhaps quote a little from the old publicity files and a few of the books; oh, yes and talk about her house. Did she do much entertaining in it?'

'A fair amount. She had some friends among the great and the good, whom she valued highly; perhaps because her origins were so very unestablishment.'

'Why didn't I think of that before? The niece is clearly not part of the establishment. It could help enormously. Using talent (unspecified) to transform a drab existence. Wonderful. Where did she come from?'

'Reading, I understand. I know very little, but presumably Marilyn would be able to tell you more.'

'Yes, I'll have to see her again in any case. Well, thank you, Ann; you have helped. I'll have a word with Eve and get you a synopsis with an adjusted word count before the end of the week. Is that all right?'

'Fine. A last glass to finish the bottle?'

'I'd better not. I thought I'd pop along and see if I could take Ms Taffle out to dinner and pick her brains a bit.' Seeing a look of astonishment on Ann's face, Willow added: 'Is that a problem for you?'

Another faint flush stained the perfect cheekbones.

'Whatever you wish, of course. I just hope it doesn't give her ideas above her station to be dining with one of our most popular writers. Do you know her office? It's the last one on the far side of the lightwell.'

Willow's eyes had grown hard, but she thanked Ann for the drink and the advice with adequate politeness. Making her way along the tortuous passages to the small, dark office where Victoria Taffle sorted out the inconsistencies and infelicities of her authors' work, Willow felt she could imagine what the woman's life was like sandwiched between their tantrums and Ann Slinter's disdain.

When Willow put her head round the door of the office, she was not surprised to see the lanky, dark, plain woman whose appeal Toby had so violently refused. Her eyes were reddened either from that encounter or from too much reading in a poor light, but there was a surprisingly satisfied smile on her face.

'Hello,' said Willow from the doorway.

Victoria looked up, frowned, sniffed, and then smiled more nervously as she stood up.

'I suspect you don't generally have time for lunch since you're so busy,' said Willow, confident that the woman would know who she was, 'and so I've come to haul you out of your den for some dinner and a short consultation about Gloria Grainger. Clearly Ann is working you far too hard, but I need your help. Will you come?'

'I ought really to get home when I've done this. I mean it's terribly kind of you, but I ought to get back. It's a rather long journey. Besides, I've still got two enormous manuscripts to read for the editorial meeting tomorrow.'

'Too bad. Telephone home to say you can't come quite yet.' Willow smiled. 'Tell them that yet another tiresome author is demanding your attention and read the first, the middle and the last chapter of each manuscript over breakfast in the morning. I'm sure that's what most editors do.'

When Victoria said nothing, Willow added:

'I'll go next door and ring up to book us a table.'

Departing without giving Victoria another chance to protest, or perhaps to have to explain that there was no one at home to care whether she returned or not, Willow tried to think of a truly luxurious restaurant where the editor's clothes would not look out of place. She remembered a tiny French brasserie on the northern edge of Covent Garden, which Tom had found, where the cooking was remarkably good, the atmosphere gentle, and the clientele quite prepared to put up with eccentricity. Taking a telephone book from a shelf behind the empty desk, Willow found the number and made sure that a table would be kept for her in ten minues.

Victoria Taffle protested once again when Willow reappeared in the office, but she refused to listen and whisked them both out of the building, where she hailed a passing taxi. When they were sitting on the back seat, strapped in by the new – and quite merciless – seat belts, Willow said gently:

'Something tells me that you haven't been treated very well recently and Ann certainly puts too much on you. I thought that perhaps I could kill two birds with one stone: pick your brains about Gloria for my memoir and, as a representative of the hated authors, make up to you a bit for what we've all done to you.'

'You're very kind,' said Victoria, but she did not sound grateful, merely depressed.

Eleven minutes later the two of them were sitting on opposite sides of a table in the soft light of the restaurant, sipping their drinks and reading the menu. Willow had ordered mineral water for herself and *kir* for Victoria.

'I think I'm probably going to have the lobster,' said Willow musingly in order to show her guest that she need not consider the price of what she ordered, 'and something first, but I'm not sure what. What about you?'

Victoria's menu hit the table with a snap as she dropped it.

'You're being terribly kind,' she said, looking more intelligent than she had before. 'I'd love to have the lobster too, if that's really all right.'

'Good. And to start?'

'Perhaps the pigeon-breast salad?'

'Good idea,' said Willow as she consulted the wine list. When the waitress reappeared Willow ordered the food, half a bottle of simple claret to drink with the salads and half a bottle of stunning white burgundy for the lobster.

'Now tell me,' she said, 'about life in publishing. I'm beginning to think I've had an altogether erroneous idea about it. It's always seemed rather . . . '

'Glamorous?' suggested Victoria bitterly. 'Most outsiders think that, but it's quite the reverse for us. Some of the authors are different, of course. They do have glamorous lives.'

'Actually, I was going to say "leisured". I gather I was wrong.'

'Good heavens yes! You obviously can't imagine what it's like. The actual productive work on the manuscripts is really laborious and has to be done with maximum concentration. You can rarely achieve that in the office, so you have to do it at home. Only nowadays working at home on Wednesdays, which always used to be the routine, is frowned on so you have to do it at night and at the weekend. If you try to do it where people can interrupt and telephone, you tend to make idiotic mistakes that make people furious. You get blamed by the authors if you change things they particularly like, but if any mistakes are left in the finished book, you get blamed for that too. The author who made the mistakes in the first place never comes in for a reprimand, or hardly ever.'

'Are you sure?' asked Willow, unconvinced by Victoria's paranoia. 'That seems most unjust.'

'Oh, yes, I'm sure. Haven't you read those reviews that say things like X has been ill-served by his editor who really ought to have known that fourteenth-century Chinese merchants always wore yellow shoes, or whatever it is. It really isn't fair.' Her face had more colour in it and her reddened eyes looked much more alert.

'How are we supposed to be experts on everything we have to edit? Most non-fiction editors have to tackle everything from self-help to . . . oh, anything: diet, plumbing, needlework, archaeology, psychiatry, all sorts of historical figures whose biographies are published, the decorative arts and so on.'

'But surely for most of those you'd have specialist referees at least.'

'Not these days, I'm afraid,' said Victoria laughing in a patronising way that made Willow's sympathy falter for a moment. 'There's never the money for that, or the time usually. I suppose academic books are still read for facts, but we don't publish technical stuff: just ordinary non-fiction.'

'Are there no compensations?' asked Willow curiously just as the pigeon-breast salads were laid in front of them.

'Oh yes,' answered Victoria, 'there are. There are some truly professional authors – usually the ex-journalists – who are positively pleasant to deal with. And just occasionally there's a book that I really like; not often, but, say, once a year.'

She cut a piece off one of the slices of pigeon and speared it with her fork. Holding it half-way between her plate and her mouth, she added:

'I suppose what I hate most about it is being held responsible for the awfulness of the books I've worked on when I had no say in having them taken on in the first place and have hated them all along. That and having to explain to the authors of mediocre books why we're not spending anything on publicity and that they've sold only about two copies since publication, or – worse – that we've had an average of fifty returns a week. That's utter hell. And when they ask plaintively whether one likes their book, that's worse still. Because of course one doesn't – usually.'

'Oh dear, oh dear,' said Willow, unable to suppress a smile. 'How little we authors know of the anguish our books cause.'

Victoria ate the piece of pigeon and then reloaded her fork with salad.

'You know, it may sound exaggerated, but "anguish" is the right word. It's real torture sometimes.'

She put the salad in her mouth and when she had finished chewing she smiled. For once she ceased to look victimised.

'I must admit that I have thought of writing a kind of survival guide for authors with a glossary of all the codes we use.'

'Such as?' Willow was not certain she wanted to hear, but could not resist asking.

'Oh, things like: "We've shifted your publication date from September to February. We think the book will do better then." ' Victoria's tone had led Willow to feel extremely glad that her books were still published in September.

'And what does that mean?' she asked.

'That the book in question hasn't a hope of selling.' Victoria's eyes positively glittered with mischief and Willow knew that she was enjoying the vicarious revenge on the people who made her working life so hard. 'There are lots more, of course, but I won't bore you with them now.'

'I wouldn't be at all bored,' said Willow with feeling.

'All right. Then there's: "Your book is most beautifully written but it needs a braver publisher than us," which either means that we think it's pornographic or that it won't sell more than a couple of hundred copies. Or: "It doesn't quite work as a novel," which usually means "we don't think you can write for toffee." '

'I see that I'll have to listen for the unpalatable truth behind everything Ann says to me now.'

'Oh, you don't have to worry. Everyone approves of your books because they make money. And another thing: authors need to know why their editor changes from great enthusiasm after she's first read the book to qualified liking and then brooding silence.'

'Why?' asked Willow, watching the mischievous smile return to Victoria's face.

'Someone else, someone powerful in the sales department probably or the marketing director, has read the manuscript and sneered at it. When your editor is never there to answer her telephone and takes days to ring you back, then you know she's being personally criticised because of your awful book by all her colleagues.'

Her face had grown animated as she talked and she had begun to look alert and intelligent.

'Did you suffer from that over Gloria's books?' Willow asked.

'Not exactly. Everyone knew how much I hated them. But I did try to duck her telephone calls – with disastrous results.'

'Really?'

'Yes. I could never get any work done with her ringing up to complain twice a day or ask for the latest sales figures, but she soon wised up to what I was doing and demanded that I give her my home number.'

'You didn't, surely, do that?' said Willow.

'Well, she asked me point-blank if I was refusing to give it to her, and I simply couldn't say "yes". I thought of lying and giving her someone else's, but I realised it would just get worse and worse, so I did.'

'And did she ring you often at home?'

Just then the waitress came to take away their salad plates and return with the lobster, succulent pink-and-white slices lying in a pool of orange-yellow sauce, like a particularly luscious sunrise.

'God yes!' Victoria seemed unaware of the sensory delights of the food that had just been put in front of her. 'She sometimes rang at half-past six in the morning, because I'd got into the habit of leaving the phone ringing while I had breakfast, knowing it was probably her. She just took to ringing earlier and earlier each time.'

'That must have been difficult,' said Willow, looking at the other woman with both sympathy and a wild surmise. She mocked herself out of it at once. No one would commit a murder merely to stop early-morning nuisance calls. 'Couldn't you have stood up to her?'

Victoria looked at her with a horrible mixture of shame
and resentment in her grey eyes. After a while she shook her
head.

'No, it seems I couldn't. And I got so tired.'

'I can imagine, but at least you can sleep in peace now.'
Willow ate the first bite of her lobster and sat for a moment
with all thought suspended, simply tasting and feeling.

'Yes, but I'll probably lose my job,' said Victoria with what
Willow knew to be unwarranted pessimism.

She took a mouthful of food and quickly swallowed it
without apparently chewing or tasting any of it. Willow
thought that she might just as well have been Eeyore
miserably eating thistles, and had to suppress a smile.

'Why's that?' she asked.

'The only reason I was ever promoted was because Gloria
insisted on having a senior commissioning editor in charge
of her books. Ann and the others still treat me as a line
editor. They've been longing to keep me out of the editorial
meetings ever since I started going to them. None of the
other editors share my taste in novels and Ann never lets
me commission the non-fiction titles I want. They can't
demote me, so they'll probably sack me. And it's impossible
to get publishing jobs these days. There are literally
hundreds of experienced editors out of work.'

Beginning to feel impatient with such a deluge of gloom,
Willow had to admit to herself that Victoria was both
intelligent and quite realistic about her position and abilities.
Ann was right: her judgement was clearly sound despite her
lack of confidence. Willow quickly ate some of the
vegetables from a plate at her side and tried to help her
towards a little optimism.

'Well, perhaps you'll suddenly find a wonderful new
author who will save the firm in the way that Gloria once
did,' she said.

For once Victoria looked positively superior and completely sure of herself.

'You must be joking! For one thing no important agent is
going to send me any decent stuff, because they all want

Ann to handle it. Obviously her authors get bigger advances and bigger publicity budgets than any of ours, and so I only get offered dross that's been turned down by everyone else in London.'

'Perhaps if you cultivated some of the agents a bit, they'd send you better things. What about mine?'

'Eve Greville wouldn't send me anything she thought remotely publishable. And she's right, because if she ever did send me something, when I came to present it to the editorial meeting the others would all spit on it just because it is mine.'

Remembering Ann's saying that Victoria could never defend her own judgement, Willow tried once more to encourage her.

'Couldn't you persuade them? Explain to them why you're so keen on the book? In the civil service I quickly discovered that having the right ideas is less than half the battle: persuading colleagues to accept them is far more important.'

'All my colleagues despise my judgement, even though I'm usually proved right in the end. Then I remind them. But they hardly ever admit it.'

'But don't you try to persuade them in the beginning?'

After a moment's thought, Victoria said, sounding a little surprised:

'I don't suppose I do. I tell them what the book's about and why I think it's good and then if they're stupid enough not to see why we ought to buy it, it's their fault. Not that it happens often. Most of the books I get offered are such utter crap that I know why everyone else has turned them down.'

'Perhaps it's easier blaming your colleagues' poor judgement than fighting for your own?' suggested Willow, seeing why Ann found her subordinate so difficult to like. The long face tightened. Victoria finished her lobster and sat in obstructive silence.

'But none of that is really what I need to know,' said Willow with a smile, still wanting to show Victoria that she was contributing to her own miserable position in the pecking order and to offer her a way of improving it. 'Tell me about Gloria – not about her impossibleness, but about her character and her life. Do you know anything about her past?'

'Not much, but there was a story she used to tell to writers' groups and sales conferences and things, which went as follows: life at home was very bleak; no one understood her; her only pleasures were found in imaginary friendships with fictional characters in books she read; they were often unsatisfactory in one way or another and so she set about creating her own. It does make sense of a sort. First within the books and then in the life they bought for her she could be queen of all she surveyed.'

Willow nodded.

'Yes, that does make sense. I see that Ann is right about your good judgement.'

A doubting smile improved Victoria's face.

'Did she really say that? Ann Slinter? About me?'

'Yes. You see, Victoria, people do have more esteem for you than you seem to have for yourself. I think you need to work on that for a bit.'

There was silence as Victoria obviously battled with her dislike even of such tactful, well-meant criticism. Willow, who had her own similar loathing, felt profoundly grateful that her imagination had saved her from wallowing in a morass of pessimism and resentment like Victoria's.

As they left the restaurant, Willow said:

'Have you far to go? Would you like to share a taxi?'

'No, it's all right. I get the train from Euston. I can easily take the tube there from Leicester Square.'

'That's quite a hike from here. I'll take you in my cab.'

'No, it's all right. I like to walk.'

'Even in the dark with all the muggers around?' Willow was surprised; physical courage did not seem to fit in with her picture of Victoria.

'I'll be all right, really,' she said with one of her best smiles. 'I don't think that muggers frequent my route and no one's ever molested me yet and I do have one of those shrieky alarms and . . .'

'And?'

'And apparently they frighten both two- and four-legged predators. It's the dogs that make me most afraid.'

'I don't altogether blame you,' said Willow, watching an unleashed bull terrier walking demurely at the side of its owner.

'Don't they look cuddly?' said Victoria, shuddering.

'Not to me.'

Victoria thanked Willow for the dinner, adding:

'You've been very kind to me. I'd really love to work on one of your books, but I don't suppose Ann would ever let me.'

'I'll have a word with her,' promised Willow, thinking that Victoria would probably find something to dislike about her and her books pretty quickly. 'Perhaps you could edit the memoir.'

7

WHEN WILLOW GOT HOME THAT evening, depressed and irritable, she saw that there were four messages on her answering machine. Dropping her coat on one of the cream sofas, she pressed the replay button and listened.

'Willow? This is Eve. What's this Ann's just told me about your altering the length of the Gloria piece? We need to talk. Ring me first thing in the morning.'

Feeling rebellious, Willow made a note and then listened to a more hesitant voice:

'Oh, er, hello. This is Marilyn Posselthwate. We met when you came to talk to me about my aunt. I've been wondering . . . That is, would you like to come to her funeral? Her executor is back and has phoned me to explain all the things we've got to do for it. There's so much to be arranged that we can't have it until Friday.'

The contrast between that voice and the next was enough to bring a slight smile to Willow's tight face as she listened to Tom.

'Will, me here. Sorry for behaving like a bear. We still haven't enough for an arrest and I'll be working late tonight. But do ring me if you feel like it. Only if you want of course. I should be home by tenish.'

The last message made her smile widen.

'Willow? It's Richard Crescent. I haven't seen you for ages. What about dinner? Or that lovely play everyone talks about with a woman musing about her past in a convent? Or a nice violent film? Whatever. It would be great to see you.'

Ignoring Eve, because of the time, and the two men, Willow rang Marilyn Posselthwate.

'It's really kind of you to invite me to the funeral,' Willow said after she had introduced herself, 'but are you sure you want a stranger?'

'You're hardly that. After all Aunt Ethel's publishers want you to write about her and so it seems like a good idea. I've been phoning quite a lot of people to sort of make it worth doing all the things Aunt Ethel wanted. Quite a few have said they'll come, even Samantha Hooper.'

Willow smiled at the awe in Marilyn's voice.

'I'd heard she once worked for your aunt. I gather you like her books.'

'I think they're wonderful. They've got so much page-turn, don't you think?'

'I've only read two,' said Willow, amused by Marilyn's bit of publishing jargon, 'but I agree: they did keep me hooked from the first page to the last.'

'Well, will you come to the funeral?'

'I shall if I possibly can. What time will the service be and where?'

'Friday at three-thirty. Before that there's the official time for what the undertakers call viewing in the chapel of rest.' Marilyn's voice became much less hesitant as it sharpened into complaint. 'Apparently she insisted that she's to lie in state for two full days surrounded by about a million pounds' worth of hothouse flowers.'

'Goodness,' was all Willow could think of to say.

'The funeral will be in the church on the green here and she's to be buried at Mortlake,' said Marilyn more calmly. 'That bit's for family only. There'll be a formal tea here for everyone else while she's being actually buried and then champagne later.'

'It all sounds quite elaborate,' said Willow tentatively.

'I know. It's typical of Aunt Ethel to go over the top like this. And it's frightfully inconvenient for everyone.'

'She is dead, you know, Marilyn,' said Willow before she could stop herself.

'We wouldn't be being put through all this if she wasn't. But at least that'll be it. After Friday, she can't impose on any of us ever again.'

Listening to the satisfaction in Marilyn's voice, Willow wondered again if she could possibly be speaking to Gloria's murderer. There was absolutely no doubt that Marilyn was glad to be rid of her aunt, but was there any more to it than that?

'She always did want more than other people have,' Marilyn went on angrily. 'Two days in the chapel of rest, surrounded by a hundred lilies and even more roses. Special singers and musicians at the funeral. You'd have thought she was born royal or something, instead of working class.'

'Good heavens!' said Willow, interested in Marilyn's contempt. 'I've been wanting to ask you about her childhood. Did she talk about it much?'

'No.' Marilyn was either wholly uninterested or frustrated at having her complaints cut short.

'How odd.' Willow allowed her voice to drift upwards, making a question of her two words. The idea of cycles of abuse filtered into her mind again.

'Not really. She despised her whole family. I suppose that's why she hated me so much. She tried to forget she ever came from a two-up two-down in Reading. I wish I'd had the power to fix the funeral. I'd have had her buried back there quick as a flash.'

'I see,' said Willow, feeling her sympathies for Gloria returning fast. She herself would never return to Newcastle if she could help it and well understood Gloria's desire to leave her past behind. 'I'm getting some idea of how to pitch my memoir of her, but I did wonder if I could come and talk to her secretary some time soon.'

'Well, yes, if you like.' It was odd how pleasant Marilyn's voice could sound when she was not talking about her aunt.

'Come any time. Patty and Susan will both be here again tomorrow, because Susan is still handing over all the things she did while Patty was ill.'

'Thank you. I'm not quite sure when I'll be able to get to Kew, but if you don't mind the uncertainty, we could leave it that I'll be with you some time tomorrow.'

'That's fine. Goodnight.'

'Oh, by the way?'

'Yes?'

'What is the name of the executor who rang you up?'

'Gerald Plimpton.'

'Aha. I see. Thank you, Marilyn. The other thing I was going to ask is whether you think your father would be prepared to talk to me about your aunt's childhood.'

'I don't suppose he'd mind,' said Marilyn still sounding quite pleasant. 'But he has no phone. He will be at the funeral tea on Friday so you could talk to him then. Okay?'

'Fine. Thank you. Good bye.'

Willow thought that at last she might be able to get some useful information. Ann Slinter had told her that Gerald Plimpton cared about Gloria, and, as her executor, he would be in a position to disclose all sorts of useful facts about her estate and her heirs.

Knowing that it would be useless to ring Ann's office at that time of night and determined not to be the kind of unbearable author who telephoned her publisher at home, Willow put down the receiver and wandered into her writing room, thinking about Gloria Grainger and her household.

'From Reading Slum to Kew Green' seemed a possible title for the memoir, but when she had written it down, Willow frowned in distaste.

'Dull and clumsy,' she said aloud.

After several other attempts she came up with 'Beauty and the Beast', which had just the kind of ambiguity she liked. It summed up not only the basic plot of Gloria's novels but also played with the paradox of the beautiful house and the misery that her tyranny seemed to have created in it.

95

Smiling once more, Willow removed the plastic covers from her computer, switched it on, and opened a new file under that title. Blinking at the black-and-white screen, she tapped in private headings for the four sections into which she was planning to divide her piece: The Climb; The Pinnacle; The Descent; The Accusation.

The cursor flickered under the last letter and she wished that she could remember more about the fairy tale. There must be more relevant headings to be drawn from it, she thought. Planning to pick up a collection of folk tales next time she was in a large bookshop, Willow shrugged and filed the insignificant document.

When the screen was blank once again, she typed the headings for another document, which was beginning to interest her far more than the memoir: Suspects, Motives, Opportunities, Means, Alibis.

Having thought about the headings for a moment, Willow entered the names of Marilyn and Posy with their possible motives. They might both seem unlikely killers, but the possibility that Gloria had been murdered by someone was coming to seem more and more likely. Too many people had been glad to hear of her death. Too many of them had benefitted by it.

It was frustrating not to be able discuss the case with Tom, Willow thought, as she stared at her empty columns, and even more frustrating not to be able to interrogate her suspects openly. Eventually she filed her embryonic report of the case and, remembering that she had not told Mrs Rusham that she would be out for dinner, went to see what she had left in the Aga.

Having discovered an interesting variation on the traditional shepherd's pie in the bottom oven, Willow rescued it. Seeing how shrivelled and black it had become, she scraped it into the kitchen bin and put the encrusted dish into the sink to soak. When she had finished, she made herself a cup of mint tea.

She took it into the drawing room and tried to ring Tom as he had asked her to do. His machine answered her call.

' "Tenish" seems to have been an underestimate,' she said into it as nicely as possible. 'I hope that means you've got your confession. I'm after one, too. I'm perfectly certain now that I was right. It is quite possible that Gloria Grainger was deliberately killed.' Willow thought for a few seconds as the tape wound silently on and then added crisply: 'It'll be like old times to swap notes of our successful interrogations. See you soon. 'Bye.'

She cut the connection and then telephoned Richard Crescent. He answered in person.

'Richard, it's Willow.'

'My dear, how nice! How are you?'

'Not bad at all even though I've let Elsie Trouville talk me into doing a job for her at the Home Office when I ought to have freed myself from all that by now.'

Richard laughed.

'And I always thought you were tough enough to withstand anything.'

'I've always been able to deal with bullying and contempt,' said Willow, 'but she used reasoned admiration and I've discovered I'm a sucker for that. What about you?'

'Oh, give me reasoned admiration any time.'

'Idiot! You know I didn't mean that.'

'I know.' Richard was still snuffling with laughter. Then his voice changed as he went on: 'I'm fine really. Little Emma and I have discovered we don't share quite as much as we once thought we did. The whole situation is marginally bleak. We'll both survive it, I suppose.'

I see, thought Willow, remembering the way Richard had succumbed to young Emma Gnatche's longstanding heroworship. So that's why you're ringing me. Aloud she said:

'Poor old you. Well I'm delighted to help you get over it, although I'm not too keen on the idea of a violent film.'

'Nor you are. Silly of me. It was Em who liked them; I've never understood why. What would you like to do?'

'Perhaps just dine and catch up?' she suggested before remembering the gaps in her knowledge of what might have happened to Gloria Grainger. 'Oh, no. What I'd really like most of all is to meet a barrister. D'you know any well?'

'Not again!' Richard sighed theatrically. 'Willow, you are the worst exploiter I've ever come across. Here am I, longing to retrieve our old friendship, and you just want me to get at some information for you. Wretch!'

'But you do know a barrister, don't you? You must. They're just your sort of people.'

'I have come across one or two, mainly at the commercial bar. What do you want one for?'

'Libel.'

Richard roared with laughter again.

'You're not telling me that you're being sued over one of your *romans de concierge*, are you?'

'Certainly not.' Willow sounded careful of her dignity. 'But I do want to find out about it.'

'There's a chap called Sebastian Borden I know a bit; he prosecuted a libel case last year, even though it's not his speciality. Would he do?'

'He sounds fine.'

'Okay. I'll fix something – probably a drink at El Vino's – with him and ring you back. You will dine with me afterwards, won't you?'

'I'd love to, Richard,' said Willow, adding: 'I've missed you during your Emma months.'

'Me, too. It's curious isn't it?' He sounded sad and Willow felt the first concern for Emma stirring in her.

'Is she all right? Ought I to get in touch?'

There was a pause before Richard said slowly:

'I think I'd leave it to her if I were you. She precipitated the parting, if that's what you'd call it, and she seemed to be rather afraid you'd be angry with her for "letting me down". I was probably always too old for her.'

'Dear oh dear. Well, I'm sorry it didn't work, Richard.'

'Not half as sorry as I am,' he said. 'I really . . . oh, you know.'

'You really cared about her?' she said, feeling all her real affection for Tom surging through her. 'I know you did.'

'Still, chin up and all that. I'll ring you when I've spoken to Sebastian. Good night, Willow.'

She replaced the receiver, wishing she knew whether Tom still had any feelings left for her. The old days of living in deliberate detachment from other people had been so very much easier, she thought. Then she had often been angry, but never hurt.

It came to Willow as she stood with her hand on the telephone that what Tom was doing was really hurting her. Panic-stricken by the admission and completely unable to think of any way of dealing with it, Willow left the telephone and picked up a handful of the paperbacks her publishers had sent round. Work could probably protect her better than anything else.

She concentrated hard on Gloria's books, noticing that they were all quite thin and that the covers were very dated. Each one showed a misty water-colour of a slender blonde with indistinguishable features posed against some romantic landscape. In some she was wearing a ball dress; in others beach clothes or occasionally a professional-looking suit; but in all of them there was a storm behind her, or a jagged mountain or endless butter-yellow sand dunes.

Willow flicked through the pile, deciding that they could contain no more than seventy thousand words each, perhaps half the length of her own novels. She chose three to read and lay full length on one of the down-filled sofas with *Buttercups for the Bridesmaids* in her hands. An hour and a half later she had finished it, her face creased into an expression of mild distaste. Skimming through *The Juice of the Pomegranate* and *Fortunes of Flora*, she began to share some of Posy Hacket's dislike of the books.

Superficially they were almost charming – if sentimental and not very well written – accounts of the tribulations of good, innocent girls. Each heroine fell in love with a wild or cruel man, whose essential sweetness was revealed only because of her gentleness and devotion.

All of them were astonishingly or delicately beautiful with straight little noses and lustrous eyes and at some stage in the story they all had smiles of frank openness, whatever that was. They all, Willow also noticed, wore something made of iridescent silk. In one book it was merely a scarf, in another an evening dress, but in the third it was the heroine's hair 'long and black, gleaming like iridescent silk'.

Willow smiled at each repetition, knowing how easy it was to fall into the trap of over-using a particular, if unimportant, phrase in book after book (her own was 'long, thin thighs'), but she was irritated that all the heroines longed for marriage as a reward for their sufferings and always achieved it on the last page, as though it marked the end of their real lives.

As she thought about the basic plot, she did remember a little more about the original version. In *Beauty and the Beast*, she thought, the heroine saved not only the beast but also her father from the results of his own fecklessness. It was as though the first story-teller as well as Gloria believed that women's greatest achievement – their destiny even – was to submerge their own selves in order to rescue damaged or damaging men.

'Bloody Hell!' she said loudly, dropping the last of the books on the floor. She told herself that it was absurd to connect Gloria's bizarre philosophy with her own doubts about Tom and what his brooding anger might mean.

Silently reprimanding herself for mixing work and emotion, Willow picked up the books again and concentrated hard on passages that had particularly struck her. Beneath the clichés and the formulaic romance, there seemed to be a subtext of salacity and suggested violence, which went some way to explaining Posy's exaggerated horror of the novels.

When she had finished reading, Willow puffed up the cushions behind her head, thinking about the woman who had written them and whether the fantasy of taming harshly cruel men with pure adoration was her own, which she had merely been unable to put into practice, or whether it had started with an adult memory of nursery renderings of the fairy tale. Willow also re-read Posy's article.

'Why?' Willow asked herself aloud, wishing even more strongly than before that she had been able to talk to Gloria at least once to ask the questions that kept nagging at her. 'Why did she want women to be so submissive? How much of what she wrote was from her unconscious and how much deliberate?'

When Willow eventually stopped trying to put herself into the mind of the dead woman, she went into her bedroom, relieved that she would be able to swing her legs across the entire width of the big bed without having to worry about kicking Tom. Later she arranged herself with maximum comfort and let almost random thoughts swim in and out of her consciousness until she slept.

The next morning she woke slowly with a smile on her lips, still half occupied with her dream of lying on velvet grass in the hot shade of the large beech with her legs dangling in the mill pond outside her house. As sharpness returned to her mind, she laughed. The grass in her garden was rough and thistly. It would be years before it could match the softness of her dream.

Lazily, comfortably, she got herself out of bed, bathed and put on a black knitted dress she had bought from a young designer whose clothes seemed cut for comfort as much as elegance. When she was ready she pulled open the thickly lined chintz curtains in her bedroom and saw that the street outside was covered in snow. The road already had brown tracks along it where the early delivery lorries and the commuters' cars had been driven, but the pavements were still pristine.

An elderly woman bundled into a heavy fur coat stumbled across Willow's view, pulling a small, hairy brown dog behind her. It stopped to investigate something at the foot of a parking meter and the woman rounded on it and shouted something. The words did not reach Willow, but the sharpness did. The dog persisted in its sniffing for a moment and then allowed her to pull it away.

Why did the woman snap? Willow asked herself, still

trying to imagine what it had been like to be Gloria, who had treated her niece at least in much the same way. The woman in the street might be cold or afraid of slipping in the snow; she might be in pain from her legs or her back; but it seemed to Willow to be more likely that she lived alone and had become accustomed to expressing every minor irritation, secure in the knowledge that the lapdog would not retaliate, just as none of Gloria's household had ever retaliated.

Had anyone in her seventy-two years come close enough to her to make her question her tyrannical behaviour? Did it creep up on her as she grew richer or had she always cared nothing for the feelings of people around her? Did she realise how horrible they thought her or did she consider herself to be like the sweet, yielding, gentle heroines of her books? Or had she perhaps expected to be saved and rescued by the sweet understanding of someone else? Was she hoping that the young women who worked for her might play the part of the dutiful daughter, seeing through her harshness to the vulnerability within?

Brushing her short hair once more, Willow ignored a faint, subterranean sense of something wrong and went to see what Mrs Rusham had produced for breakfast.

'What an original idea!' she said as Mrs Rusham put a plate of angels on horseback in front of her.

'I know you would never eat stewed prunes,' said the housekeeper, 'but I felt that you needed them. The bacon ought to make them palatable. Your letters are there.'

She left without waiting for a comment, which was lucky because Willow was torn between amusement and outrage that her housekeeper thought her costive. The uncomfortable idea that Mrs Rusham might dislike her as much as Marilyn had loathed her aunt returned for an instant until Willow began to eat. The soft prunes, impregnated with the salty fat from the bacon, tasted wonderful and reminded Willow that Mrs Rusham could hardly do her job so well if she hated it or felt exploited.

After breakfast Willow set to work to sort out her thoughts. The two parts of her quest were becoming inextricably muddled. For the memoir she needed to talk to someone about the childhood from which Gloria had so effectively removed herself. But for her investigation into the death, Willow needed to know much more. There was one new and potentially useful source of information for both parts of the quest.

She rang Ann Slinter and asked for Gerald Plimpton's telephone number. Ann gave it to her at once, but she also said:

'Do be tactful, won't you? Gerald knows what I think of Gloria's ghastly books and her behaviour but he still cherishes some kind thoughts about her himself. She was always nicer to men than to women.'

'I'll be all charm and sympathy,' Willow promised. 'Thanks, Ann.'

Gerald Plimpton sounded much less fragile than Ann had suggested and immediately agreed to see Willow and tell her all she wanted to know about Gloria Grainger's early success, for the memoir.

'Why not lunch with me at the Garrick today?' he said.

Despite her promise to be charming, Willow could not quite bring herself to accept the invitation, but she was reluctant to antagonise him by explaining her distaste for a club that had so resoundingly refused to admit women members.

'That's sweet of you,' she said girlishly, 'but couldn't I give you lunch in the flat? My housekeeper is a really good cook and it's both warm and comfortable here.'

'So's the Garrick,' he said, 'but I'd be delighted to accept. Thank you.'

'Excellent.' Willow gave him her address, adding: 'We'll expect you at about one then.'

Knowing that nothing broke the icy composure of her housekeeper, whatever her private feelings might be, Willow was not troubled by the thought of imposing a guest on her at such short notice. Wandering through to the impeccable white kitchen, Willow told her about him.

'Very well,' said Mrs Rusham. 'And what kind of food would you like?'

'Goodness, I'm sure you're better at deciding than I. He invited me to his club, so he probably likes things like oxtail and treacle tart.'

Another minute smile cracked the seriousness of the housekeeper's face as she nodded.

'There's no time for oxtail, but I could easily prepare a mixed grill followed by apple meringue. With some split almonds sprinkled on the meringue as it cooks it becomes a little less obviously a nursery pudding. Potted shrimps to start might be suitable.'

'Mrs Rusham, what would I do without you? It sounds perfect.'

'Thank you. I had better go to the butcher straight away unless you need me for anything else immediately?'

'No, thank you.' Willow smiled, aware of something very like affection for the dour, efficient woman, who had never yet divulged her Christian name. 'I'll deal with the telephone and any deliveries.'

In fact there were no interruptions, and Willow had plenty of time to read all her notes before meeting Gloria's executor.

8

GERALD PLIMPTON ARRIVED POLITELY TEN minutes late, dressed in a dark-grey suit that managed to express formality without giving any suggestion of an office. His hair was pale grey and the slackening skin of his face and neck betrayed his age, but his carriage was upright and his voice firm. His tie was dark and noncommittal, which made Willow, who had half expected to see the salmon-and-cucumber stripes of the Garrick tie, think that he might have understood her reluctance to eat there. It was a while before she realised that he was probably wearing it in recognition of Gloria's death.

'How do you do, Mr Plimpton?' she said as Mrs Rusham brought him into the drawing room. 'Can I offer you some sherry? Or would you rather have something else?'

'Sherry sounds delightful. Thank you.' She poured him a glass of an almencista sherry she particularly liked, but, aware that she was going to need all the tact and dissimulation she could muster, chose mineral water for herself.

'I spoke to Ann Slinter after you telephoned me,' he said as they sat down on opposite sofas, 'and she told me something of your difficulty.'

Willow raised her eyebrows and smiled enquiringly.

'In finding people to speak kindly of Gloria Grainger,' he explained.

'Ah, yes,' said Willow. 'So far I have managed only to talk to people who were frightened of her or had some reason for active dislike.

'So few people really knew her,' he said sadly, reawakening some of Willow's sense of identification with Gloria.

As she smiled at him, he added: 'This is wonderful sherry.'

'I'm glad you like it. It's one of which I am particularly fond.'

'How strange and charming to find a woman of your age interested in something as unfashionable as sherry.'

'I've never been enormously interested in fashion except when I need it for a character in one of my books. May I ask you quite frankly what you thought of Gloria's novels?'

Gerald Plimpton crossed his long legs.

'I don't see why not. They could never have been my chosen reading matter, but they were skilfully directed at a particular market and highly successful in their day. That the market has changed I understand well enough, but I do not believe that writers like Gloria deserve all the opprobrium that is flung at them by feminists these days.'

'Or by journalists like Posy Hacket?' suggested Willow.

'Indeed.' His still-goodlooking, faintly familiar, face was as wintry as the weather outside. 'I thought her piece in the *Readers' Quarterly* very unkind indeed and it hurt Gloria badly. I'm not sure that I have ever heard her as upset as the day she read it. She telephoned me at once.'

'Was it you who suggested that she should sue?'

'Good heavens no! The idea of writers suing each other fills me with horror. It gives such a very bad example, besides wasting an inordinate amount of time and money. Any unnecessary involvement with lawyers is to be avoided in my view.'

There was so much distaste in his face that Willow wanted

to ask about his own experiences of the legal profession, but before she could give rein to her curiosity, she saw Mrs Rusham at the drawing room door. Willow nodded to her and then turned back to her guest.

'Shall we lunch? It seems to be ready.'

She led the way into her small green-and-white dining room, where Mrs Rusham had clearly been busy. The table was newly polished and there was a low silver bowl of Christmas roses that Willow had not seen before.

'What a charming room!' said Gerald Plimpton as he sat down and shook out his napkin. 'It's a pity that you and Gloria never met. You obviously share her interest in English furniture.'

'Yes, indeed. There are some lovely pieces in her house. I was impressed by them. But you were telling me about her reaction to the libel case. Why do you think she was so upset by the article?'

'Wouldn't anyone have been?' asked Plimpton. 'Wouldn't you?'

'No, I don't think so. Angry perhaps, as I was when the same journalist savaged me, but I don't think I'd have been emotionally upset. It was presumably the suggestion that she was inciting violence to women that troubled Gloria so much.'

'I'm not altogether certain that I want to discuss that,' he said with new coldness. 'It's hardly relevant to your memoir.'

'Ah,' said Willow, her curiosity burning. 'What a pity! I was wondering as I read some of her books last night whether perhaps she might have had a closer experience of actual violence than most of us. That could explain both her books and her clearly less-than-kindly treatment of subordinates.'

Willow watched Plimpton's face and thought she detected a slight warming in his eyes.

'I do feel,' she went on, 'that, if it were so, referring to her experiences in the memoir might be an effective way to counter the kind of accusations Ms Hacket made.'

Mr Plimpton drank a little of the Chablis Mrs Rusham had provided to go with the potted shrimps and then helped himself to a piece of thinly buttered brown bread.

'Was she ever married?' asked Willow, making him smile.

'No. And not for want of offers.'

'Then was it her father? Or perhaps her brother, which might explain why she and his daughter got on so badly. This is not prurient curiosity on my part. I genuinely want to understand her so that I can write something real.'

'Ann was right about your intelligence, I see.' Gerald drummed his long fingers on the well-polished mahogany table and then looked directly at Willow. 'You're right in a way, although she never said that either man ever hit her. All she told me was that her father was one of those men who cannot prevent himself beating his wife.'

'How horrible!'

'Yes, it is. Gloria rarely spoke about it, but it undoubtedly informed her whole life as well as her work.'

'And do you think that her novels were the result of wishful thinking?' asked Willow, adding as soon as the idea occurred to her: 'Or perhaps a way of telling her mother that she could have prevented the violence if she had behaved differently – more self-sacrificially perhaps?'

'I don't know,' said the elderly publisher, 'and I never asked her any questions about it. The subject arose once as she tried to explain to me why she could not bear the thought of . . . of a close relationship.'

Willow, who had heard from Ann about the many male writers who seemed to believe that they had *droit de seigneur* over their female editors, knew that she could never ask the distinguished-looking elderly man at her side whether he had had similar feelings about his female authors.

'She was clearly very fond of you,' she said, going as far as her conscience would allow.

'Why do you say that?' The coldness had returned to his voice and made Willow glad she had said nothing more direct.

'Marilyn Posselthwate has told me that her aunt had

named you as executor of her will. People don't normally do that unless they have warm feelings for, and complete trust in, the person they have chosen.'

He smiled slightly.

'Perhaps. Splendid potted shrimps. I've always liked them.'

'I'm so glad,' said Willow, who had thought them dull. Mrs Rusham must have been listening at the door for she came in just then to remove their plates and bring in the mixed grill, garnished with grilled tomatoes and small bunches of watercress. She also collected from the sideboard a small eighteenth-century decanter into which she had earlier poured a half bottle of Saint Emilion.

'Can you tell me something about the will?' Willow asked when her housekeeper had gone. 'I assumed that her solicitor would refuse to divulge anything at all about her and so I haven't even bothered to ask.'

'Why do you want to know? Surely you can't expect to put that kind of information in your book about her?'

'I wouldn't include it specifically,' said Willow quickly, 'but I need to know in order to put into perspective the sort of woman she really was. For example, Marilyn believes that her aunt disliked her so much and exploited her so badly that she will inherit nothing. I find that hard to believe of the woman you have described with such warmth.'

'I see what you mean. Well, perhaps I can go so far as to tell you what the solicitor has already explained to Marilyn: she is among the major beneficiaries, as indeed am I. I am afraid that that is all I can tell you until the will has been read after the funeral.'

Willow knew when she met an unmoveable resolve and started to eat her mixed grill, thinking about the space beside Marilyn's name in the 'Motive' column of her computer document. She also thought about the size of Plimpton's inheritance and the fact that he was the only person to have spoken kindly of Gloria. Wondering if his advertised affection might not simply have been a blind, she asked him anodyne questions about what Gloria had been like in her youth and in the days of her great success.

Gerald Plimpton spoke readily of his admiration for his author, for her professionalism and her charm, making Willow curious again only when he mentioned Gloria's sense of humour.

'That is something no one else has mentioned,' she said, 'and something I have not picked up from her books. What form did her humour take?'

'Well, she could tell an excellent joke at a party – thoroughly professional timing and never too long or too dirty – and she undoubtedly enjoyed stringing along the pompous or the arrogant to make fools of themselves.'

'Ah, a sense of humour but an unkind one, perhaps?'

'Yes, perhaps.' Mr Plimpton smiled. 'But how kind should one be to the pompous and the arrogant?'

'Good point. What did she look like? I've just realised that I have seen no photographs of her at all, which is extraordinary.'

'Not really. She considered the modern habit of slapping author photographs on to jackets, posters and so on thoroughly vulgar. And she rather disliked the way she was ageing. In her youth she looked very like her niece, if slimmer and rather more confident. She always longed to be taller.'

'But she was pretty?'

'I'd have said so, and increasingly well dressed as she earned more royalties.'

'Her niece suggested that she suffered from a certain *folie de grandeur*. Would you agree?'

Once again a smile transformed the severity of his face. He touched his lips with the damask napkin and looked around the elegant, well-furnished room.

'What successful novelist does not?'

Willow laughed to hide a mental wince. 'Don't you think that rather than *folie de grandeur*, it is often a mixture of a cloak for self-doubt and a natural development of spending so much time alone?'

'No,' he said bluntly.

They both heard the telephone ring and Gerald Plimpton

made a graceful gesture with his right arm, suggesting that Willow should pay no attention to him if she wished to deal with the call.

'My machine will cope if Mrs Rusham's busy,' she said. 'What else ought I to know about Gloria before I actually start writing?

'She was an excellent and generous hostess. The last year or so she was really too tired for late nights, but in her heyday, her dinner parties were some of the best and her invitations highly prized.'

'By?'

'By her friends,' he said, the ice back in his voice.

'And who were they?' Willow was determined to pursue it despite his snub. 'Besides yourself, of course. Ann spoke of "the great and the good" but I never really know what that means.'

'And you a civil servant! It means precisely what you think: politicians, Conservative naturally, judges, the occasional permanent secretary, the glamorous medical consultants, the more important journalists, a few Royal Academicians, one or two High Anglican churchmen. That sort.'

'None of whom objected to her books?'

'Her books were not relevant to her friendships.'

'That seems strange,' said Willow, knowing perfectly well that her own books were wholly irrelevant to her difficult current relations with Tom or her past affair with Richard Crescent. 'Or perhaps they never read any of them.'

'That, I suspect, is likely.'

'Did you?'

'I was her publisher.'

'Which even I know does not mean that you actually read them.' Willow had decided that she had played the ingenue for long enough and switched into her more customary critical persona.

'You're right, of course,' he said with a charming, self-deprecatory smile.

Willow suddenly realised why he looked familiar. It was

his photograph that stood in an elaborate silver frame on Gloria's bedside table.

'I read some of the first book,' he was saying, 'when it was recommended by a junior member of the firm and I thought it showed possibilities. After that, I must confess I left them to my lady editors.'

After they had both laughed at his admission, they managed to eat the apple meringue and drink the coffee Mrs Rusham made without annoying each other again.

When he had gone, thanking Willow for her hospitality, she added his name to her computer document and made a list of the few solid facts he had given her. The most important, apart from the hints of violence in Gloria's childhood, seemed to be that Marilyn was to inherit something at least.

Willow picked up the telephone receiver and dialled the number of the house in Kew. Marilyn answered and said she would be delighted to answer any more questions Willow might have.

'Thank you,' said Willow. 'And if I came this afternoon, might I have a chance to see the secretaries too?'

'Of course. Any time before half-past five.'

That settled, Willow replayed the earlier message and found that Richard had arranged to meet his barrister friend in chambers at six o'clock that same evening.

'We'll go on for a drink at El Vino's and you can interrogate him there,' went the message, adding that Richard expected Willow to dine with him afterwards as 'a fee for the introduction'. Thinking that with all the eating and drinking she was having to do she would soon be having a heart attack of her own, Willow rang his office to say that she would try to get there in time but might be a little late as she had to drive out to Kew first.

9

THE DOOR WAS OPENED BY a middle-aged woman, who spoke in the soft accent of the West of Ireland. She introduced herself as Mrs Guy, adding:

'Marilyn told me you'd be coming. She'll be back soon, but she had to take Peter to the hospital just after she spoke to you. She won't be long.'

'That's fine,' said Willow walking into the hall. 'But it must be very serious. Last time I was here, he went on his own, I think.'

'He always went alone before madam died. Marilyn had to be in the house then. Come on in now, and I'll be putting the kettle on while you talk to the girls downstairs,' she said, shutting the door behind Willow. 'He hated it and so now she takes him. But he won't let her wait for him there, so she'll be back soon. Shall I take you down to the office now?'

'That would be kind,' said Willow, hoping that Marilyn would not be back before she had a chance to pump Mrs Guy as well as the two secretaries. 'Marilyn said you were very fond of her aunt.'

'Oh, to be sure I was. Come on down this way. The basement stairs are a bit steep and the light's not so good, so be taking care now. She was good to me, you know, and I'll miss her. She made me laugh.'

'D'you know, you're the second person today who's said something like that, which is funny – I mean strange – because her books aren't amusing at all,' said Willow, obediently watching where she put her feet.

'Well no, but they wouldn't be, would they now? The fans, as she always called them, they wouldn't have liked that at all. They liked their love stories straight, she told me once. They wouldn't have been standing for any sarcasm.'

'That sounds rather as though she despised them.' Willow occasionally despised her own readers but was ashamed of it.

'Well she did and she didn't. Here we are.' Mrs Guy opened a white-painted door and put her head round, saying: 'It's Miss King.'

The door was opened more widely from the inside and a tall, well-built young woman with magnificent shoulders and very blonde hair appeared, holding out her hand.

'Do come in. Patty and I are ploughing through vast amounts of paper, so I hope you'll forgive the mess. I'm Susan Robinson by the way and this is Patricia Smithe.'

Willow smiled at them both, noticing that Patty Smithe looked as though she had been genuinely ill. Her triangular face was sweetly pretty, but her skin was greyish and there were heavy bags under her dark eyes. Susan pulled forward the one comfortable-looking chair in the big, gloomy room.

'Do sit down, Ms King,' she said.

'Don't you get depressed working down here all the time?' asked Willow, seeing how little light came through the barred windows and how oppressive the low ceiling made the room. It was not how she had intended to start the interview, but it served her well. Susan laughed and answered her with more warmth than she could have expected.

'Gloria believed absolutely in keeping her employees below stairs, but on very good days Patty was occasionally allowed through the back kitchen into the garden during her lunch hour. Weren't you?'

'Provided she wasn't having a lunch party,' agreed Patty, not smiling at all.

'She does sound rather difficult to work for,' Willow said, trying to gauge the precise degree of resentment in Patty, who interested her more than Susan, even though it was the latter who had been working for Gloria at the time of her death.

Patty looked nervously back at the papers in her hands. She put them down on the desk and smoothed out the crumples.

'Well yes,' she said, pushing her heavy brown fringe away from her face and making it look much less triangular but just as sweet. 'She never seemed satisfied with anything I did and sometimes . . . I really think that sometimes she didn't tell me the right thing.'

'I don't understand,' said Willow, instinctively looking to the other woman for a translation.

'Like many bullies,' said Susan, dropping her hand protectively on her friend's shoulder for a moment, 'she engineered situations in which she could criticise. Unfortunately, Patty let her do it.'

'Well, I could never really be sure that my memory was right. Susan always tells me I'm dreadfully wet.'

'You two seem to know each other well,' said Willow, wondering at the obvious bond between them.

'Oh we do. We share a flat,' said Patty with a weak smile, 'which is why Sue knew that I was desperate a couple of weeks ago. She persuaded me to go sick.'

'I see; and you stepped into the breach.'

'That's one way of putting it,' said Susan, moving away. 'I've been working as a temp since I walked out of my last job four months ago, and it struck me that if I could see exactly what Gloria did to her secretaries I could help Patty a bit more than just listening to her in the evenings.'

'And did you discover anything?'

'Sure.' She shrugged her swimmer's shoulders, looking more than a match for any unreasonable employer. 'She played the most idiotic games, dictating something she didn't mean and then pretending that I'd got my shorthand wrong when she checked my typing. Sometimes she'd give me the wrong name for the person I was supposed to be telephoning. That sort of thing.' Susan laughed. 'She pretty soon discovered that I wouldn't stand for it and after a bit we got on quite well. I even came to enjoy some of the games.'

'I can't think how,' said Patty, shuddering. 'I was always terrified of her and the harder I tried to get things right, the worse it became until I really was making mistakes. I did once try to stand up to her, as Sue told me I should, but it just caused a horrible row.'

'Why on earth did you stay working for her?' Willow asked, uncomfortable in the presence of such misery.

Patty got up and stood with her back to the others, peering up at the light through the barred window.

'I suppose because I thought I'd be just as useless anywhere else.' Her voice wobbled and she took a deep breath: 'At least I had a job, and one near the flat. I can't bear public transport and you see I can walk here. I like the house, too. We did sometimes . . . I mean, occasionally, she'd invite me to lunch in the dining room and show me things she'd bought and be quite kind to me. I suppose, looking back, I was hanging on, really, waiting for more of that kindness.'

'Another victim,' said Willow to herself and was appalled to realise that she had mouthed the word distinctly and that Susan had read her lips.

'I don't think that's fair,' she said sternly, making Patty turn to ask:

'What's not fair?'

'What Gloria put you through.' Susan spoke kindly before turning back to Willow and saying much more briskly: 'Now, how can we help you, Ms King? I'm sure you've got lots to do and we certainly have, sorting out all these papers for Mr Plimpton and the lawyers.'

Noticing that Susan was almost patronising in the way she protected her weaker friend, Willow asked questions about the libel case, which added nothing to her knowledge. She went on to the subject of Gloria's books and discovered that Patty quite enjoyed them although Susan thought they were dreadful.

'Did you have much to do with them, Patty? In your work, I mean.'

'Well, I had to type them out for her, of course. Sometimes from her handwritten version; sometimes from dictation. And occasionally I had to ring up Weston & Brown for her, but nothing more than that.'

'Whom did you deal with there?'

'Vicky Taffle. You ought to talk to her.' Patty's gentle voice hardened noticeably. 'She could tell you even more about Gloria than I could.'

'Oh?' said Willow, hoping for more. 'Why's that?'

'Well Gloria was sometimes quite nice to me. From what Vicky said, she never saw that side of her at all. All she ever got was rows and criticism. She had an awful time.'

'But then, presumably, it was diluted for her by all her other work,' said Willow. 'She must have been dealing with other writers, too.'

'Yes, of course,' said Patty so quickly that it seemed she must be afraid of being punished for the tiniest disagreement. 'How silly of me!'

'Not really,' said Susan, once more touching her shoulder. 'Even during the weeks I've been here, Gloria did seem to monopolise Vicky's attention.'

'And what about Gloria's friends?' Willow asked when that topic had been exhausted. 'Did she see them often?'

'Quite often. She'd really given up having big parties,' said Patty, 'but they came to small lunches and things still.'

'What about dropping in?' Willow hoped that she was sounding appropriately casual. 'For instance, did anyone come to see her on the last day of her life?'

'There was only Mrs Guy and me here that day,' said Susan, looking surprised. 'Patty was still laid low in the flat.'

'Isn't that sad?' said Willow. 'She had a lonely death.'

'Perhaps, but there was nothing strange about it. Lots of her days were like that. She often didn't leave the house if it was as cold as it was last week and she certainly didn't have visitors every day. But she wasn't exactly alone. Marilyn spent the day at her beck and call as usual.'

'But no visitors?' Willow risked arousing their suspicions in her need to establish exactly who could have had the opportunity of tampering with Gloria's medicines or in some other way hastening her death.

'Well, there was a delivery of something that Mrs Guy took in; wine, I think. But that was all.'

'Surely Peter Farrfield came across,' said Patty, laughing. She turned to Willow. 'He was always wheeling himself over or ringing up for one of us to help him if he couldn't get his chair up the slope. Some days he was better than others.'

'No. For once I don't think he was here at all,' said Susan, frowning. She shook her head. 'No, I'm sure he didn't come over, but you could always check with Mrs Guy if it's that important. Though, come to think of it, I'm not sure that he's been in the house at all since I started working here. But I could easily have missed him.'

'Oh, it isn't important,' said Willow hastily. 'I'm just trying to get a picture of her last day. It really does seem sad to me.'

Susan raised her eyebrows and tightened her lips, but she said nothing.

'Could you have missed anyone else?' Willow asked, trying to sound wistful. 'I'd like to think she had had at least one friend.'

'No,' said Susan abruptly. 'I didn't go out to lunch on her last day. Mrs Guy made me a sandwich and a cup of tea, and I'd have heard the front door bell. I always do. I suppose someone might have come after I'd gone back to Patty in the flat, but Marilyn never mentioned anyone.'

'I'll ask her. But there is one thing I don't want to ask her about in case it upsets her,' Willow said in order to divert any suspicion of her reason for wanting to know such trivial details. 'Did her daughter spend much time here in the house?'

'Oh, she was never allowed in the house at all,' said Patty, apparently oblivious to anything odd about Willow's questions or Susan's reaction to them. 'Gloria loathed children, and she found the whole idea of Sarah disturbing. Marilyn used to hope things would change, but she never dared actually bring the child over here without permission and she never got that.'

'She did come once, though,' said Susan more readily. 'Just after I'd started here. Gloria was unbelievably angry. It was quite the most exaggerated thing I've ever seen. Sarah had come across to see her mother about something urgent one afternoon when she'd got back from school. Gloria was in the hall when she came through the garden door and even I could hear the vituperation from down here. She said some shocking things. Sarah burst into tears and a door banged and that's all I heard. Marilyn was obviously upset when I next saw her, but she never mentioned it and so I didn't either.'

'Do you get on well with Marilyn?' asked Willow, waiting to see which of them would answer.

'Fairly well,' said Patty, shrugging, 'but I don't think we'd ever be friends or anything. We did try not to work each other up when Gloria was being difficult.'

'How admirable,' said Willow with some sincerity. Patty smiled at her gratefully and seemed to relax. 'And Mrs Guy?'

Patty's face tightened up again and she looked at Susan.

'She tended to act as Gloria's spy,' said Susan frankly. 'They were as thick as thieves, you see, and if one of us was a few minutes late in the morning, Mrs Guy would always notice and go running up to tell Gloria.'

'Gloria wouldn't necessarily know that you were here then?'

'Oh no. We had to use the basement door rather than the one upstairs to get in and out. I never had any contact with her until she buzzed for me to go up with the post. What about you, Patty?'

'No. She never wanted me until about ten, although I was always here by nine.'

'Who let you in?'

'I've got a key,' said Patty, looking surprised at last.

119

Willow smiled and glanced round the gloomy office, with its grey haircord carpet and old green filing cabinets.

'Quite a contrast with upstairs,' she said, thinking that Gloria had been playing Marie Antoinette to her staff's *sans coulottes*.

'Yes,' said Susan coldly. 'But that's the sort of thing she particularly enjoyed.'

'You're being very frank,' said Willow to them both impartially.

'I suppose we are.' Susan was once again their spokeswoman. She shrugged her splendid shoulders. 'I detest the thought of hypocritical respect just because someone's dead.'

'So do I,' said Patty, looking shy. 'It would be so awfully dishonest to pretend that we liked her just because we're safe from her temper now.'

'No one has yet done that,' said Willow, smiling at her, 'except possibly Gerald Plimpton. Do you know him?'

'Oh, yes,' said Patty, smiling quite freely. 'He used to come to lunch a lot, even recently when she didn't see very many people.'

'Really? When was the last time he came?'

Patty reached for a large diary and flicked through the pages.

'The Tuesday before Christmas. I remember he brought her a present, quite elaborately wrapped in silver paper and gold ribbons, and stayed to lunch. It was quite a celebration, I think, because she'd ordered champagne.'

'But, Patty, didn't you tell me that he looked furious when he left?' said Susan.

Willow was intrigued to notice that Susan was carefully emphasising the number of people who had been upset by Gloria in her last few weeks. It suggested that Susan might have understood the nature of Willow's quest and wanted to ensure that no suspicion was attached to Patty. That in itself made Willow wary.

'Is something the matter?' asked Patty gently. 'You look as though you've got a headache.'

'I'm fine,' said Willow quickly, wishing that she could be more open about her suspicions and ask her questions directly. 'You were telling me about Gerald Plimpton's rage.'

'Well, yes, we were. It's true that he did look cross,' said Patty obediently. 'She sent for me to see him out and he was quite curt with me, which was odd, because he was usually very kind.'

'I thought he was charming when I met him,' said Willow, trying to organise her distracting thoughts and concentrate, 'and he spoke very warmly of Miss Grainger. Are you suggesting that was hypocrisy?'

'No, I shouldn't have thought so,' said Patty, for once not looking towards her stronger friend for guidance. 'He was very fond of her and generous with presents and flowers and things. He brought her a huge bunch of red roses that day as well as the parcel.'

'Was she angry too?'

'She was nearly always angry.' Patty sighed, looking very pretty and very fragile. 'In fact it was the things she said to me that afternoon that made me . . . I mean, it was after that that I felt so ill.'

'And I'd refused bookings that week because I wanted to do some Christmas shopping and so I leaped at the opportunity of seeing what really went on here,' said Susan quickly. 'You know, your memoir isn't going to please people like Plimpton if it includes all our complaints.'

Willow produced a fairly convincing laugh.

'This is simply probing for background,' she said, gesturing to the notebook in which she had been scribbling bits of what they told her. 'But it'll come in useful, I expect.'

'Well I hope so. Yes, Mrs Guy?' Susan's voice had changed. Willow turned round to see the cleaner holding open the door.

'The kettle's boiled and Marilyn said I was to give Miss King tea if she wasn't back from the hospital.'

'Thank you, Mrs Guy,' said Patty, making it clear that she thought she was talking to an inferior, which surprised

Willow. 'Is there anything else you want from us at the moment?'

Willow shook her head.

'You've given me useful confirmation of things I've already heard,' she said, very conscious of the presence of one of Gloria's few defenders in the room with them. 'Thank you for talking to me.'

She shook hands with them both and preceded Mrs Guy out of the room.

'Would you like to have tea in the drawing room?' Mrs Guy asked. 'Or would you rather come and have a cup in my kitchen? It's warm there.'

'The kitchen then,' said Willow with what she hoped was a frank and open smile like the ones Gloria's heroines always produced in difficult circumstances. 'I've already frozen myself in that drawing room once.'

Mrs Guy pulled out a chair for her at a traditional wooden kitchen table, scrubbed until it was dry and pinkish white. The units round three walls of the room were covered in shiny yellow Formica, and the floor was of patterned linoleum that looked as though it had been designed in 1951 for the Festival of Britain. But every part of the old-fashioned kitchen was scrubbed clean.

'You do keep this house well,' said Willow, sycophantically. Mrs Guy turned and shot a look at her that was infinitely sharper than her creamy voice.

'To be sure and wasn't it a little thing I could do in return for all she did for me?'

'It's good to hear someone speak of her so kindly.'

'There's a lot of people owed her a great deal more than they gave, I can tell you.' Mrs Guy sounded suddenly much less Irish as well as more severe.

'Really? Who?'

'Those girls in there for instance. They never worked hard enough to please madam, but then young people nowadays don't know what work is, do they, Miss?'

'Marilyn at least seems to be fully conscious of what she owed her aunt,' said Willow, enjoying the diplomatic ambiguity of the sentence. Another sharp glance from Mrs Guy suggested that she, too, had noticed it. She made tea in a blue pot and when it had stewed for a minute or two poured a cupful for Willow.

'It wasn't so much her I was thinking of as those girls and Peter Farrfield.' The Irishness was returning. 'Wasn't he living for nothing in the cottage, eating dinner with madam as often as not, and relying on her to see him right if his case went badly for him?'

Mrs Guy poured her own tea, added two spoons of sugar and sat down opposite Willow, who was looking puzzled.

'You'll surely have heard about his case?' said Mrs Guy with the pleased smile of the inveterate gossip who has found an interested and ignorant listener.

'No,' said Willow. 'I've never met him and Marilyn didn't mention any case. All she said about him was that he was fond of Miss Grainger and that he was in a wheelchair.'

'Yes, the poor man. He was in a car smash, you know. Terrible it was, but he was lucky: the other driver was killed.'

'I see,' said Willow slowly. 'Then it's an insurance matter?'

'That's right. The company's been a long time deciding whether to pay his claim or not.'

'But why? I thought most car accident claims were straightforward. What happened?'

'All I know is that it was on an empty road, in the light and there was no rain or oil to make them skid, and yet the two of them collided face to face. And the other man died. The two companies are fighting about which one will pay the claims, madam said.'

'Claims?' repeated Willow. 'Oh, you mean that the other man's estate is claiming, too.'

'So madam told me. And it could go against Peter if he isn't very lucky indeed. I think that's why he kept himself so close to madam. He was going to need her if he got no money.'

'But he would have got it,' said Willow automatically keeping the conversation going as she registered the fact that Gloria had been surprisingly frank and open with her cleaner. 'It's only a question of which company had to pay up. It's irrelevant to him which, apart from his no-claims bonus, I suppose. Tiresome that he has to wait of course.'

'He had only third-party insurance. Madam told me that, too.'

'Did she?' Willow's tidy eyebrows were tucked neatly into her forehead as she frowned. It seemed unlikely from everything she had heard of Gloria Grainger that she would have sat gossiping with her charwoman, however 'good' she had been, without some strong reason.

As Willow watched the Irish woman's sharp dark eyes, she cursed herself for sounding so doubtful. A useful fountain of information should never be capped simply because the source is dubious.

'How long had you known her?' Willow smiled as she asked the most anodyne question she could invent.

'Nearly twenty years I've been coming here and you get to know a person well in that long. Oh, I tell you I'm going to miss her.' Mrs Guy's eyes were softening again.

'She was lucky to have you.'

Mrs Guy drank some tea, looking almost as though she could not trust herself to say any more. Willow, conscious of time passing, did not want to upset her and turned the conversation back to Marilyn and her relations with her aunt.

'Well all I can say is that madam was very patient with her.'

'Really? I'd understood that Ms Posselthwate did everything for her aunt.'

Mrs Guy snorted. 'She took her time about it all and she skimped, too, whenever there wasn't someone watching her. She was always going off across the garden to see if Peter was all right if he wasn't over here bothering madam, or to check that the child had been brought back from its school.'

Willow thought about Marilyn's shiftiness when questioned about the precise events of the evening her aunt died and wondered if she had just heard the simple, only mildly discreditable reason for it.

'Did Mr Farrfield look after the child then?'

'Well and wasn't it the least he could do for her? Living free and all?'

There was a slight sound behind Mrs Guy. Willow looked up and over the charwoman's head and saw Marilyn, her face white and furious. Willow wondered how long she had been standing there. Seeing the doubt in her face, Mrs Guy turned and Willow watched her shoulders stiffen.

'There was no need to bring Miss King down here, Mrs Guy. Whatever would my aunt have said to you?' Marilyn sounded infinitely more assured than Willow had heard her at their previous meeting or on the telephone. 'A tray of tea in the drawing room would have been more suitable, don't you think? Will you come up now?'

Willow stood slowly, not wanting to antagonise either woman.

'Thank you for the tea, Mrs Guy. You were most hospitable. And you were right: it's beautifully warm down here.'

The Irish woman smiled at her and then raised her eyebrows in an expression of ludicrously exaggerated deference, which Willow assumed was directed at Marilyn's back rather than at herself.

Marilyn took her up to the drawing room, which was just as cold as it had been during her earlier visit, and offered her the same velvet-covered chair.

'How did you get on with the secretaries?'

'Fine, thank you,' said Willow automatically, wondering how to ask the questions that were filling her mind. 'Although, I'm still puzzled about a lot of things.'

'Really? Is there anything more that I can tell you?' asked Marilyn.

'Well, yes, I think there might be. Last time we were sitting here, I felt that you were holding back something to do with the evening your aunt died. Do stop me if I'm intruding, but you seemed to feel as though I was about to accuse you of something.'

Marilyn flushed and shook her head. Willow was interested to see that she was also biting her upper lip.

'No, it wasn't that at all. At least, in a way I suppose it was. I feel as though I failed her, you see, although the doctor says it wasn't my fault.'

'I've understood that. Is that all that was worrying you? Surely not?'

Marilyn's flush died and Willow thought that there was a hardness about her eyes that had not been there before. It could have been simple obstinacy or a dislike of being cross-examined, but Willow thought that there was more to it.

'Come on, Marilyn. You seem to have looked after a difficult relative with exemplary patience. Can't you just tell me what was making you defensive? I have heard it suggested that you sometimes went home to the cottage when your aunt expected you to be here. Is that all it was?'

Marilyn continued to say nothing.

'You're making me curious, you know. All sorts of ideas are occurring to me, which I'm sure are exaggerated.'

'Oh, all right,' said Marilyn pettishly. 'If you must know, I do feel a bit responsible. She did ring once, but I was in the toilet and I wasn't going to rush out. She'd been difficult all day and I thought she could jolly well ring again. But she didn't, you see, which made me wonder afterwards if it had been her bell at all. I thought it might have been the front door, but there was no one there. When I didn't hear another bell at all I waited until half-past nine and then crept up and, like I said, she seemed to be asleep. But, you see, she wasn't.' She gasped suddenly and pulled a tissue from her sleeve to mop her eyes.

Willow's suspicions had been so tickled up that she could not believe there were any real tears to be dried.

'The awful thing is that I now know that she might have rung that one time and been trying to get me to call for Doctor Trenor. He says it wouldn't have made much difference and he also reminded me that she could have called him herself. There's a telephone by her bed. You must have seen it.'

'Yes, I did,' said Willow, well aware of how easily modern

telephones could be unplugged from their sockets. 'I see. I apologise for distressing you. Tell me one thing more: had she seemed at all ill during that day or was it only tiresomeness?'

'Mostly. She'd complained of being breathless, but then people with hearts often do. Doctor Trenor told me. Oh and she said she'd had a terrible headache all night the day before, if you see what I mean. She said it felt as though she'd been hit on the head.'

'I see. Well, thank you; you've been very frank and I'm grateful.'

'You will still come to the funeral, won't you?'

'Why ever not?'

'Well, I'd hate you to think that . . . not to come because you thought I hadn't done enough for her. And I'd hate your book to . . . '

Willow, who had had her share of doubts over things she had told journalists and other interviewers, thought that she understood.

'All right, I promise I won't write anything about the way you looked after your aunt.'

'Thank you,' said Marilyn, smiling again. 'You've been very kind. I'm sorry to have been so silly. It's just worried me rather a lot, although Doctor . . . '

'Trenor says it wasn't your fault,' said Willow crisply. 'Yes, I've got that bit. Shall I see myself out?'

10

WILLOW ARRIVED AT SEBASTIAN BORDEN'S chambers in the Temple late, wishing that she had had time to go home first. Her clothes felt crumpled and her makeup smudged, but they mattered less than her need to mull over what she had been told in Kew before the first impressions confused themselves in her mind. She also wanted to brief herself for the meeting ahead by re-reading the things Posy Hacket had said about the libel case.

Climbing breathlessly up the stone stairs, Willow asked a dark-suited woman who brushed against her the way to Mr Borden's room. She followed the directions and found herself in a medium-sized office furnished with several deep armchairs, a large desk and stacks of books and pink-taped briefs. A gown hung on the back of the door with a red brocade bag, rather like a luxurious laundry bag.

Thick curtains of the same good red hung undrawn at the sides of a window that looked out on to a murky lightwell. Willow looked round the comfortable, untidy room in appreciation and smiled at the two men, who had leapt to their feet.

Struck by their unnecessarily exaggerated gesture of deference, Willow was about to ask them to sit down when the stranger behind the desk said:

'At last! I'm panting for my glass of wine. And I'm sure Richard is, too.'

He was a tall man with narrow shoulders and an academic-looking stoop. Willow graciously apologised for keeping him waiting and introduced herself. Richard came to where she was standing in the doorway and kissed her.

'Good to see you, old girl.'

'Come along,' said the barrister impatiently.

Willow moved aside, and he led them out of his room and down the stone stairs into King's Bench Walk. Even her long legs struggled to keep up with the barrister's as she and Richard followed him through the cold darkness to El Vino's.

Most of the chairs were occupied by well-dressed lawyers of both sexes attempting to cap each other's stories of cases brilliantly won or cruelly lost. Sebastian strode ahead and turned and waved triumphantly to the other two. They made their way between the chair backs and settled at a small table right at the back of the room.

'You know it really is good to see you,' Richard said, putting a hand over Willow's for a moment. 'Heavens you're cold. I didn't realise you hadn't any gloves.'

Willow looked down at her slender hands and noticed for the first time that the second finger of each was white and stiff.

'Hell! I must have left my gloves in Kew. I was in such a rush.' She massaged the whitened fingers, trying to force blood back into them. 'I didn't even notice they were cold.'

'Sebastian,' said Richard, but the barrister was deep in a discussion with the waiter about which wine to order. 'He knows all about your books and is riveted at the thought that the next one is going to include a libel case.'

Willow laughed, pleased with Richard's misapprehension, and waited until the question of the wine was settled. When it had been dealt with, Sebastian turned to Willow and she saw that when he smiled his long serious face seemed to grow younger. His eyes even began to reflect some of the confident jollity of the other drinkers.

'I've ordered quite a nice claret. Youngish. Is that all right for you?'

'Splendid,' said Willow, trying to gather her wits and warm her hands and not listen to an extraordinarily funny account of the defence of a series of doctors accused of sexually molesting their female patients that was being given by a man behind her. Regretfully she stopped her ears to the richly entertaining sound of a born raconteur and concentrated on the business of the evening.

'Now what can I do for you?' asked Sebastian Borden. 'My wife will be intrigued to hear that I'm about to figure in one of your books.'

Accustomed to choosing her own words carefully, Willow noted the barrister's skilful use of 'intrigued' and deduced that his wife disapproved of Cressida Woodruffe's novels.

'It's a simple question really. Does a libel case die with its owner, if you see what I mean?'

'In this country? Yes, but not necessarily everywhere in Europe or in all the American states.'

'Ah,' said Willow, thinking about what Posy had said and wondering if her ignorance of that salient fact could possibly have been genuine. 'That's exactly what I thought; after all how could you reasonably claim that someone suffered as a result of his reputation being impugned once he was dead?'

'Precisely. Is that all you wanted to know? How disappointing!'

'No, indeed,' said Willow, looking at him carefully. 'I have plenty more but I didn't want to bore you with the whole list at once. Do many libel cases end with the sort of immense damages that one reads about in the newspapers?'

'No. They're mostly on a scale of five to twenty-five thousand pounds. But it depends very much on the reputation of the plaintiff and the seriousness of the libel.'

'Good Lord!' said Richard, interrupting. 'Does it really? I seem to remember huge sums being paid for all sorts of things that are more in line with prep-school insults than serious attempts to destroy someone's professional reputation. Wasn't there one actor who sued because a journalist had written that his bulbous nose and prognathous jaw made him look more like a failed boxer than a figure of high tragedy?'

'I think you'll find that most of the really big sums are awarded for serious libels. A lot of them are too big, of course. Juries have got used to the idea that tabloid newspapers can afford to pay out hundreds of thousands and some of them seem to assume that private individuals can do it, too, particularly when they're "toffs" or whatever the modern equivalent is.'

' "Stinking capitalists", I should think,' said Richard, laughing as richly as the defender of the allegedly dirty doctors behind him.

'Oh, stop pretending to be ninety, the pair of you,' said Willow, irritated as she always had been by the games Richard played with his old school friends. Sebastian Borden looked at her with coldness in his small eyes.

'What else is it that you wish to know?' he asked, articulating each word with immense care as though she were a particularly stupid client, or perhaps deaf. The wine was brought, tasted and poured before she was able to answer.

'What sort of damages a novelist might expect to be awarded against a journalist who had accused him,' she said, determined to disguise the real case by changing the pronoun, 'of inciting a particular group of people to commit violent assaults.'

'Racially motivated?'

'No,' said Willow.

'Pity. Incitement to racial hatred is easier to assess. A famous novelist?'

'So so. Probably not one of the literary establishment.'

'It's hard to guess what juries will do these days, but I'd have thought if his case succeeded he might get anything between eight thousand, say, and a hundred and fifty, and costs, of course.'

'Good Lord! What an enormous spread! How does anyone dare defend anything?' Willow asked, appalled at the risk she and every other writer took by publishing anything at all.

Sebastian Borden laughed.

'Not many people do dare to sue,' he said. 'You need a pretty bottomless purse either way and there's no legal aid for libel.'

'How sad for you.'

Richard, hearing the sarcasm and hint of anger in Willow's voice tried to intervene, but before he could say anything Sebastian had laughed again.

'That's debatable,' he said. 'Legal aid rates are pretty low, you know. That's why most of us get out of crime as soon as we can.'

'Untroubled by your social conscience,' said Willow, trying to appear charmingly teasing.

'You manage to conceal yours pretty well in your novels.'

'We all work for money,' Richard contributed cheerfully, refilling all their glasses and signalling for another bottle. 'Biscuits anyone, to soak up the hooch?'

'Good idea,' said Sebastian, leaving Richard to order.

'So what do the most successful juniors at the criminal bar make these days?' asked Willow.

'I suppose about fifty thousand a year if they do nothing but crime. Otherwise, a hundred thousand more but there are plenty of expenses to soak up a lot of that.'

'Like the biscuits,' said Richard, deliberately trying to reduce the tension he could feel in Willow.

'It's a strange system, isn't it?' she said, staring at the wine in her glass. 'There are those young men in prison awaiting trial who hang themselves because the prison service can't afford enough staff to prevent their being bullied and yet the barristers who could have defended them get paid more in a year than they're likely to see in a lifetime.'

'That's life,' said Sebastian, clearly still very annoyed. 'We barristers have all worked a great deal harder than most of those clients will ever do, and lived through penurious and often frightening pupillage, to achieve enough skill to defend them. They're jolly lucky to have counsel prepared to do it when they could earn a great deal more elsewhere.'

He looked down at his watch and leaped to his feet, saying:

'Will you both excuse me? My wife will slaughter me if I'm late for dinner again. Perhaps next time you're researching aspects of the bar you'd like to come to chambers a little earlier in the day. I'd be delighted to show you round.'

Willow thanked him for his helpful information and settled back in the deep leather chair with a sigh of relief when he had left them.

'Phew!'

'What were you up to, Willow?' asked Richard. 'I haven't seen you so spiky for years.'

'Sorry,' she said shortly, admitting to herself that she did in fact feel pricklier than she had for some time. Perhaps her difficulties with Tom were making her regress. Memories of her old life returned and with them her deliberate refusal to feel anything at all except anger. Her skin crawled as she thought of what else might be lying in wait in her subconscious mind.

'What's up, old girl?'

'Nothing. My mind was wandering. Old age perhaps. Sorry to have upset your friend. I hadn't meant to do anything except pick his brains about libel, but I've been reading quite a bit recently about what goes on in our prisons. I'm becoming appalled at the whole business of who gets what out of our judicial system and the rarity of real justice – or the possibility of reforming criminals by imprisoning them. I'm surprised you don't feel even more angry having seen it all from the wrong side.'

'Sebastian has nothing whatever to do with the prison service.' Richard's voice was harsh enough to make Willow reluctant to push him any further. 'There are a lot of injustices in this world of ours, my dear, but the profits of barristers versus the misery of criminals in gaol is not one that's going to keep me awake at night.'

'Isn't it? That makes me happy for you.' Willow caught sight of Richard's expression and added: 'I get irritable when

I'm called "my dear" in that avuncular fashion both you and your friend used. Let's get out of here and away from the law. I think I've had enough of it for one day.'

'What do you think makes barristers less worthy of their hire than rich merchant bankers like me or novelists like you?' Richard asked, irritable in his turn.

Despite his annoyance, he held her coat for her with all his usual conventional politeness. Willow negotiated her arms into the sleeves, managing to laugh at what he had said.

'Fair comment,' she said, tucking her hand into his arm as they left El Vino's and gasping at the cold, 'but I won't take back what I said.'

'Oh, Willow,' he said, bending to kiss the top of her head, 'I've missed your bracing criticism these last months and I suppose I've lost the knack of dealing with it.'

'That's very chivalrous, Richard. I know I behaved badly, but he got my goat.'

'So I saw. Where do you want to eat?'

'Wherever. You choose.'

He took her to an old favourite that they had used at least once a week in the days when they were lovers. As they ate the once-familiar food and relayed old jokes to each other, Willow felt herself relaxing properly for the first time since she had returned from her mill. Well aware that it had once been Tom who had been able to provide that relaxation for her, and that it was the very fact that she and Richard were no longer conducting a love affair with each other that made it possible, Willow nevertheless enjoyed it.

Life was so easy, she thought, when you did not have to worry about the feelings of the person opposite you, and she smiled at Richard with an open warmth that led him to stretch out a hand to her. She touched it briefly but withdrew so quickly that he shrugged and turned to ask for the bill.

'Richard, you're a good friend,' she said, deliberately unaware of the significance of the shrug.

'But that's all, I take it?'

'I don't think one can ever drink at the same spring twice, do you?'

'That's one of those phrases that sound profound but are actually meaningless,' he said, 'although I get your drift. It's been good to see you. I've been hanging around the kindergarten too long and letting it get under my skin. I ought to have had more sense.'

'Don't be so hard on yourself. Emma had adored you for years and you were . . . wounded. It's hardly surprising you took the comfort she was offering.'

'Yes, but it's disconcerting to realise that one has reached middle age and has come to prefer the company of one's . . . sorry. Can't think what I'm saying.'

Willow laughed.

'You could have substituted "one's friends to one's lovers",' she said kindly, 'if you thought "one's fellow geriatrics" was a trifle insulting.'

Richard laughed with her.

'I wasn't actually going to say that.'

'Probably not,' she agreed, watching him pay the huge bill, 'but it must have been pretty pejorative or you'd never have blushed like that. It was a charming sight. Are you coming back for a drink?'

'Why not?'

'Mrs Rusham will kill me if you leave any clues to your presence. She's been pining for you terribly and if she'd known I was seeing you she'd have cooked you a hamper of delicacies and insisted on waiting in the flat to see you.'

'She's a good woman, Willow, and a remarkably faithful employee.'

Willow, who knew that perfectly well, glared at him, thinking: I must be cracking up completely if I'm feeling jealous of my housekeeper's crush on Richard Crescent.

'Come on,' she said aloud.

Richard obeyed and ten minutes later parked his car in the first available space in Chesham Place. They walked across the fifty-odd feet of slippery pavements to her front door, hanging on to each other's arms for safety. As they reached the house in which Willow had her flat, a man got out of a car parked across the road. Willow looked up, startled and immediately wary.

'Tom? What's the matter?' Then she remembered. They had had a longstanding date for dinner that evening.

'Are you quite mad?' she went on. 'Didn't it occur to you hours ago that I couldn't make it? Why didn't you go home?'

'Didn't it occur to you that it would have been only polite to let me know you couldn't make it and stop me worrying about you?' Tom turned away from her without waiting for an answer and said in his usual voice: 'Hello, Crescent. How are you?'

Richard looked at his erstwhile rival and recognised something of his desperation. He took off his gloves and held out a hand. After a moment's hesitation Tom shook it.

'Desperately grateful to Willow,' said Richard with a frank and open smile of his own, which Willow registered in irritation. 'She's been advising me on my dealings with Emma, who's just decided that I'm years too old for her after all.'

Tom looked from one to the other and in the eerie light of the streetlamps reflected up from the dirty snow he seemed to flush slightly.

'Are you coming to join us for some whisky?' asked Willow, not best pleased to see Richard lying in order to protect Tom's feelings, but thinking it too absurd that they should all be standing freezing in the snow, making each other angry.

'Not if I'm intruding,' Tom said at once, trailing his coat in a way that made her want to hit him.

Not wanting to dignify his attempt to force reassurance out of her, Willow took her icy right hand out of her coat pocket in order to find her key and open the front door.

'Come on both of you or we'll all freeze to death,' she said.

Frowning, she led the way into her flat and to the warm, firelit, flower-scented drawing room.

'Richard, will you pour Tom a huge Leapfrog and yourself whatever you want while I go and soak my numb hands in hot water?'

She disappeared into her bathroom and locked the door behind her so that she could be alone to deal with the mixture of feelings that was making her seethe. It was true that in her growing interest in how Gloria Grainger had really died, she had quite forgotten her date with Tom, but his sitting in the car outside her flat like an irate father or a private detective made her furious.

Whatever they had shared, he had no right to spy on her. Worse, his masochistic waste of time and suffering was too obviously designed to make her feel guilty. He had no right to that either.

When she had eventually recovered her temper she went back into the drawing room to find the two men as cosy together as though they were in some all-male club. They both stood up as she shut the door behind her with something of a snap and Richard carefully waited for Tom to ask her what she wanted to drink. Well aware of her determined independence, he did nothing of the kind.

Willow went to the drinks' tray and poured herself a tiny glass of green chartreuse, thinking that the taste of wormwood was highly suitable to her mood.

'Women, eh, chaps?' she said at last.

Richard stiffened but Tom laughed and she remembered all over again why she liked him so much.

'Absolutely, Will,' he said, apparently back to normal. 'And fair's fair: you talk about "men" with that particular artifically thin, mean, mocking voice women use when they're objecting to something supposedly characteristic of our sex, don't you?'

'Oh, all the time,' she agreed with a smile. 'Good to have you back.'

Richard sighed silently and drained his drink.

'I'd better be off. It was a good evening, Willow. I'm only sorry it was at Tom's expense.'

'Don't worry about me,' said Tom with enough warmth to make Willow confused all over again. 'I can take it in a good cause like yours.'

She got up and escorted Richard to her front door.

'You did a lot for me this evening,' she said quietly. 'Thank you.'

'Getting you the legal research so easily and for nothing, you mean?'

'No. You've every right to feel cheated, but I didn't do it deliberately. I hadn't understood quite how sore I've been feeling and being with you was . . . '

'Like zinc-and-castor oil on a baby's bottom? I know.'

'Actually I was going to say "comforting", but a nappy-rash ointment would do just as well. You're funnier than I remember, Richard. Don't lose heart – or touch – hm?'

'All right. Thanks for having dinner with me. I liked it.'

'Good. And if your friend Borden says anything about how awful I was, you can always say I'm only a distant acquaintance.'

He patted her face.

'Never that. However cross you made and make me, I'd never do that. I'm dead fond of you, old girl.'

'What a tribute! Good night, Richard.'

'Tom really cares for you, too,' he said abruptly. 'Don't let him get your goat too much. He . . . he doesn't look happy.'

Willow could not say anything. She felt as though she were on some wild emotional sea-saw. Having no experience of the effects it was producing in her, she was alarmed. When Richard had gone she went slowly back to Tom.

'How's the case?' she asked in order to keep her mind off the sea-saw.

'We got the confession today, thank God,' he said.

As she heard that, Willow had second thoughts about Tom's motives for waiting so long in the street and remembered that she had been trying to mend whatever had been broken between them. She stopped half-way to the sofa and smiled helplessly at him.

'I am really glad, you know. I do understand that it was getting you down.'

'And I suppose I have been behaving like a louse. I snapped at you badly, didn't I, Will? Was that why you stood me up tonight?'

'No. That was a mistake. I've got so involved in this Gloria Grainger business that I've been rushing from one meeting to another. Richard and a legal chum of his were the last.'

Tom laughed, sounding slightly strained, and came to put an arm tentatively around her waist. When she did not move away, he kissed her.

'Sorry. I'd been assuming that you've been using me as a teaser for him; now I think that it could be the other way round. It's doing wonders for my faltering self-esteem.'

'Teaser?' Willow said distantly.

'Ah, you don't know anything about the breeding of race horses then?'

'No,' she said with some of the old crispness. 'And I suspect it's just as well.'

11

A S SOON AS SHE HAD finished her wonderfully solitary breakfast, Willow telephoned Posy Hacket.

'Hello, this is Posy Hacket's telephone,' sang the machine that answered. 'I'm sorry I'm working just now, but if you leave a message I'll ring you back as soon as I knock off.'

As soon as the beep had sounded, Willow said:

'Hello, this is Willow King. I'm sure your lawyer has already told you that a libel case can't be inherited. I happened to be sitting next to a barrister yester—'

'Hello? It's Posy here. Sorry, I've got into the habit of letting the machine answer in case it's something I don't want to deal with. You are kind to ring. Yes, my solicitor has told me. It's been a terrific relief.'

'I'm sure, although her heirs might not have pursued it even if they could have done,' said Willow, still not quite convinced of Posy's supposed ignorance of the law. 'None of the possible people seem too keen on her. I've been trying to find out who they are for my memoir, but apparently she left strict instructions that none of them was to be told anything until after the funeral. That's this Friday.'

'I see. No one's told me. Not surprisingly, perhaps.' Posy Hacket was silent after that, and Willow felt forced to say:

'There is something else that you might like to know.'

'Really? What's that?'

'I've discovered during my researches that Gloria Grainger was herself a witness to, if not actually a victim of, male violence, which might explain the bias of her books, even if it doesn't excuse it.'

'Hell!' said Posy again. Willow waited for a while and then said:

'Posy? Are you still there?'

'Yes, I'm here. How do you know?'

'I spoke to an old friend of hers and got it out of him – not without difficulty.'

'I'm not surprised. For some reason w— people are always ashamed. As though suffering it is somehow worse than perpetrating it. Who was it, her husband?'

'She never had one. It was her father.'

'I wish I'd known . . . Except that she should bloody well have known better. If she knew . . . Oh, bugger it all! God, how one gives oneself away! I'd be grateful if you'd not tell people. I know theoretically that there's no actual shame in having been beaten up, but I still feel it.'

'I'm so sorry,' said Willow carefully.

She was glad to know that there had indeed been a personal reason for Posy's loathing of Gloria's books, but she was not certain quite how much significance she could give it.

'I won't say that I had no idea because it had occurred to me. I feel nothing but sympathy for you.'

'I'm not sure that I want your sympathy – or anyone's. But thank you all the same. Good bye.'

As Willow sat with the telephone receiver in her hand, she wished that she had been able to watch Posy Hacket's face as they talked. It was hard to judge quite how deep her loathing had been and consequently how realistic her place among the suspects.

The idea that Gloria might have been murdered no longer seemed at all exaggerated, but Willow knew that no one else would be convinced until she could offer not just her own growing certainty but also hard evidence of who had killed Gloria and how.

The first thing she would have to do was talk to Gloria's doctor and find out the truth about her heart condition as soon as possible. Willow flipped through the pages of her notebook and found the doctor's name and address. His telephone number was listed in the directory and she dialled it. The telephone rang and rang until a bad-tempered male voice said:

'This is the doctor's surgery but he is not on duty at the moment. Appointments may be made between ten and twelve-thirty. Surgery is from four-thirty and emergencies should be referred to 081-873 6945. This machine does not take messages.'

At first Willow had thought that she was being answered by a recorded message, but by the time the voice had reached the emergency telephone number, she realised she was connected to a human being in spite of the last sentence.

'Doctor Trenor?' she said quickly before he could cut the connection. 'My name is Willow King. I am not a patient. Marilyn Posselthwate gave me your name. Have you a moment even though you're off duty?'

There was a short, gusty laugh.

'So you weren't taken in by my impersonation of the broken answering machine?'

'No, I'm afraid not. It was the irritability of your voice that gave you away. People dictating into machines tend to sound bland or throttled, but never angry.'

'I see. Young Marilyn has told me about you and warned that you might be in touch. What can I do for you?'

'Well, I hoped that we might meet so that I could ask you questions about your late patient, the sort of questions that I have found myself unable to put to either her friends or her relations.'

'I expect that would be all right, always bearing in mind medical ethics and confidentiality.'

Remembering what she had heard about the allegedly

'dirty' doctors the previous evening in El Vino's, Willow almost laughed. She managed to control herself and promised that she would always consider medical ethics when she was putting her questions to him.

'Splendid. Then what about meeting this morning? As you've heard, I am not on duty just now.'

'Unfortunately I am. What you might call my day job demands my appearance at the Home Office in fifteen minutes. But I'll be free this afternoon. If your surgery is not until four-thirty, perhaps we could meet before that.'

'Hmm. I've several house calls to make, but I'll have to eat. Lunch in the Maids of Honour in Kew Road at . . . when could you make it?'

'Quarter past one,' said Willow, only just suppressing a sigh at the thought of yet more food. She would have to stop Mrs Rusham cooking whatever she had selected for lunch.

'You're on. I'll see you then. I shan't have much time and so if you're late I'll simply start eating. Acceptable?'

'Fine.'

Everything seemed under control when Willow reached her office in the fortress in Queen Anne's Gate and listened to her staff reporting on what they had done since she had last been there. They all seemed thoroughly on the ball and capable of doing exactly what she had asked. She congratulated them more warmly than she would have done in the days when the civil service was her entire life.

Sandra, the Higher Executive Officer, reported that the Directorate of Prison Affairs had suggested that Willow should visit a tough prison called Great Garden in Berkshire, whose governor was a member of the new committee. An appointment had been made for Friday at eleven o'clock.

Remembering that Gloria's funeral was to take place at three-thirty that afternoon, Willow asked that the appointment be shifted back to nine so that she would have enough time even if there were bad delays getting back into London.

Willow then turned to Raymond Beete, who had already drafted his position paper on the existing educational opportunities in Great Britain's prisons. He had also talked to a prison psychiatrist about the possibility of commissioning a report on the changes that he believed were necessary within the education system to assist in the preservation of the inmates' mental health. What he had not yet done was sound out any members of the Prison Officers' Association about their reaction to any changes in the system.

'Good. I think it's far too early for that yet,' said Willow, giving Raymond her full attention. 'Now tell me what you've discovered so far.'

As they talked, she became so interested in the points he raised that she was surprised when he said it was twelve forty-five and that he must leave for an important meeting. Her own appointment with the doctor in Kew seemed to be in jeopardy and so she hastily locked away her papers, told Sandra that she had to leave but that she could be telephoned at her flat later if anyone needed her, and ran out of the building into Petty France. A taxi was passing the door of the Home Office and she hailed it. The cabby stopped with a wail of his brakes.

She gave him the address of the restaurant in Kew, adding: 'And hurry. I'm horribly late.'

'Okay, Miss, have you got everything?' he said, leaving his brakes on.

'What?' asked Willow, furious. 'I asked you to hurry.'

'If you're in that much of a hurry, Miss, you've probably forgotten something,' he said infuriatingly. 'Money, briefcase?'

'I've plenty of money.' She felt as though she should physically hold the anger inside her head. 'Please get a move on.'

'Suit yourself,' said the driver, setting off. Talking over his shoulder, he then proceeded to tell her horror stories of passengers who had reached Heathrow before they discovered that the crucial document they needed in the States had been left in their office, passports mislaid, and tickets left on the hall table.

Willow, her temper rising with every yard they travelled, decided that she would crack completely before they reached Kew and diverted him towards Chesham Place, so that she could pick up her own car. The detour might make her late, but at least it meant that she would arrive with her self-control intact and her mind alert.

She handed the cabby a five-pound note, not caring that the fare was only half that or that he was furious at losing the chance of a much larger one, and shoved her key into the door of her own car.

As she was sitting waiting at a set of lights in the Cromwell Road fifteen minutes later, she wished that she had succumbed to the blandishments of a cellular-telephone salesman she had once summarily rejected. If she could at least reassure Doctor Trenor that she was on her way, he might wait for her. As it was he would probably have eaten and gone by the time she reached the Maids of Honour.

The thaw was beginning and the hard impacted snow on the roads had been reduced to mounds of watery brown slush. It was easier to drive over, but looked so depressing that Willow would have preferred the dangers of the icy snow. She reached Kew and found a parking place quite quickly, but it was half-past one by the time she walked into the restaurant and looked around for the doctor. Either her fears had been reasonable or he, too, was late.

Willow found the table he had booked and when a waitress in a blue-and-white overall came to take her order, she asked whether he had left a message for her. The waitress went to consult her colleagues and reappeared with the comforting news that there had been no messages for anyone that day. Willow sighed and ordered herself the set lunch of soup, roast and pudding, because it seemed such remarkably good value. While she waited she looked around the room, which seemed pleasantly countrified with its pink-washed walls, wheel-back chairs and open fire.

Amused and relaxed by her surroundings, she took her leather-bound notebook out of her bag and started to write up accounts of her discussions in Kew the previous afternoon and her telephone call to Posy Hacket that morning, as well as an analysis of the possible extent of Posy's anger and its consequences.

The soup was brought before Willow had time to finish her analysis, let alone consider the implications of what Gloria's secretaries had told her. That there were several serious implications seemed certain to Willow and she let her mind play about with them as she drank the soup.

She had finished it and had managed to eat quite a lot of her large plate of meat and vegetables by the time she was interrupted by a familiar, bluff voice:

'Miss King?'

Willow looked up and saw a large freckled man in late middle age dressed in a baggily cut suit of hairy green-brown tweed and highly polished, heavy, brown brogues. He would not have looked out of place in a farmhouse on Dartmoor. Willow was amused at the idea that he must consider Kew to be 'country' rather than town and wondered what his younger patients thought of him.

'Yes,' she said, putting her knife and fork together and getting out of her chair. 'You must be Doctor Trenor. What can I get you?' She smiled at one of the waitresses, who came straight to the table.

'You're buying are you? Something to be said for feminism after all. Hah! I haven't time for a whole lunch so I'll have two of their little pasties and some cider.' He pronounced 'pasties' in the West Country way with a long 'a', and Willow was glad that she had picked Dartmoor as his natural setting.

She put her notebook away into her handbag and watched the waitress walk out into the shop-part of the room. She was back four minutes later with a plate of pasties and a glass of cider.

'Thank you, my dear,' said the doctor, raising his glass to her.

Willow winced, but he seemed not to have noticed.

'Aah, it's good to sit. Sorry I was late: one elderly patient had had a bad fall last night and I had to arrange to get her

146

checked over at X-ray in the local hospital. Now, what is it you think I can do for you?'

'As Marilyn has probably told you, I am writing a memoir of Gloria Grainger for her publishers,' said Willow, her coverstory fluent and convincing.

The doctor nodded. She wondered what he would have said if she had told him she was gathering evidence to prove that his late patient had been murdered.

'I understand that she became increasingly difficult during her last years and I assume that that must have been because of her state of health. Can you confirm that?'

Willow sat with her pen held ready on a clean page of the notebook, like an efficient, old-fashioned secretary.

'Not really,' said the doctor through a mouthful of pasty. He swallowed and collected the crumbs that clung to his lips in an immense white linen handkerchief, which he then thrust into his pocket.

Willow thought of pointing out the flowered napkin that had been laid beside his plate but decided against it.

'She'd suffered from angina for some time, but it did not give her permanent pain – nothing like patients with arthritis, for example – and it hardly inhibited her from doing anything she wanted since she was not a particularly active woman.'

'Then how do you account for her behaviour?' Willow smiled as though in eager expectation of a medical lecture.

'Young Marilyn could have given you just as good an account of that as I. There was no medical reason whatsoever for her aunt's temper and intolerance. She was probably the most selfish woman I've ever come across, and that's saying something I can tell you.' He stopped and drank. Then he added: 'If you ask me, her problem was that she had far too high an opinion of herself.'

'Goodness me! Do you talk about all your patients so frankly?'

'Certainly not. Miss Grainger's dead. And her relatives are fully aware of my views. Indeed, so was she. I often told her that she should control her temper for the good of her health if not for the happiness of her household. If you want to know, I think that young Marilyn has had hell's own delight between her aunt and that wretched young man of hers. She's too good to live.'

'I see. Yes, I thought she seemed rather put upon.'

'Put upon!' The doctor seemed to explode and the crumbs from another mouthful of pasty flew across the polished wooden table. Willow moved backwards, out of the line of fire, wondering how far the doctor's devotion to Marilyn might have taken him.

'That's putting it mildly,' he said when he had restored his crumby handkerchief to his pocket once more. 'She spent her days and much of her nights running between the two of them, taking orders, cooking meals, clearing up after them, soothing them when they couldn't sleep. She was permanently tired, I suspect, and her aunt's death has been a mercy for her, whatever does happen about the will.'

Willow looked at the big man opposite her. His reddened face and his bulging eyes showed how angry he was. She could not decide whether his feelings had got the better of his discretion or whether he was so unsuspicious and innocent that he did not see the construction that could have been put on his comment about the will.

'I'm sure you're right,' she said, attempting a soothing voice.

Motives for wishing Gloria dead were two-a-penny, but there was still no hard evidence to prove that she had been killed.

'What was it that actually killed her aunt?' asked Willow in search of it.

'Heart failure. Haven't they told you that much?' The doctor sounded thoroughly impatient.

'Yes, but I never know quite what it means. Did you do a post mortem?'

'My good woman, when you've a patient of her age with a history of angina, a gross appetite for all the wrong kinds of food, a violent temper, and a refusal to take any kind of exercise, you do not bother with an autopsy. The cause of death is perfectly obvious.'

Willow crossed her legs and finished her pudding.

'Yes, I think I see,' she said with a deep frown. 'It's just all so difficult for a lay person to understand. Were you surprised at her death?'

'I've just answered that question.'

'Oh, yes of course. Silly me. You said she over-ate, didn't you?'

'Yes, and whenever young Marilyn attempted to feed her less dangerous food – cut back on the cream and butter and so forth – there was the most terrible scene. I've had that poor child on the telephone to me in tears more than once, asking what to do.'

'She certainly seems to have relied on you a great deal,' said Willow, remembering what Marilyn herself had said about the doctor.

Willow wrote down a précis of everything he had said and then put away her notebook, intending to show him that she had finished asking questions about Gloria Grainger.

'Can I get you some pudding?'

'Not for me, thanks, although the buns here are some of the best in London. But I need coffee. I expect you do, too?' asked the doctor, beckoning to the waitress.

'Good idea.'

Willow spent the short interval before his attention returned to her phrasing and rephrasing her next question.

'Tell me about Marilyn. She seemed so overshadowed by the idea of her aunt that I didn't really feel I got to know her.'

The waitress came back with their coffee and the doctor waited until she had gone.

'She's had bad luck,' he said and poured cream into his coffee. 'Her mother died when she was fifteen and, reading between the lines, I don't think she got much comfort or support from her father. He may simply have been devastated by his wife's death. It happens. And hers was pretty long, drawn out and painful, I understand. Well, poor little Marilyn got her comfort the only way she could and fell pregnant. Hence dear Sarah.'

'Poor child,' said Willow with only moderate sympathy, drinking her coffee black.

'As you say,' he said looking at her with slightly more approval. 'With typical guts, she refused either to have an abortion or give the child for adoption and set about trying to find a residential job that would permit her to have the child with her. She spent a couple of terms at a boy's prep school, where she was wickedly exploited, until her father wrote to his sister asking for help.'

'So he did have Marilyn's interests at heart,' said Willow, who had been imagining another violent and difficult man.

'Presumably. He was just not a very adequate parent for a teenage girl without a mother. But in this case, he persuaded his sister to give her niece a job and a home. Marilyn has always been aware that she owes the old girl a lot, but I keep telling her she's paid it back with interest. I suspect she arrived in Kew hoping for a bit of the mothering she'd lost and found she'd stuck her nose in a viper's nest.'

'It must have been awful,' said Willow kindly.

'You're right there. Her aunt believed that she'd kicked the dust of Reading off her feet, but she still had enough resentment and spite to take it out on her niece once the girl was in her power.' He finished his coffee, withdrew his huge handkerchief, shook crumbs all over his tweed trousers and wiped his mouth. 'Resentment is the most destructive of human emotions.'

'More so than ordinary hate?' asked Willow, interested and thinking about both Posy Hacket and Patty Smithe.

'I'd have said so. Hate is hot and straightforward. Resentment is more like dry rot: eating slowly away at the fundamental fabric, destroying everything but the surface, which is left looking quite sound. Horrible!'

'I must think about that.' Willow was intrigued by the glimpse of an offbeat imagination she would never have suspected in so conventional a man. 'It's an interesting proposition. Perhaps you're right and her aunt's death has really been quite a mercy for Marilyn.'

'I hope she gets her just reward.' The doctor looked at the

large watch on his broad, hairy wrist. 'I must go. Good of you to give me lunch. I hope I've told you what you wanted to know.'

'Yes, I rather think you have,' said Willow, rising to her feet and holding out a hand. The doctor shook it.

'The only other thing I wanted to ask is are you Mr Farrfield's doctor as well?'

'No, thank the Lord. Watching one selfish bloodsucker drain young Marilyn was bad enough. Two would have been intolerable.'

'Is he really as bad as that?'

'Well, he's a selfish young bugger anyway. Sorry. Forgive my language. Selfish young rascal. He treats her as though it was her fault he's in a chair, but she was nowhere near the crash. He was driving the car himself, they tell me, and he owes her a lot for taking him in. Why she puts up with him, I can't think.'

'Perhaps he's the father of her daughter.'

'Perhaps he is.' The doctor looked disapproving. 'In which case, I'd have said she had even less reason to put up with him. None of our business though if he is or if he isn't. Good day to you.'

'Good bye.' Willow sat down, interested in his clumsy but clearly deep admiration for Marilyn.

Looking through her notebook for what Marilyn had said of him, Willow wished that she had taken her dictating machine to all her interviews so that she could have had a record of the precise words people had used. She had left it behind because of the inhibiting effect it tended to have on people unused to being recorded, but it would have helped.

Finding her written account of her first conversation with Marilyn, Willow did notice one direct quotation. Deciphering her own scrawl with difficulty, she read:

'I don't know what I'd have done if I hadn't had him to help me when Aunt Ethel became too difficult.'

12

HAVING RUNG THE DOORBELL OF Gloria Grainger's house ten minutes later, Willow was disappointed to be faced once more with Mrs Guy. Aware that the cleaner left the house every day at half-past five, Willow knew that there was no point in asking her any of the questions that might elicit the truth about Gloria's death.

It was clear that whatever had been done to her must have happened after she had gone up to her bedroom on the night she died, unless someone with the freedom of her room had previously tampered with the last pills she took. No one would admit to doing that, however skilfully the questions were put to her.

'Good afternoon, Miss King,' said Mrs Guy with a cheerful smile, not looking at all like a killer.

Willow smiled back in what she hoped was an encouraging fashion.

'Hello. I'm sorry to disturb you again, but I was passing and I dropped in on the off-chance that I could have a word with Marilyn, but I take it she is out. Do you know when she's expected back?'

Something moved behind Mrs Guy's eyes and her mouth tightened into an angry rosette.

'She's not out at all. She's upstairs on the telephone. Will you wait in the drawing room?' There was so much emphasis on the last two words that Willow laughed.

'I knew that you weren't minding my kitchen, whatever she said. Come along in.'

'Thank you. I didn't mind it at all. It was warm.'

Mrs Guy laughed as she showed Willow into the bitterly cold drawing room and then stopped. Her face suggested that she was struggling with a desire to say something.

'Can I help at all?' asked Willow.

Mrs Guy looked carefully up the stairs and came back into the drawing room, shutting the door behind her.

'We've had a terrible scene here today,' she said, her eyes bright with interest, 'and I'd never mention it except that I think you ought to know.'

'I?' Willow was torn between intense curiosity about anything that went on in the house and anxiety that Mrs Guy might have somehow divined her daily increasing suspicions.

'Marilyn found Peter over here this morning, going through her aunt's papers,' said Mrs Guy impressively.

'He wasn't?' said Willow, genuinely shocked into an interrogatory protest.

'He was,' answered Mrs Guy at once. 'And what do you think of that now?'

'But how did he get down to the basement? Did one of the secretaries help him?' Willow thought of Susan's powerful shoulders.

'Oh, no. He wasn't after any of the office papers. It was her own ones he wanted, that she kept in the study.'

Willow could not remember being shown anything like a study on her first tour of the house.

'Where's that?'

'It's the door just across the hall.' Mrs Guy pointed at the closed drawing room door as though they could both see through it.

'Oh, I see. Marilyn didn't show me that. And what did Peter find?'

'I don't know,' said Mrs Guy sadly, but she cheered up as she added: 'but Marilyn caught him at it and she gave him what for all right. They started going at each other hammer and tongs. Hammer and tongs.'

'But what do you think he was trying to find?'

'A copy of her new will of course.'

'New?'

'The one she only changed a while before she died.'

'And how do you know she did that?' Willow could not help remembering the secretaries' accusation of spying.

'Didn't she tell me so herself just before Christmas?' said Mrs Guy with dignity. 'When she said she'd be leaving me the twenty-five thousand pounds.'

Before Willow could apologise for her doubting tone of voice or ask any more, the drawing room door opened to reveal Marilyn, her face flushed and pretty.

'Mrs Guy,' she said with even more authority than she had shown the previous day, 'you have plenty to do downstairs.' The charwoman left the room, obviously not as surprised as Willow was by the change in Marilyn.

'Forgive me for disturbing you yet again,' said Willow as the door shut behind Mrs Guy. 'I was lunching with Doctor Trenor at the Maids of Honour and I felt I couldn't simply leave the area without seeing how you were.'

'That's really kind of you. I feel so . . . oh, so many things that I could burst, you know. You wouldn't come for a walk with me, would you? I don't think I can stay in the house any longer. Have you time?'

'Well, yes. I'd like that,' said Willow, surprised by the unlikely friendliness but determined to hear exactly what had been going on. 'I'm delighted to see you so much happier. What's happened? Or mayn't I ask?'

'Of course you can, but wait till we're out of here. There won't be any flowers, but why don't we go into the botanic gardens? I can afford it now.'

Willow, who had only ever heard the gardens called 'Kew' was amused at the formality of the title, and nodded.

'My boots aren't very robust,' she said, looking down at

them and remembering how much they had cost. She noticed with regret that there was already a faint white salt line above the sole.

'Don't worry. Most of the paths are hard and we can go and stroll in the palm house. They won't be at risk at all. Come on.' She almost waltzed out of the room and reappeared with a heavy woollen coat over her arm.

'Now what is it?' asked Willow as soon as they were within the great gilded iron gates of Kew Gardens and had paid their entrance fee. 'I'm consumed with curiosity.'

Marilyn, who had been walking briskly towards the long, gracefully mounded bulk of the palm house, stopped as though she could not both walk and tell her news. She faced Willow, her eyes blazing.

'Sarah and I are safe now and for ever.'

'I don't think I understand.'

'Aunt Ethel has left me three hundred thousand pounds and a trust for Sarah that will pay for her clothes and school fees and all sorts of extras until she's eighteen. Isn't it amazing and wonderful?'

'Yes indeed. Astonishing after what you've told me. But how do you know? I thought you said that neither the solicitor nor your aunt's executor would tell anyone the contents of the will until after her funeral.'

Marilyn started to walk again. Willow saw that her eyes were less excited and her mouth turned down once more.

'Yes, but we had a bit of trouble here this morning and I rang Gerald Plimpton to explain what was happening.' Marilyn stopped talking until they had reached the doors to the immense greenhouse. She hauled open one of the heavy doors, gesturing for Willow to precede her.

The wet heat seemed to hold Willow back for a moment, but she pushed through the barrier it created and sniffed the peculiar, unforgettable smell of warm vegetation, decomposition, damp, and something else she could not pin down. Condensation streamed down the smeared glass all around her, lying in terracotta-coloured pools on the white iron of the ledges and dripping from the floor of the gallery.

Marilyn followed her in and breathed deeply.

'I love this place,' she said, her voice gentle for once and her eyes dreamy. 'When I first came to live with Aunt Ethel I was very unhappy, but I'd bring Sarah in her buggy on my afternoons off and life wouldn't seem so bad. It was much cheaper then, of course.'

'I'm glad,' said Willow. 'You were about to tell me the rest of what it is that's made you so happy today.'

Marilyn turned, beaming.

'Aunt Ethel's left me the house as well as the money. Can you believe it? She's left me the whole exquisite house as well as three hundred thousand pounds.'

'Congratulations.'

'Thanks. What's so marvellous is that now that the house is mine I can decide who stays and who goes. I've told Mrs Guy she's to leave at the end of the month so that I'll be free of her interfering, inquisitive face at last.' Her voice was sharpening as she spoke. 'And I've told Peter to get out of the cottage at once.'

Aha, thought Willow, perhaps the sacking explains the charwoman's relish for the argument she overheard.

'And so you've got it all. I am pleased for you. And Doctor Trenor will be delighted. He was singing your praises all through lunch.'

'Was he?' Marilyn's smile was full of affection and gratitude. 'He's been very good to me, even before . . . But you're wrong.' A faint shadow dulled her excited eyes. 'I haven't got it all, nowhere near, although I've got more than I ever dreamed of. Mr Plimpton told me the rest, too. He thought it wouldn't be fair to make me think I was what they call her residuary legatee.'

'Oh, who is that?' asked Willow.

'He is, but there are other people getting a bit too. Mrs Guy will get twenty-five thousand, which is at least twenty-thousand too much if you ask me, and the doctor gets the same and so does Patty Smithe. At least we think she does. The wording says "if she should be working for me at the time of my death", and technically she was, although she hadn't been to the house for nearly two weeks. Mr Plimpton gets quite a lot of the furniture and most of the paintings as well as whatever's left over. But he doesn't think it'll be all that much after the tax has been paid and the others have had their legacies.'

'Well that sounds most suitable.' Willow could not imagine that Gerald Plimpton would have participated in a murder for the furniture and the residue of the money, but it was possible that twenty-five thousand pounds could have been enough to excite someone's greed, and three hundred thousand and a beautiful house were infinitely more than the gains of many murderers whose parole forms she had read at the Home Office.

'But I'm surprised,' Willow went on aloud without too great a delay, 'that Mr Plimpton should have told you all the details. You seemed so sure that he wouldn't.'

'I know.' Marilyn's face changed. 'He was reluctant even after I'd told him about all the trouble this morning. But eventually I made him understand.'

'What did happen?' Willow knew that she sounded abrupt, but her curiousity was pricking furiously.

'Peter and I had a terrible row,' said Marilyn in a matter-of-fact way, 'and I told him to get out of the cottage. He said I wasn't in a position to throw him out of a house that wasn't mine and that would probably be his as soon as all the probate business had been dealt with.'

'You mean he thought your aunt was leaving it to him?' Willow hoped that she did not sound quite as astonished as she felt.

'So he said. He thought she'd promised to leave him the cottage and the house months ago. When he said it, it seemed horribly likely.'

'But why, Marilyn? Why do you think she liked him so much? After all he was your friend, and you've told me often enough that she treated you really badly. Why should he have been different?'

'I used to think,' said Marilyn, 'that she just did it to spite me, which would be utterly typical of her. It's the kind of

157

thing she'd enjoy. But recently I've been wondering if it wasn't simpler. He used to butter her up all the time, flirt with her, tell her how magnificent she was and just like Queen Elizabeth I.'

'Good heavens!' said Willow, amused. 'He must have seen himself as the Earl of Essex. Talk about *folie de grandeur!*'

'I don't know about that. But it's what he used to say to her. I heard them at it often. It makes me feel quite sick to think of it!'

'I'm not surprised,' said Willow, not altogether truthfully. She was extremely surprised that Marilyn should have continued to house and feed a man who sucked up to her hated and tyrannical aunt in such a way.

'I nearly hit him this morning when he told me all over again how much she adored him, and I knew I couldn't bear to stay in the house any longer if it really was going to be his. When I told Mr Plimpton all about it, he decided I ought to know the facts about the will after all. And so then I told Peter, which was absolutely the best thing that I've ever done.'

'That was lucky then.'

'I say, shall we go up?' said Marilyn as they reached the foot of the spiral staircase up to the gallery. 'I never can when I've Sarah with me. She gets awful vertigo.'

'Let's,' said Willow, moving to let the other woman lead the way.

They walked up the steep, twisting stairs in silence, concentrating on their feet until they reached the gallery, from where they could look down at the wonderful mixture of greens and browns of the leaves below them. The scent seemed different up there, less musty, and the air was fresher and cooler. Willow asked no questions, following her guide in silence. Eventually, Marilyn stopped and leaned her elbows on the broad iron rail of the gallery's edge. Her face looked hard. Staring down at the spreading leaves of a squat tree below her, she started to bite her lips.

'Isn't that a marvellous sight?' Willow pointed to the second staircase that could be seen rising out of the dense forest to their left, almost smothered by the leaves of what looked like a giant bamboo. 'It's like something out of a weird dream of pursuit and escape.'

'Why?' Marilyn's voice was flat and incurious, but Willow answered her question, trying to explain her own moment of vivid imagination.

'If you ignore everything except the trees, you can imagine being in some steamy tropical forest, trying to get away from your pursuers – slavering dogs, perhaps – and suddenly you see that graceful white staircase and start flying up it away from all the hell on the ground.'

'But you wouldn't. If you could get up it, so could they and their dogs.' Marilyn's literalness made Willow sigh.

'It was just an idea I had.'

'Oh. Well, anyway, when I told Peter to get out and accused him of only living with me to weasel his way into my aunt's affections, d'you know what he said to me? He said that no one would ever have wanted to live with a dreary, suburban skivvy like me for any other reason.'

Her outrage, which at last seemed justified, stopped Willow's wandering thoughts.

'What a shit he must be,' she said more frankly than she usually spoke to Marilyn. 'I'm not surprised you were angry.'

A faint light flickered in Marilyn's brown eyes.

'Not half as angry as he was when I told him that he had to go and why. He was so sure, you see. But he was wrong.' Her voice rose again as she added: 'In spite of all those candlelit dinners I had to watch them at, and all his horrible charm, she liked me best.'

Willow was both amused by Marilyn's childishness and disturbed by her spite. They leaned on the white iron railing, watching a steady drip of condensation making a pool on the floor below. Willow began to wonder for the first time whether Marilyn had shared more than her physical appearance with her aunt. Downtrodden though Marilyn had been, perhaps now that she had the power that money always brings she would take the same pleasure her aunt had found in punishing other people for her remembered sufferings.

'How did you and Peter come to be sharing the cottage in the first place?' Willow asked, setting off towards the downward spiral staircase.

'I asked Aunt Ethel if he could live with Sarah and me after he came out of hospital,' said Marilyn more calmly. 'He wrote to tell me that he needed us then, you see, even though he hadn't wanted to have anything to do with us before.'

'That sounds,' said Willow carefully, 'as though he might be Sarah's father. I'm sorry if I sound intrusive.'

'I thought you knew he was.' Marilyn laughed shrilly. 'But I don't know why. How could you have known?'

'Did your aunt know?'

'I never told her,' said Marilyn after a pause. 'It always seemed better that she shouldn't know for certain, whatever she might have guessed.'

'Why?'

'Oh, because she had a lot to say about the horribleness of men and she might never have let Peter live with us.'

'Well, she'd have been right about him, wouldn't she?' said Willow.

Marilyn looked startled for a moment and then nodded.

'Well, yes,' she admitted, 'but I didn't know that then. She never asked about Sarah's father, you know, not once. And we'd already been living in the cottage for five years before Peter came. There didn't seem any point telling her.'

They reached the stairs and Willow started down, thinking how pleasant it was to be in the palm house alone. The only other time she'd been in there had been one Saturday afternoon when people had had to queue for the stairs and children's shrill voices had bounced off the glass sides and roof, punctuated by the exasperated commands of their fretful parents.

'Perhaps he told her he was Sarah's father,' said Willow, half to herself, 'and that's why she got so angry just before Christmas and decided to change her will.'

There was a slithering sound and a curse behind her. Willow half turned to see something coming towards her, but before she could do or say anything, she was hit forcefully across the shoulders. Falling forwards, Willow saw the steep spiral stairs surging up towards her. Panic-stricken and beyond thought, she flung out her right arm towards the decorative banister. One of her gloved fingers banged into a leaf-shaped panel and was bent agonisingly back on itself. Despite the pain, she just managed to get a grip of the banister.

But the speed of her fall pulled her fingers away. She desperately tried to hang on, her teeth gritted and every muscle fighting for safety. Her shoulder was ferociously wrenched and she felt herself falling towards the harsh greyness of the steps. They seemed to plunge downwards for miles ahead, a sickening spiral of fear. Flinging up her hands to protect her head and face just before the impact, Willow felt the steps crunch into her thighs and stomach and breasts and elbows.

Her body slithered agonisingly on, blood rushing into her head and making it intolerably heavy. She tried to swing herself across the stairs to stop the terrifying fall. Her half-protected head cracked against one of the banister rails and she gasped.

The next twist in the spiral allowed her to jam one hand against the broad central pillar. Her leather glove pressed against the white-painted iron and slowed the descent a little. Her body was still moving, but for a moment she thought she might be safe.

A split second later, her hand was struck heavily by one of Marilyn's booted feet and her neck by the other. Marilyn's whole weight fell on to Willow's body, forcing her head further down. On they fell as though they were on some hellish version of a helter-skelter. Scrabbling with her hands for purchase to stop the momentum, Willow scraped her palms even through her gloves and banged her head and bruised her ankles.

At last she managed to get both hands round one of the

plain rails. Gritting her teeth against the force and the pain, she let her body swivel and slammed her booted feet into the central pillar and eventually managed to get herself the right way up and her feet in front of Marilyn so that she, too, could fall no further.

The blood seemed to recede from Willow's painful head, leaving it aching. She leaned her back against one of the heavily moulded iron banisters and caught her breath. Looking up, she realised that they had fallen only about fifteen feet. It had felt like fifty.

Breathing in deep, tearing gasps, she managed to say with all the sharpness induced by real physical terror:

'How could you be so stupid? Why didn't you hang on to the sides?'

There was no answer.

'Marilyn?' she said even more sharply. 'Are you all right?'

Twisting her painful body, Willow levered herself upright enough to look at the other woman's face. It was yellowish white and completely expressionless, the eyes closed and the mouth slack. A large dark bruise was already forming on the side of her forehead. Realising that Marilyn must have knocked herself out when her head hit one of the hard steps or the banisters, Willow let some of her anger go and tried to think.

Waiting until her own breathing was almost normal, she stood up, feeling all her bruises and wrenched muscles, and took off her coat to prop Marilyn safely against the banisters. When she was certain the other woman could not fall again, Willow made her way down the rest of the twisting stair, holding on to both rails and stepping carefully around the worn, slippery patch in the centre of each tread.

She was trembling by the time she reached the bottom and felt horribly dizzy. Only the thought of fresh air made her able to loosen her hold on the iron rails so that she could walk on out of the steamy heat.

Breathing great gulps of painfully, wonderfully, cold air, she ran down the hard asphalt paths towards the main gate. Her breath hurt her throat as it was forced upwards by her pumping heart and there was a stitch in her side to add to her increasingly sore bruises. She was sweating from the effort but her body was bitterly cold.

At last she reached the gatehouse and a welcoming woman with short hair and a helpful smile. In the face of her incredulity, Willow gasped out her story and asked for help.

'Is it bad enough for an ambulance?'

'No, I shouldn't have thought so,' Willow said, leaning against the wooden sides of the hut, panting. 'I can't see how she can have broken anything, since I was underneath her and I'm only bruised. But she's too heavy for me to lift on my own and her house is way down towards the bottom of the green. Can you help?'

'I can't leave the gate, but don't worry. I'll get you some help.'

'I know what we ought to do,' said Willow, wondering how she could have forgotten the doctor's devotion. 'Ring Doctor Trenor's surgery and see if he's there. Tell him Marilyn Posselthwate has had an accident. She's a patient of his. I haven't got his number, but it'll be in the book.'

'It's all right, I know the number.' The dark-haired woman smiled again. 'He's my doctor, too. You'd better come in and sit down.'

'I must go back to her. If he can't come, will you let me know somehow?'

'All right. You go on back.'

Dr Trenor came running into the palm house twenty minutes later, by which time Marilyn had come round briefly and complained of a headache and bruises and then apparently sunk back into unconsciousness. He flung himself on his knees at her side, saying furiously over his shoulder to Willow, who had descended the stairs again to get out of his way and was waiting at the bottom, sitting on the edge of the nearest flower bed:

'What have you done to her?'

Willow's mind started working again. Knowledge of the changed will flashed past pictures of the doctor's intense anxiety and Marilyn's stated affection for him, her inheritance, his loathing of Peter Farrfield, his certification of the death without any kind of post-mortem examination, his anatomical knowledge, Marilyn's clearly desperate need to be free of her aunt's temperament.

'Nothing,' said Willow with what she felt was remarkable coolness. 'She did it. She slipped somehow and banged into me and the two of us went tumbling down. I'm bruised but she's the only one to break her crown.'

It was not until she saw the doctor's outrage that she realised she had been quoting from 'Jack and Jill' and thought she must be lightheaded herself.

'Sorry,' she said quickly. 'I'm a bit shaken. She was awake a few minutes ago and seemed perfectly normal, if bruised. I'm not sure if she's fainted or what.'

'Yes; I see. Stay there. I'll attend to you later.'

He touched Marilyn's face, calling her name over and over. Willow disobeyed his instruction, wanting to know exactly what Marilyn's first words to him would be.

They were disappointingly banal.

'What happened?'

'You fell,' said Doctor Trenor, holding her hands. 'But as far as I can see there's no serious damage. Can you sit up?'

She did as he asked, wincing. When he asked her very gently what hurt she stretched out one of her arms. Willow noticed for the first time that she had remarkably small hands.

'It's my wrist. It really hurts.'

He manipulated it carefully and said she'd sprained it.

'It won't kill you, luckily.'

She managed a shaky laugh and he added: 'Come on, young Marilyn, up with you. Miss King and I will help you back to the house and I can give you a proper examination there and some strapping for the wrist.'

'Willow? She was falling, too. Is she all right?'

Willow moved out of the shadow of a large tree with fern-like leaves and smiled slightly. She was still angry, and the terror of facing that plunge downwards had not left her, but there seemed no point in yelling about her feelings.

'Luckily my injuries seem to be superficial. Nothing hurts badly except my shoulder and that's probably just wrenched.'

The doctor handed her the coat she had used to wedge Marilyn against the banister. Willow put it on, wincing as she moved her right shoulder, while he helped his patient to her feet. With him on the side of her sprained wrist and Willow on the other, they moved slowly along the central aisle of the glasshouse and out into the cold once more.

It took them fifteen painful minutes to get back to the main gate, where Willow offered to fetch her car so that she could drive Marilyn the hundred yards or so to her house.

There they discovered that Mrs Guy had already gone, even though it was only twenty-past four. Being under notice, she must have decided she no longer needed to work a full day. There was no sign of Peter Farrfield either. Under Marilyn's instruction the doctor telephoned the cottage, but there was no answer.

'Selfish toad's probably sulking somewhere,' he said angrily.

'Or drinking in the pub,' said Marilyn bitterly. 'That's what he usually does when we've had words.'

'What about the secretaries?' said the doctor. 'Can't one of them make you some tea while I get you to bed?'

'Don't let's worry them,' said Willow quickly. 'I can do that. I know where the kitchen is.'

Neither of the other two protested and so Willow left them walking slowly up the stairs towards the second floor, amused to think of herself with the freedom of the house. At the head of the steep basement stairs Willow stopped, suddenly assailed with what she assumed must be vertigo.

The mixture of dizziness and swooping fear was not something she had felt before. Pressing her hands flat against the wall and not looking down, she started her descent, wincing at each step as she jarred her bruised body.

Poking about in the cupboards in search of cups, a teapot and a milk jug, she saw that Gloria had owned two sets of china: one, presumably for her own use, was modern

Sèvres; the other was a basic, heavily glazed, dark-brown farmhouse set. Willow chose the French porcelain for the tray she soon carried upstairs.

Listening for voices on the top-floor landing so that she could select the right door, Willow heard the doctor say:

'But it's all yours now. You can have as much heating as you want and you can tell everyone else to go to hell if that's what you feel. So what if it ruins the furniture? You have the power in this household now and you need not put up with anything. It's your turn at last, my child.'

Willow knocked on the door with the edge of her tray. The doctor opened the door and took the tray from her.

'Now,' he said, laying it down on the empty dressing table, 'would you like me to look at your injuries?'

'It's all right,' said Willow, rubbing her shoulder and ignoring the dizziness that still plagued her. 'I can move it, so it can't be dislocated. The rest is only bruises and scrapes. If it were anything more I'd not be able to walk. But thank you.' She turned to Marilyn, who was looking fragile and appealing in the big spare bed. 'Do you need any help with your daughter before I go?'

'She's with a friend today. I sent her there before I tackled Peter this morning. Oh, dear! They'll be bringing her back to the cottage and the front door's locked. I don't let her have a key any more because she always loses them. If Peter isn't back, she won't be able to get in. She may not think to come round to the Green and ring the bell here because she was never allowed to in the old days. I'd better phone . . . oh, no, that's no good either. Liz said she'd take them swimming and come straight back here from the pool. I'll have to go to bed over there.'

Marilyn struggled with the blankets, which the doctor had tucked tightly into the mattress.

'No, you don't. That wretched, cold, damp, hen house would be bad for you,' he said. 'We can make some other arrangement.'

'Why don't I simply go across the garden and leave a note for your daughter on the front door?' said Willow, not averse to seeing how easy or otherwise it might have been for Peter to get his wheelchair from the cottage to the main house.

'Good idea,' said the doctor as Marilyn relaxed. 'Get your friend to bring her round here. Now, my dear child, will you be all right for a bit? I ought to get on with my calls.'

'I'll be fine,' said Marilyn without thanking him.

'I'll look in again this evening, make sure everything's all right and that you've got something to make you sleep. Don't get out of bed until you have to. You need rest. Good bye, Miss King. I'm glad you're all right. Thank you again for my lunch.'

'It was a pleasure.'

When he had gone, Willow seized the opportunity for which she had been angling.

'Shall I fetch you some writing paper so that you can write a note to your friend for me to stick to the cottage door?'

'That would be kind. There'll be some in Aunt . . . in my study downstairs. It's opposite the drawing room.'

Willow left without another word. The study was as exquisite as the rest of the house. Both the panelling and shutters had been painted a soft creamy colour and the polished floor was partly covered by an old French rug woven in muted pinks and greens. The furniture was restricted to an impeccable walnut secretaire with an upright chair in front of it and two old wing chairs on either side of the delicately carved chimneypiece. The curtains were of old-rose and cream silk, looped back with twisted cords.

The desk was open and the flap was covered in a mass of jumbled papers, which Willow was certain Gloria Grainger would never have allowed. Looking carefully but quickly through the top layer, Willow realised how furious Peter Farrfield must have been when he searched through it. The papers were all either fan letters or photocopies of adulatory reviews. There was nothing either legal or financial there at all.

Frustrated herself, Willow reached into one of the compartments at the back of the desk and brought out a neat bundle of engraved writing paper. As she left the room she noticed that there was a draught-excluding piece of wood about an inch and a half high at the threshhold. That would not have been enough to prevent any wheelchair-bound person getting access to the room, but the three steps she could see between the hall and the door into the garden must have presented more of a problem.

Marilyn wrote her note and gave Willow the key to the back door of the cottage, which could be reached only from the garden of the main house. As she walked along the brick path between the immaculately kept flowerbeds, Willow noticed all the unevennesses and shallow steps that might have impeded someone in a wheelchair. They were not enough to have made such a journey impossible without help, but it would have been hard.

Having climbed the gentle ramp up to the back door of the cottage, unlocked the door and left it ajar, she went into the spartan kitchen. There she found a baize-covered noticeboard with several spare drawing pins. Taking two, Willow went out into the narrow hall and the door that opened on to the street. She pinned Marilyn's note to the outside of the door, before shutting it carefully. As she was slowly walking back towards the kitchen and the door that would lead back into Gloria's garden, she heard the unmistakable sound of a footfall upstairs.

'Hello!' she called, surprised but not nervous.

A tousle-haired young man dressed in jeans and a blue guernsey appeared at the top of the stairs. His broad face looked astonished.

'Hello,' he answered politely enough in a deep, pleasant voice. 'Who on earth are you?'

'A friend of Ms Posselthwate,' she said in her best civil-service voice. 'She asked me to leave a note on the door for her daughter. And you?'

He hesitated for a moment and then smiled pleasantly again.

'Poor old Peter asked me to come and pack up his things. I gather he's fallen out with his young woman and so I've taken him in. Someone had to volunteer to pick up his stuff.'

'Oh, I see,' said Willow, still puzzled. 'Why are his things upstairs?'

'He slept up here,' said the young man, pointing to a rail that ran along the stairs and led to a padded chair Willow had not noticed.

'Ah. Shall I give Ms Posselthwate a message for you?'

'Oh no, don't worry her. She's got enough on her plate from all I've heard.'

'I'm afraid I can't let it go at that,' said Willow, conscious of everything she had heard and suspected about Peter Farrfield. 'For all I know you could be a burglar.'

'Me?' said the young man, his face breaking into a delightful smile as he flung his arms wide. 'Come on up and see what I'm taking.'

Willow did not move. She had that much sense; or perhaps the memory of having been thrown down one staircase had sharpened her always strong self-protective instincts.

'Oh, all right. I'll bring the cases down and show you the contents. I won't be a minute.'

Willow looked for the telephone she knew must be somewhere in the hall or kitchen. She found it on the untidy dresser in the kitchen, but before she could pick up the receiver, the young man was back. He laid two old-fashioned suitcases on the formica-topped kitchen table and flung back their lids. Piles of obviously male clothes covered shoes in one case and books in the other. The only incongruous item was a squash racket.

'Poor man,' said Willow pointing to it and suppressing a groan as the movement pulled at one of the bruises on her back. The young man smiled again.

'I know. And he used to be so active. It's rotten luck. He said he'd give it to me.'

'I see. Now why not come across to the house and make yourself known to Ms Posselthwate? Then everything will be in order.'

'I'd rather not actually,' he said with an attractive air of confiding that brought a reluctant smile to her lips. 'You can bear witness that I've taken nothing that's not Peter's and I don't want to complicate her life any more. Tell her, if you will, that he'll be all right with me. I'm Martin Smith. She'll know. I'll be in touch when the dust has settled.'

He held out his right hand. Reluctantly Willow accepted it. She was concerned but could think of no reason – or way – to force him to see Marilyn. He shut the lids and swung the two heavy cases down off the table as though they were filled with nothing more than empty paper bags. Willow made a mental note of his great upper-body strength.

'So long,' he called over his shoulder.

'Before you go,' said Willow firmly, 'you'd better give me the front-door keys he lent you. I'm sure Ms Posselthwate would prefer to have them under her own control.'

The young man hesitated again, then tucked one heavy case under his left arm and took a pair of keys out of his right trouser pocket.

'Fair enough,' he said. 'Here.'

Willow took them and followed him to the front door to make certain that it was double locked behind him, before walking painfully back across the garden to report to Marilyn.

'Martin Smith?' she said, her face a study in astonishment. 'I've never heard of him. And he's going to look after Peter?' She put one small hand up to hold her forehead as though the ache in her head was preventing her from thinking. At last she looked up again at Willow.

'I don't understand.'

'I'm sorry,' said Willow. 'I couldn't think how to hang on to him, short of physical means and he was obviously a lot stronger than me even when I haven't just been . . . fallen down an iron staircase.'

'What did he look like?' asked Marilyn, tugging at the taut blankets in an effort to get out of bed. 'Ow!' she screamed as she bent her sprained wrist again.

'Careful,' said Willow. 'He's gone now, anyway. There's nothing you can do. He was not very tall – I'd say about five feet ten – but he looked immensely strong, particularly in the

170

arms and shoulders. He had thick, untidy dark-brown hair. I didn't notice what colour his eyes were, but his smile was very attractive. He was wearing jeans and a dark-blue guernsey. He had a deep and rather pleasant voice. What's the matter?'

There was an expression of intense concentration in Marilyn's eyes.

'Was the guernsey darned at all?' she asked with a half smile that Willow could not read.

'Good heavens, I don't know!' Willow was irritated by the question but she did her best to remember exactly what she had seen. 'Actually I think there might have been a darn. Yes, that's right: the colours didn't match. That must be why I registered it. It was green and towards the cuff on one arm. I think the left.'

Marilyn's colour was fluctuating like an arty film advertisement for vanilla ice-cream covered with raspberry sauce.

'That bloody, lying, exploiting little bastard!' she said at last, her voice exploding into an uncharacteristically raucous shout on the last word.

'Who?' asked Willow just at the moment when she realised the answer. 'You mean that was your supposedly wheelchair-bound friend himself?'

'It must have been. Unless he'd lent his jersey to another short, dark, smiling man with a deep voice.' Marilyn pushed her heavy hair away from her face. 'I darned it for him all in a hurry one weekend when I couldn't get out to the shops to buy dark-blue wool.'

'But he was moving without any trouble at all,' said Willow. 'How could it have been him?'

'It must have been. There can't be two men who look like that. But we can settle it one way or the other. I've got a photo of Peter in my bag. Will you get it?'

'Yes,' said Willow, when Marilyn had offered her the small colour print, which looked as though it had been taken for a passport. 'That's him. So he's not disabled after all. Well, well, well.'

All sorts of new possibilities crowded into her mind.

'He must have been pretending to be crippled to get money out of his insurance company,' said Marilyn, making Willow irritable all over again.

'Come off it,' she said at once. 'How could he possibly have been doing that? You can't even submit a claim for personal injury without doctors' certificates and a police report, let alone expect to get any money. Besides, wasn't Peter's story that there was another driver involved who died? No one could invent that for an insurance company without being exposed as a liar instantly.'

'Well, I don't know, do I?' said Marilyn pettishly. She looked up at Willow through her eyelashes. 'I've never driven a car.'

'It's much more likely that he was simply trying to charm money out of your aunt. Do you know if she gave him anything while she was still alive?'

As she asked that, Willow became concerned for Marilyn's blood pressure. Her face was so flushed that it looked almost purple and her eyeballs seemed to be swelling as they protruded between the lids.

'Probably. I'd never thought of it, but it makes sense of a lot of things, doesn't it? And to think that I was paying for everything for him all the time. It's not fair. I . . . '

'All right, all right,' said Willow, trying to soothe her. 'Obviously you never even thought of doubting him.'

Marilyn shook her head, her lips firmly closed.

'It's irrelevant now in any case. He must have realised that the goose that layed the golden eggs was dead and, since he must have known he'd get nothing out of you after the row, decided to cut his losses.'

'When you said he was a shit,' said Marilyn viciously, 'you were flattering him, weren't you? Think of everything I did for him. Lifting him in and out of his chair, taking him to hospital . . . No wonder he'd never let me stay while he actually saw a doctor. The whole bloody thing was fake. God! I feel a fool.'

'There's no point in thinking about it now,' said Willow, becoming aware of something alarming that was rising up from her subconscious mind. It seemed to her then that anyone who was reckless enough to allow a man to live in her house ought not to be surprised if he turned out to be a criminal. The very extravagance of her generalisation appalled her, and so did its implications.

'I ought to go now,' she said hurriedly. 'Will you be all right?'

'Yes,' said Marilyn, hunching her shoulders under the blankets. She remembered her manners enough to add: 'Thank you. You have been kind to me.'

'That's all right,' said Willow, far more concerned about her own affairs than any of Marilyn's. 'Good bye.'

13

W ILLOW DROVE AS FAST AS possible back to Belgravia, watching the rush-hour traffic flooding out in the opposite direction and trying quite hard to confront the significance of her own suppressed emotions. Her head and all her muscles ached, and one part of her mind rejected everything the other part suggested.

When she reached the flat she sighed in relief to be home, alone. Fires had been lit in all the rooms. Christmas roses and bowls of white and yellow forced hyacinths added freshness to the air, and the light everywhere was mellow and calm. Mrs Rusham was in the kitchen, preparing dinner, and everything was as it should be.

Willow stood in the doorway of her drawing room, breathing in the scents of the hyacinths and the fire, relieved that the money that made her secure was her own, earned by her, owed to no one and expected by no one. She was perfectly safe, she told herself, and wondered why the statement seemed so unconvincing.

'Would you like tea now, Miss King?' Mrs Rusham's voice made her employer jump. 'I am sorry to have surprised you.'

'Yes, thank you,' said Willow, unbuttoning her coat so that she could disguise her residual fear. 'It's a bit late to eat, but a cup of tea would be lovely. Could you get rid of these for me?' She handed the housekeeper her coat and gloves and went to sink into the softness of one of her big sofas, letting her head flop back on to the cushions.

Mrs Rusham brought in tea on a large Victorian black papier mâché tray, decorated with overblown painted roses and mother-of-pearl lozenges, which Willow had recently bought because it amused her.

'Is there anything else you need?' asked Mrs Rusham. 'I have put the newspapers and the second post on the telephone table. Your dinner's in the Aga and there should be plenty. I've laid the table. If there's nothing else, I'll be on my way.'

'Thank you, Mrs Rusham, that seems splendid,' said Willow, noticing that despite her refusal of food, her housekeeper had provided scones keeping warm over hot water beside small dishes of clotted cream and strawberry jam and a plate of egg-and-cress sandwiches. 'I'll see you tomorrow.'

When she was alone, she decided that she could manage to eat a little, despite her late lunch, and split a scone and spread it lavishly with cream and jam. She enjoyed the crunchy lightness of the scone almost as much as the rich sweetness of its topping. The smoky, tarry taste of the Lapsang Suchong tea, sharpened by lemon, made the perfect contrast and she even toyed with the idea of eating all three scones before common sense returned to her.

Laughing, she let her mind revert to the investigation, trying out first one explanation of Gloria's death and then another. None of them seemed convincing, not least because Willow did not have enough facts about the state of Gloria's body when it was discovered.

Wishing that she knew more about forensic medicine, Willow decided to get some professional advice. She fetched the telephone and punched in the number of Dowting's Hospital in South London. When she was answered, she gave her name and asked for Doctor Salcott, an old acquaintance who had often given her useful medical information. She was told that he was 'on the ward' and was being bleeped. In four minutes she heard his voice:

'Willow! You know that's the oddest name. I still can't help thinking of you as Cressida. It comes much more naturally.'

Willow laughed.

'Hello, Andrew. How are you?'

'Much the same as usual: furious with the Minister of Health, furious with the chief executive of the hospital, furious with my wretched patients, furious with my accountant who can't find a better way of dealing with the fees my foreign patients pay, and so on.'

'Oh, the traumas of consultant status! Don't you wish you were still a humble registrar?'

'Certainly not. I've never been humble in my life and I don't intend to start now.'

When they had first met, Willow had found his relentless masculinity and rollicking humour hard to take, but since then she had discovered that real discernment and intelligence lay behind them. She was rather proud of her own tolerant appreciation.

'What can I do for you this time?'

'Hearts,' she said. 'You're good at hearts, aren't you?'

'Stuffed with prunes and bacon and steamed in the pressure cooker for forty minutes? Yes, all my friends enjoy them. A touch of coriander often helps.'

'Idiot! Cardiology rather than cookery.'

'Oh, how dull. A professional question. All right, but you'd better be quick because the bleeper's going again.'

'Is there any way a heart attack can be induced by someone wanting the patient to die?'

'I'll have to get back to you. The answer's too long to give while the bleeper's going. Bye for now.'

'Good bye, Andrew. When?' said Willow into an empty telephone. She replaced the receiver and sighed, turning over her letters to see if there were any that looked at all interesting. One with her agent's distinctive typing on the envelope reminded her that Eve was still waiting for a call.

Willow looked down at her watch and, seeing that there were still ten minutes until the end of Eve's working day, picked up the receiver again.

'Eve. Me: Willow.'

'About time, too. I wish you authors would clear things with me before you go messing up my deals with your publishers. Purely editorial matters are of course a matter for you and Ann to discuss alone, but anything that affects money or agreements really ought to come through me. It saves confusion, if nothing else. She's been on to me wanting to cut your fee for the synopsis because you've told her the book will have to be shorter, and I didn't even know what she was talking about. It made me look a fool.'

'I'm sorry.' Willow recognised the justice of the complaint. 'You're right and I won't do it again. As it happens, I think I may have found enough new information to bulk up what I'm going to write. The synopsis . . . '

'Is already overdue.' Eve's voice was crisp and cold, like a fresh lettuce thought Willow irreverently, relieved that she could still amuse herself with verbal games. 'Ann has pointed out that if they don't get the complete manuscript within the next two months, there will be no point in even trying to publish it. Gloria will be not only dead and buried, but also forgotten within six. At the rate you're going with the synopsis, you'll never do it.'

'I'll try and do as much as I can tonight,' Willow said, wondering whether she had the energy for anything except sleep, 'and fax it to you as soon as possible tomorrow. Perhaps I'd better ring Ann to reassure her. Would you permit that, Eve?'

'There's no need to be sarcastic. I think it's a good idea. Calm her down and possibly discuss the direction you're planning to take. That ought to keep her on your side,' said Eve, beginning to sound more relaxed. 'But don't forget when you've got Gloria out of the way, you've still got a new kind of novel to invent.'

'And a committee looking into prison education to keep under control,' said Willow completely sobered. 'Why did I

177

ever agree to that? I've even said I'd go to Great Garden prison on Friday morning and be shown the educational facilities and some of the work that's getting done. God knows when the new novel will get sorted. But I promise I'll deal with the Gloria synopsis as soon as possible. And I'll ring Ann now.'

'I should hope so too. You've never been this unprofessional before. Something seems to have gone to your head.'

'How odd. I have just fallen on it. Perhaps I'm concussed.'

'Don't fall into that particular trap, Willow.'

'Which?'

'Using up your creativity to produce excuses for late delivery,' came the tart answer. 'It's the beginning of the end: I've seen it too often to mistake.'

'I have in fact just fallen down the spiral staircase in the Palm House at Kew and I'm covered with huge black bruises, and in fact reeling from shock.'

Willow suddenly realised that that was actually true. She felt extremely wobbly. No wonder her subconscious mind had been throwing up bizarre ideas. Perhaps she need not worry about them after all. Much more lightly she added:

'But I'll take your warning to heart.'

She said good bye before Eve could do more than sketch an apology, and immediately telephoned Weston & Brown. The receptionist put her straight through to Ann's office, but it was obviously a bad time to have disturbed her. She snapped out a brief greeting and then said:

'Look, I really haven't time to talk now. Is it about the synopsis?'

'Yes. Eve thought . . . '

'Could you come in and talk about it tomorrow? I've a free half-hour in the afternoon, at half-past three. Could you make that? I'll have time then to concentrate on it, but just now I have to go. All right?'

'All right,' said Willow since there was really nothing else to say.

She went into her writing room and tried to work, but was not successful. Two hours later, she was sitting at her desk with her head in her hands, thinking about going to bed really early, when she heard her front door bell ringing. Something about the dinner that Mrs Rusham said she had left in the oven began to make sense. Willow pushed herself up off her chair and went to open the front door. A sharp pain surged through her shoulder muscles as she raised her arm to the latch and she gasped.

Tom was standing outside her door with a bottle of champagne in his hand.

'I thought we'd celebrate,' he said.

'Perfect,' said Willow, blinking as she wondered whether her continual failure of memory when it came to dates with Tom was as sinister and Freudian as she feared. Then she decided that her exhaustion gave her enough of an excuse for forgetfulness that evening. She put a hand on her forehead.

'I've been working and my mind's still half on what I've been writing,' she said. 'In a minute or two I'll be in celebratory mood, too.'

Tom frowned and Willow tried to make herself imagine what he might be feeling instead of simply assuming that it was anger.

'You know where everything is,' she went on. 'Can you sort yourself out while I get my mind in order?'

Tom looked carefully at her and seemed to decide that her blankness and slow voice were not designed to wound but were merely a function of her mind being on her work.

'I'll bung this in the fridge and lay the table,' he said easily. 'Don't rush. There's plenty of time.'

'Thanks,' said Willow, 'but don't worry about the table. Mrs R. has done it.'

'Why not have a bath? I know you like one between work and food. I've still got today's papers to read.'

She smiled at him, her eyes a little more alert than they had been but still vaguer than usual.

'I'd like that. You have good ideas, Tom.'

'I know,' he said, ruffling her neatly arranged hair. 'Are you all right?' he added as she flinched. 'You look at bit battered.'

'I fell and banged myself this afternoon and various bits of me are rather painful, but I'll live.'

'You'd certainly better have a bath then. Would you rather I went away?'

Willow looked at him carefully. The very fact that he had offered to leave made it unnecessary for her to accept and so she shook her head, wincing again as the movement exacerbated the pain.

Emerging half an hour later, damp and still aching but much more alert than she had been, Willow found Tom lying on one of the sofas, his shoes conscientiously left on the floor beside the three newspapers he had finished. He was asleep. She stood looking at him, noticing the deep lines around his mouth and between his eyebrows. It was absurd to read mood into a sleeping face, but she thought it possible that he looked worried rather than angry. Her own part in their difficulties, which she was just beginning to unravel, troubled her.

'Tom,' she said and when he did not wake laid one of her hands on his forehead. His eyelids lifted at once and he smiled.

'I do like having my head held.'

'Lucky you,' said Willow, removing her hand at once. 'It always makes me think of being sick. Come and have dinner. Are you hungry?'

'Come to think of it, I am. I don't seem to have had much time for eating the last few days.'

'I thought you were looking a bit weedy. Hasn't everything been sorted by your man's confession?'

'A lot of it, but the Crown Prosecution Service isn't happy with the supporting evidence we've got. A confession isn't enough these days: it's too easily retracted,' said Tom, leading the way into the kitchen, where he picked up an oven cloth and proceeded to remove a dish from the bottom oven of the big Aga.

'It's a carbonnade of beef,' he said, smiling at her over his shoulder. 'I peeked earlier – luckily, because Mrs R. had left a note asking you to finish it off with mustard-spread bread. I did that about half an hour ago.'

He carried the dark-red enamelled dish through into the dining room, leaving Willow to collect a bowl of salad and the unsuitable champagne from the fridge. She opened the bottle while he dished up the carbonnade.

'Here's to a successful conclusion of our various tasks,' she said, holding up her gently singing glass.

Tom picked up his, looked at her over it and then nodded.

'Success to us both,' he agreed and drank. 'Talking of which, how is your work on the old novelist going?'

'Not too badly actually,' said Willow, cutting into one of the half-crisp, half-soggy pieces of toasted, mustard-spread French bread. 'I've virtually written the synopsis in my head and it'll get typed up tomorrow.'

Willow looked at him speculatively and decided that he was just relaxed enough to be able to give her some of the help she needed in working out what had really happened to Gloria. She found that she also wanted to share her discoveries with him.

'And I have become completely convinced that she really was murdered,' she said more tentatively than she usually spoke to Tom.

'I might have known it,' he said, frowning horribly at her like a pantomime villain.

She laughed and was glad when he smiled back. It looked as though they were beginning to get back to their normal pleasure in each other's company.

'I'm glad you are yourself again, so that I won't have to remind you that you once came to me for help when you were convinced against all the odds that several apparently unconnected deaths were the work of a single murderer.'

'Well, I was right,' he said with an indignation at least as theatrical as his grimace had been.

'And I am right now. I know I am. Listen, Thomas. I'd like your opinion if you could give it to me uncorrupted by anger or sentiment.'

181

'I think I could probably manage that,' he said, starting to eat.

He looked up at her every so often as she described what she had learned, guessed or imagined. When she eventually came to the end of her story, he laid down his knife and fork.

'So, you're suggesting that the novelist could have been killed by her niece for the money, by the doctor for love of the niece, by the niece's boyfriend for the money because he didn't realise she'd changed her will, by the charwoman for money, by the secretary out of hate, by the secretary's friend out of protectiveness of the secretary, by the journalist out of hate or fear of the libel action, or by Uncle Tom Cobbley and all.'

'I love the way you take my ideas so seriously,' said Willow, trying to look seductively at him.

'Did you know that cats do that to express a lack of aggression?'

'Do what?'

'Narrow their eyes at other cats – or people.'

'No, I didn't actually. But do be serious for a minute, Tom. The least obvious suspect is Mrs Guy the cleaner. Despite the money, I'd have said that she had the most to lose by Gloria's death, and I think their affection sounds quite genuine. Mrs Guy is the only person who's been made at all miserable by the death.'

'Since she's the least likely, I'm amazed that you don't suspect her most.' The mockery in Tom's voice and eyes was not unkind, but Willow disliked it all the same.

'You can be intensely irritating sometimes. I'm serious, you know,' she said.

'All right. I can't think why. The whole scenario seems ludicrous. You must see that.'

'Actually I don't and I don't think you would if your mind was working properly.' The ache in her head had started to nag again.

'Oh well, if you are determined to believe it was murder, I suppose you'd better tell me who your most obvious suspects are.'

'The niece and the doctor, probably working in tandem.' Willow was too absorbed in her thoughts to see Tom's real reluctance to listen to her suspicions or to wonder about it.

'They had the greatest opportunity and possibly the strongest motive. The doctor adores the niece and she has just inherited a fortune. Her aunt changed her will two weeks before she died. She'd told Mrs Guy about her legacy and so it's quite possible that Marilyn knew about hers, too, and was lying when she told me she had no expectations. Perhaps she wanted to ensure that her aunt died before she could make any more changes.'

Tom sighed. 'It's possible, I suppose, but I can't see that you've any evidence at all. It's pure speculation.'

'Well she did push me down the spiral stairs at the palm house in Kew this afternoon,' said Willow indignantly.

'What?' asked Tom sharply. 'You said you'd fallen and banged yourself. You are mad, Willow. Are you all right? Have you seen a doctor?'

'Yes to both,' she said, not bothering to explain that she had not allowed Doctor Trenor even to look at her injuries.

'You do frighten me sometimes,' he said, sounding breathless. 'All right. So you're not injured. Well, thank God for small mercies. Now where were we? Yes, you being pushed down the stairs. Are you sure that was deliberate?'

When Willow shook her head, he smiled, looking much happier.

'There you are then,' he said. 'Once again you've nothing substantial. Anyway, I'm surprised to hear you talking about spiral stairs. You've always told me they should be helical.'

'Don't mock me,' she said crossly and then laughed with him, thinking that she recognised an attempt to resuscitate an old joke and perhaps retrieve some of the old freedom. 'You're right, of course, but ever since you took to teasing me by calling them stelical haircases, I've given up in despair.'

Tom got up to put his arms round her, apologising when she winced. He stroked her hair and kissed her white forehead.

'Thank you for admitting that at least something I've done or said has influenced you,' he said as he went back to his chair. It was not as light as it should have been and it locked on to all the peculiar ideas that had been bothering her since she left Marilyn.

'Don't let it go to your head,' she said, running away from them into trivial, self-protective teasing. 'It's a pretty minor point.'

'Yes, but it's real,' he said with relish.

That was better, more convincing, and so she smiled at him.

'But come on, Will, let's be serious for a minute. If you really think that every dead slapper who was disliked by her family has been murdered, you're off your trolley.'

Willow put down her knife and fork, happily allowing herself to be completely distracted for the moment.

'What's a slapper?' she asked, intrigued as always by new slang. Tom coughed and then laughed.

'It's what a lot of my colleagues call women; it's a fairly derogatory expression, implying a considerable degree of roughness.'

'I must say it sounds pretty derogatory.'

'All right, just suppose she really was killed,' he went on, ignoring the digression. 'How do you imagine the heart attack was achieved?'

Willow finished her beef and reached forward to pour herself another glass of the warm champagne.

'There must be dozens of ways: tampering with the drugs she took for her angina or making her furious about something, or making her struggle physically, I imagine. I'm sure I've read somewhere that angina can be brought on by violent effort, and I'm just as sure that it can be fatal. Or they might have induced a heart attack in some other way. I'm waiting for my medical source to produce suggestions.'

'Do you really think that a respectable and respected doctor would have done something like that?'

'I can't see why not. A medical qualification doesn't turn a human into a saint, any more than a police uniform sanctifies a thug. I can't see why there shouldn't be just as many rotten apples in the medical barrel as in any other. Although in this case I don't think the doctor did it with his own hands, because he wasn't in the house at all on Gloria's last day. I asked the secretaries. But it's possible that he might have told Marilyn how to do it and then deliberately ignored the evidence when he came to certify the death. He didn't do a post-mortem.'

Tom grimaced, shaking his head. When he saw her face change from intent to obstruction, he reached across the table for her hand, rubbing his thumb up and down her fingers.

'But don't you see, Will, the very plethora of suspects suggests the whole thing's nonsense?'

'No, I don't see that at all. Rather the reverse. It's the number of people who hated and feared her that's made me certain she didn't die by chance – or of natural causes.'

He looked at her and tried to think of a way out of the muddle of feelings in which he was lost. Shaking his head and trying not to sound as irritable as he felt, he said:

'I'm not trying to criticise you, Will. As you've pointed out I'm in no position to do so and even if I were I'd try not to. I know you hate that more than anything else.'

'I don't know that I do,' she said, aware that she was lying, but not wanting to admit to anything that he might construe as a weakness.

Tom's face grew tight in front of her eyes. He dropped her hand. He looked suddenly very tired and much older. After a heavy silence, he said slowly:

'I do wish that after all this time together you could – just occasionally – admit that you feel things.'

Troubled, because she had several times admitted to feelings that left her horribly exposed, Willow frowned. All their attempts at light-hearted teasing had failed, and she was not ready to confront the darker things that she was beginning to glimpse within herself. For all her sophistication and confidence, she felt terrified. She knew at last that it was not Tom who was frightening her but something of her own. Unfortunately that knowledge did not help her.

'I know, I know,' said Tom, rubbing his hands over his face when she did not speak. 'It's not my place to say such things. I merely love you and, irritatingly no doubt, wish you could be happy. I know that you have not the slightest desire to be either happy or loved, but it is frustrating sometimes to realise how little valued one's strongest feelings can be.' Tom's voice, which had begun in his usual measured, quiet way speeded up towards the end of his statement and began to sound extremely angry.

Willow moved back in her chair, her always pale face whiter than usual. The cheerful casualness of her evening with Richard Crescent seemed even more attractive in memory than it had been in fact. She looked away from Tom's hard face, wondering whether anger might not be easier to accept than love. A sudden thought deflected her, but Tom interrupted it before she could say anything.

'I'm sorry,' he said, sounding defeated.

Reluctantly Willow looked back at him. He had put both elbows on the table and hidden his face in his hands. All she could see was the slightly greying, thick dark hair and the blunt ends of his strong, short-nailed fingers pushing through it.

'I do actually quite want to be happy,' she said with difficulty. Tom raised his head. There was a faint hope in his dark eyes.

'And I thought we were quite happy just now before we started quarrelling.'

'We were. I . . .' When it was clear that he was not going to say anything else, Willow tried to go on being as honest with him as her old and new fears would allow.

'Happiness does just occasionally seem dangerous. It's not . . . ' She stopped, unable to formulate the idea. She felt unsafe again. The memory of the spiral stairs racing towards her made her shake. All the sharpness and brains on which she depended seemed to have deserted her.

'What isn't it?' Tom's voice had become quite gentle again, but she thought she heard an undercurrent of impatience that made it impossible to believe in the gentleness. Willow shook her red head in frustration.

'Is it me that's the trouble?' Tom asked doggedly.

She shook her head again, hating the sensation of complete loss of control she could feel threatening her. Trying to think of her work as an antidote to all the feelings she so disliked, she frowned. Tom pushed his plate out of the way and reached for her hand again.

'Listen,' he said, looking helpless.

'I'm listening.'

'I know that you need more detachment than I want. I know that I need more physical closeness than you can bear. Do you think that there will ever be any kind of compromise for us?'

Willow stared at him, wondering if he was asking her whether they should carry on trying to achieve some kind of shared life. Memories of all the good things about him, and she had always known they were many, returned to the front of her mind. So did his months of moodiness and silence. Forcing herself to be rational, she recognised that he was trying at last to use words to deal with whatever was wrong. She had wanted him to do that for weeks and so she had to meet him half-way.

'I hope so,' she said, feeling as though her throat was constricted and her tongue swollen by something that wanted to prevent her committing herself to anything, even an attempt at compromise. 'But I don't know whether I can change as much as you want.'

As she said that, she thought that it dangerously undermined her position and so she quickly added:

'And I don't suppose you can either.'

He smiled. 'Provided you're still on for the attempt at compromise, I don't see that either of us need actually change too much.'

'Really?'

'Trust me,' he said, pleading with her.

The memory of Marilyn's discovery of Peter's duplicity and fraud flashed through Willow's mind. Gritting her teeth and knowing that she would not be able to say anything convincing, she nodded slightly. It seemed to be enough.

'Okay. Well done, my . . . Will.' He was breathing deeply, but his eyes looked steadily at her and his mouth seemed relaxed. 'Okay. Let's get back to your case. Where were we? Who's your next suspect?'

'Posy, the journalist,' said Willow reluctantly. She recognised that they had just achieved something important and she was grateful for his leaving so much unsaid. The investigation seemed a much easier topic for discussion than the other, but after what she had just done she did not think she could bear him to treat her ideas with contempt.

'However much I'd hate it to be her, it seems quite possible,' she went on warily. 'In some ways, more so than Marilyn and the doctor. Although I'm sure Marilyn's been up to something.'

'Never mind Marilyn now. You're going to tell me about this Posy.'

Tom sounded tired, or perhaps bored, but at least he was listening.

'Right. Now listen. Posy must already have spent several thousand on legal fees. I say, do you want some cheese or fruit?'

'No thanks,' said Tom, pushing his smeared plate even further away from him. 'But I'll have some more champagne to fortify me. Thanks. Now, go on.'

'If the libel case went to court Posy stood to lose a fortune in costs and a mega-fortune in damages. She'd have had to go bankrupt.'

'That's not such an enormous deal these days.' Tom drank some of his champagne and made a face.

'I think it is quite a big deal, as well as being humiliating and frightening. Okay, she'd be discharged within three years, but imagine what those years would be like.'

'She might have won the case and had her costs paid.'

'She might. But look at it realistically and you'll see she'd have been almost bound to lose.' Willow took a bunch of grapes from the dish in the middle of the table and pulled one off.

'Eve thinks that Posy earns thirty-thousand a year at most and that's before tax. That wouldn't go far on lawyer's bills after she's paid her mortgage and all the rest. In spite of what she told me about never apologising, she must have been desperately worried when it became clear that Gloria wouldn't settle for anything she could afford. Posy would have been ruined and from the little she's told me she's had more than her fair share of disasters already. Perhaps she simply wasn't prepared to take any more.'

Tom stared at Willow and shook his head, his lips clamped together as though to keep in something he badly wanted to say. Eventually he relaxed enough to open his mouth again.

'It's the same thing again; you've based your suspicion on no more than speculation about a possible motive. Surely by now you know enough of the law to know what evidence is necessary even to charge someone let alone get a conviction? Motive is irrelevant until you've proof of the killing and can put your suspect with the body at the time of death and with the means to have caused it.'

'Don't be so patronising! Of course I know.'

Tom looked at her and sighed again.

'I must be tired,' he said. 'I didn't mean to patronise you.'

'Really?'

'Really,' he said impatiently and then added in explanation: 'But I deal with this sort of thing all the time. If you knew how the Crown Prosecution Service makes us go through hoops to get adequate evidence you'd see how hard it is to give any weight to such, well, such imaginative theorising.'

'This celebration has degenerated a bit,' said Willow, blinking. She decided not even to try to talk any more about the case. 'I'm as tired as you, and my bruises are aching. Are you staying the night?'

'No, I think perhaps you need your space to yourself tonight, don't you?'

Willow let him go, and went to bed alone to sleep better than she had expected.

14

WAKING THE NEXT MORNING, WILLOW remembered that it was the last day of Gloria's absurdly extended lying in state. Despite Eve's apparently desperate need of the synopsis, Willow decided to take a little more time away from it in order to go to the funeral parlour.

When she tried to get out of bed, she found that she was so stiff and aching she could hardly move. Determined not to give in to physical weakness at least, she forced herself to ignore her bruises and her still-aching head and dressed appropriately, she hoped, in a black suit and pearl-grey round-necked shirt. The combination would do perfectly well for the funeral parlour and for her subsequent meeting with Ann Slinter. Satisfied with her reflection, Willow went to have breakfast.

She had eaten a pair of baked eggs and a tangerine and was on her way out of the front door when she heard the telephone bell. It stopped after three rings, which meant, she knew, that Mrs Rusham had picked up the kitchen extension. In case it might be something urgent, Willow retraced her steps down the hall and pushed open the kitchen door with the wrong arm. The extra strain on her wrenched shoulder brought tears of pain to her eyes. They did not fall.

Mrs Rusham, impeccable as always in her long, white cotton overall, stood with her back to the warm Aga, saying into the telephone:

'I think she may already have left, Doctor Salcott, but I'll find out. Hold on a moment.'

Willow, beckoning madly, said: 'I'm here.'

'She is still here, Doctor Salcott, I'll put you on to her.'

'Thanks, Mrs R. I'll take it in my writing room.'

Willow picked up the receiver there, saying again:

'Thank you, Mrs Rusham.' When she had heard the click of the kitchen extension, she went on: 'Morning, Andrew. Thanks for ringing back. I hope your bleeper last night didn't signal a ghastly emergency.'

'An emergency, but happily not ghastly for once. You wanted to know about heart attacks. Why?'

'Oh, the new book,' she said with her usual airy excuse.

'All right: they can be caused by all sorts of things: high blood pressure, disease such as thyrotoxicosis (particularly in women), or congenital weakness in a young person; they can be triggered by stress, either physical, for example from too much violent exertion, or mental from too much anxiety.'

'Really? That's not an old-wives' tale?'

'Nope. Stress can definitely play a part in the causes of heart failure. So can an excess of alcohol, or too heavy an afternoon sleep or the effects of an anaesthetic, or all sorts of things. I'd need more data to give you a usefully specific answer.'

'Fine, listen: a seventy-year-old with a history of angina. Is there any way they – he – could be deliberately killed that would not be obvious to his doctor or to his undertaker?'

'Oh, lots. Smothered, for example. If a patient with angina dies suddenly a doctor who had been attending him for some time would be unlikely to suspect anything untoward or do an autopsy unless there were unmistakable signs of violence on the body.'

'Oh,' said Willow, taken aback.

Her imaginary pictures no longer seemed so unconvincing. It sounded as though Marilyn could easily have killed her aunt; on the other hand so could any of the other suspects, if they had managed to get Marilyn out of the way. Willow thought of Susan's account of Gloria's last, empty day.

'What else?' she asked.

'Inducing terrific rage or physical exertion, poisoning with barbiturates perhaps, although that's easier to detect. Pity your subject's male,' said the doctor.

'Why?'

'Because a man stabbed through the heart is more obvious than a woman, particularly an elderly woman.'

'I don't understand.'

'He doesn't have a breast,' said Salcott drily, 'probably a sagging breast, to hide the mark.'

'I still don't understand. Surely a stabbing produces quantities of blood that anyone could see?'

'Not always. Think of the Empress of Austria,' said the doctor cheerfully. 'She was stabbed with a stiletto through her clothes and died hours later when the blood that had been leaking into the pericardium forced the heart to stop pumping. No one knew what had happened until they opened her up after death.'

'But she must have known she'd been stabbed,' said Willow.

'You'd have thought so,' agreed the doctor. 'I can't remember exactly what she's reported to have said. I think it was that she'd simply been punched. But I do know it was a while before she died. If an immensely thin stiletto or the needle of a syringe were used, it could be up to twenty-four hours before the heart stopped beating.'

'A stiletto or a needle, or even a hatpin,' said Willow suddenly, thinking of the collection of Edwardian hats in Posy Hacket's flat. Surely each one of them had been secured to its polystyrene stand with a spectacular pin, topped with amber, jade or jet? She also realised that if Andrew were right her questioning of the secretaries about who had visited Gloria's house on the day she died might have been useless. It could have been the previous day that mattered.

'I'm not sure a needle or a hatpin would do enough damage if it were a simple stabbing,' said Salcott. 'The heart is made of tough muscle, you know, and it contracts against pressure, precisely in order to prevent serious damage from small wounds. But,' he went on, 'if the needle were held against the beat of the heart a small puncture would soon turn into a tear big enough to cause a dangerous leak.'

Willow let her mind play with what he had told her.

'You mean that as the heart beats an immovable pin would pull down against the muscle of the heart wall.'

'Precisely. All medical students have it forcibly impressed on them that they must never, ever, hold on to a needle that has been inserted into the heart.'

'I wonder if clothes would be enough to keep it still,' said Willow.

'Depends on the clothes. I suppose a stiff corset might be enough. A hand would be better. I'm getting very curious, you know.'

'I'm sure you are, Andrew, and you've given me a lot to think about,' said Willow, wishing that his bleeper would sound before he could ask any more tiresome questions. 'Are you sure it could be as much as twenty-four hours before death?'

'Absolutely, but not necessarily. It all depends on the size of the tear and the condition of the heart.'

'Thank you. I must dash now. No: one more thing. What sort of mark would be left on the skin?'

'A small bruise and a pinprick. The size would obviously depend on the size of the weapon.'

'The kind of mark one has in the crook of one's elbow after giving blood?'

'Exactly. The greater wound would be in the heart itself. Holding the needle would not affect the size of the puncture in the skin.'

'Thanks Andrew. You're a brick. Good bye now.'

Willow put down the telephone receiver without letting him say anything more, filled with the unpleasant knowledge that she was somehow going to have to examine

193

Gloria's body, if only to banish the possibility of such a sneaky and effective stabbing from her mind.

She reached up to the shelf where she kept odds and ends of all sorts, and took down the camera she always used when she was researching places for scenes in her books. It was a small but sophisticated Nikon F601 35mm camera, with a pop-up flash and a zoom lens.

Knowing that even if she had the opportunity to photograph the body the light would be poor, Willow loaded the camera with a Kodak Ektacrome 100X film that would give her both fine definition and good detail even in a dim light. She slipped the camera into her capacious, quilted-leather shoulder bag and set off for South London.

She almost passed the door of her unsaleably damp flat, where the builders ought to be at work and thought of stopping to check that they were actually doing what they had promised. But then she decided that she had too many other problems to solve to waste time on that one.

Ignoring the flat, she drove on to the funeral directors', parked in the forecourt of their elegant building and knocked on the door. There was no answer, and so she gingerly pushed at the door and it yielded. Walking inside, Willow found herself in a long, narrow hall, silent and empty but for a pair of chairs and a tasteful arrangement of lilies on a small table between them.

All but one of the dark-grey doors leading off the narrow hall were shut and so when no one appeared, she pushed the one that was ajar and put her head round it. The room was empty except for a desk and three chairs. An elderly female voice sounded from somewhere behind her.

'Can I help you?'

It was almost as though a ghost had spoken. Willow returned to the hall and saw a tidy, white-haired woman standing at the bottom of the stairs dressed in dark grey.

'Yes, you could,' said Willow with what she considered was admirable self-possession in the circumstances. 'I have come to pay my last respects to Gloria Grainger.'

At that the woman's whole demeanour changed. She

appeared to soften before Willow's eyes and she stretched out a hand, saying sweetly:

'Yes, of course. She's in our chapel here, all ready for you. You're the first to come for her, you know. Would you care to follow me?'

'Thank you,' said Willow, who had been suddenly thrust back into her original sympathy for Gloria Grainger. The thought of her planning the absurdly elaborate lying in state in the hope that people would troop past her coffin seemed unbearably sad in the light of what the woman had just said. Marilyn's absence was perhaps understandable, given that she had made no secret of her dislike of Gloria, but there were other people who had professed affection for her.

Shouldn't good manners and gratitude at least have made some of them come? Willow asked herself.

'I'm glad someone's come for her. All those flowers! Would you like me to stay with you? Some of our guests find it a difficult experience.'

'I shall be fine,' said Willow calmly, having no idea whether or not the sight of a dead body would upset her. She could not imagine why it should, but she had never seen one.

Both her parents had always insisted that there was to be neither sentiment nor ceremony after their deaths and, when it fell to her to arrange the burial of her mother, Willow had obeyed. She had not reached Newcastle until after the body had been removed from the house for unceremonious cremation.

Willow had not mourned much in any case, since her parents had taken immense care to ensure that she would never feel the need to do so. Although she had long ago understood that their emotional austerity had made it hard for her to give affection to anyone, she was only just beginning to realise that accepting it was even more difficult for her.

'This is a ceremonial visit rather than a desperate farewell,' she went on, hoping that none of her feelings showed.

'Ah,' said the woman, hardening a little. 'In that case I'll leave you. If you want anything, just ring this bell here.' She gestured to a heavily tasselled blue bell-pull and Willow nodded.

As soon as she was alone, Willow looked around the chapel. It was discreetly decorated in shades of grey and there was a rudimentary altar opposite the door. Two vast and lavish arrangements of white lilies and cream-coloured roses towered on either side of the table. There was nothing else except the coffin, resting on a pair of velvet-covered trestles. From where she was standing all she could see was the thick, purple velvet pall that covered most of the coffin and a shock of pale-grey hair.

Reluctantly moving forwards, Willow found herself face to face with the corpse of the woman about whom she had heard so much. Gloria's face looked remarkably peaceful and very like Marilyn's, despite the greyness of her thick, straight hair. There were a few strong dark bristles on her chin, which made Willow grimace in a mixture of pity and disgust as she remembered reading that beards continue to grow after death. The cheeks seemed unnaturally full given that the flesh under the chin was slack and fell against the crêpey neck. The body was dressed in a cream-coloured satin shroud that matched the ruched lining of the coffin.

Willow was glad that she felt no horror of the body and yet she found it hard to reach out to touch the coffin. Reminding herself of what she had to discover, she quickly folded back the velvet pall to reveal a kind of lace-edged satin sheet, which matched the shroud. She folded the sheet back, too, silently cursing as it slithered away and dropped to the floor.

With shaking, sweating fingers, looking over her sore shoulder every few seconds, Willow lifted the shroud from the feet to pull it upwards and almost gagged as the whole thing seemed to come away in her hands. Then she realised that it was not a complete garment, merely a pair of sleeves attached to a kind of apron that had been tucked around the body.

Willow looked down at the corpse, her mind full not of the

horror she had feared but of terror that she would be interrupted. A police siren wailed in the distance and made her jump. The dead flesh was almost white, although the face had been pinker, presumably she told herself, made up with cosmetics. Just as Andrew Salcott had warned, Gloria's breasts hung slackly over her ribcage.

Willow's own skin began to feel very cold indeed. The body seemed to have two navels. After a moment's instinctive disgust, she realised that one was a kind of plastic stopper. She took a deep breath and put out a hand to touch the body.

Unable to prevent herself feeling as though she were committing gross sacrilege and probably blasphemy too, Willow slid her fingers under the left breast and lifted it, surprised not only by the coldness but by the weight and by the scaly feel of the skin.

Trying to detach her mind from everything but her search, she looked down at what she had revealed. There, unmistakable, was the outline of a faint yellowish bruise and in the centre a small red pinprick, just as Andrew Salcott had described.

More astonished to have found real proof of her suspicions than she would have admitted to anyone at all, Willow almost shouted aloud in triumph.

There was still plenty to be worked out, of course, not least how on earth someone had stuck a hypodermic syringe or some other kind of spike in Gloria's heart without her noticing, but the fact of her murder was irrefutable at last. Secure in that knowledge, Willow also knew that she could go forward, solve the rest and even convince her doubting Thomas of the truth.

The sound of another siren shrieked apparently just behind Willow and she dropped the flaccid breast and spun round. She was still entirely alone in the quiet dimness of the chapel. The scent of the two tall vases of roses and lilies made her feel sick, but she could not possibly waste the only opportunity she would have before the body was buried to record the evidence of what must have happened.

Desperately anxious that none of Gloria's so-called friends or her staff or relations should conquer their dislike of her enough to visit her body just then, Willow dug into her bag for the camera. Her hands seemed even clumsier than usual as she checked the film, the flash and the lens. Then, pushing the apron-shroud out of the way and lifting the breast with her left hand, Willow leaned forward. With the camera held in her right hand alone, she took three photograhs in quick succession.

Knowing that her hand had shaken, she looked round for something with which to prop up the sagging breast that had felt so heavy and flakey between her fingers. There was nothing. Sighing, Willow turned so that she was standing at the right of the coffin with her back to Gloria's head. She leaned diagonally across, hooked the left breast back with her own left elbow and with both hands on the camera took six exposures. She had to lean quite close to the dead body and was surprised that it smelled of absolutely nothing, despite having been in the undertakers' hands for six days.

At last the significance of the plastic stopper in Gloria's belly became clear. She must have been drained of all her bodily fluids and refilled with some kind of preservative.

'Ugh,' said Willow before she could stop herself. She let the breast fall back and retreated to the foot of the coffin, from where she took more shots of the entire body and the face until she had used up the film.

She thrust the camera back into her bag, which had dropped to the floor by her feet, and picked up the sheet that lay in a small, shiny heap beside it. Breathing heavily, wondering if the scent of the flowers and her own dislike of what she had done might make her actually vomit, she pulled the shroud back down over the big white, hairy body, tucking it in at the sides and rearranging the sheet. The purple velvet was still in her hands as she heard the sound of a discreet cough behind her. Deliberately not turning to find out who was standing there, she leaned even closer, gagging at her own hypocrisy and kissed the cold, rough face.

As she straightened up, she took a handkerchief from her sleeve and wiped her own face, shuddering.

'Are you all right, Miss?' asked a male voice.

Willow turned and saw a fair-haired, stocky young man in a grey suit standing beside the chapel door.

'We don't usually disturb relatives, but you've been so long, we were beginning to wonder if you'd fainted.'

'Have I?' said Willow, feeling very faint indeed, but with relief that what she had come to do was done and that she had not apparently been discovered with her hands on the naked corpse. 'It's hard to judge time when you're so . . .' She let her voice tremble and die.

'I understand,' said the undertaker in an obviously artificial voice, soothing and yet somehow disapproving. 'I'll leave you alone.'

He left the room, walking silently on his rubber-soled shoes. The closing of the door behind him made no sound, and Willow realised that if she had not been looking at him, she would not have known exactly when he had left the chapel. The thought that he might have been standing watching her as she robbed the body of its dignity made her shudder and she fled.

15

THE FIRST THING WILLOW DID when she returned to Chesham Place was to ask Mrs Rusham to remove all the hyacinths from the house and substitute some flower or foliage that had no scent. Then, when the offending objects had been taken out of her bathroom and the windows opened to let in the wet, cold air, she ran a hot bath. Eschewing the Chanel bath oil she usually used, she got into the unscented water and proceeded to scrub herself all over with a stiff loofah, which she had never used before but had kept because she liked the weird stiff look of it.

When at last she was sure that she had scrubbed off not only the sickly scent of the undertakers' flowers, but also her incorrigible shame at what she had just done, she stood up in the bath, let out the hot water and, in the full blast of cold air from the windows, rinsed herself all over with the shower attachment she had never used before.

Clean at last, and cold and uncomfortable enough to feel that she had done some kind of penance, she got out and dried herself. Throwing the suit she had been wearing on to a chair in the knowledge that Mrs Rusham would take it to the cleaners, she put the rest of the morning's clothes into the laundry basket. In their place she chose a pair of comfortable black trousers and a long polo-necked violet cashmere tunic, which clashed agreeably with her hair, and added a loose black jacket.

Smiling as she recognised her defensive retreat into thinking of nothing but her clothes, she telephoned Tom. When she was told that he was not available and that no one knew where he was, she felt that she was being fobbed off and banged down her receiver in renewed irritation.

'Your lunch is ready,' said Mrs Rusham from behind her.

'Oh thank you, Mrs Rusham,' answered Willow. 'Do you know, I really don't feel very hungry.'

'It's quite light, just a little chicken in a grape sauce. You ought to eat. You're looking rather faint, if I may say so.'

'That's only because I've washed off all my makeup,' said Willow briskly. 'All right, I'll do my best with the chicken.'

She found it hard to eat even though there was nothing wrong with the chicken. Nothing that Mrs Rusham had ever cooked had been anything but delicious. But the grape sauce tasted richly of cream and armagnac and each time Willow pushed a piece of chicken on to her fork she thought of Gloria's body and the heavy, sickly smell of the lilies. She managed to eat about half the chicken, declined pudding, and welcomed the cup of strong coffee that Mrs Rusham brought her.

She carried it into the drawing room where she sat down at the mahogany pembroke table in the window and once more tried to ring Tom Worth. Yet again she was unlucky.

Knowing that it was essential to persuade him to organise an official investigation into the murder before Gloria's body was buried the following day, Willow decided to write to him. He could hardly refuse to read an urgent, hand-delivered letter, even if he were ducking her telephone calls for some reason.

First she took her film to the nearest large chemist that promised prints within an hour. Having returned to the flat, she switched on her computer and proceeded to draft a concise report of what she had done that morning. She carefully described her discovery of the wound under Gloria

Grainger's left breast and added a short account of her conversation with Dr Andrew Salcott.

Considering that she had produced quite enough hard evidence to persuade Tom and his colleagues of what had happened to Gloria, Willow went on to list the people who had – or might have had – the opportunity to cause it. Their motives for wishing Gloria dead came last, as befitted what Tom had suggested was the least important part of any murder investigation.

Much of what Willow wrote was a repetition of the things she had told him the previous evening, but it seemed crucial to put it all into the report. Tom could then pass it on to whoever else needed the information without having to add anything himself or betray the fact that he had ignored an unofficially reported case of murder.

While the machine was printing her statement, Willow returned to the chemist to collect the photographs. It was only as she reached the counter that she asked herself whether the person who had processed her film would have realised what they signified.

Feeling defensive and therefore sounding angry, she asked whether her prints were ready, thrusting her receipt at the assistant behind the counter. The young man looked at it and turned to fumble through the heap of paper folders in a basket behind him. He obviously could not find hers for he pulled open one drawer after another. Willow bit her lips, wishing she had simply included the whole film in her letter to Tom. Even as she let herself think that, she knew it was not true. To have given away the film would have been to lose control of it, and she could not have done that.

'Here we are,' said the young man, pushing a folder towards her and not meeting her eyes. 'Eight pounds forty, please. You ordered two sets of prints, didn't you?'

'Yes,' said Willow, handing him the money and leaving the shop without waiting for a receipt. Only when she was outside did she open the folder and check that they were indeed her photographs. Seeing the accuracy and clarity of the prints and the unmistakable fact that they were of a body in a coffin, she could not understand why she had been asked no questions by the chemist.

When she got back to the flat, she put one set of the prints into a separate envelope, which she clipped to her report, and then added a handwritten note:

Dear Tom,

I now *know* that Gloria Grainger was murdered. Since I haven't managed to get you on the telephone at all today, despite several attempts, I've put everything I've got so far on paper and given you photographic evidence. We must talk. She is to be buried tomorrow and someone properly qualified ought to see the body before it goes underground.

I don't know whether she comes under your jurisdiction, but at least you'll know whom to alert.

There are still a lot of gaps in what I've discovered, and too many suspects, but I'll go on trying to whittle them down to a certainty while I wait to hear from you.

Yours, W.

She drove to Kingston, could not find a space in which to park, cursed her fellow-Londoners for their inability to go anywhere except in their own cars and drove out and round the block again, searching. Eventually she saw the indicator of a large BMW start to flash and she drew into the space behind it as it left. She parked carefully, locked the car and walked through the narrow street to Tom's office.

Having been told again that he was not available, she addressed the envelope to him, adding the words 'personal', 'urgent', and 'private and confidential', before handing it to the desk sergeant.

'It is really urgent that he gets it,' she said as he took it from her. 'I haven't managed to speak to him but I know that he needs it. Can you make sure it goes up to him at once?'

'I'll see he gets it,' said the man soothingly. Willow suppressed a smile as she thought of his possible description of her lunatic determination to get the package into Tom's hands.

'It is confidential,' she said, suddenly aware of the

possibility that someone other than Tom might open the package and then castigate him for the dilatoriness and inattention that had made her so angry during the last week. She had no wish to damage him.

'I can see that, Miss,' said the policeman.

Willow thanked him and returned to the car. It was only as she was unlocking the door that she realised it was already ten past three and that she was due to be at Ann Slinter's office in twenty minutes.

Her mind must still have been on the report because she almost ran into the back of a stationary bus half-way to the A3. Telling herself that if she could not see something that size and that colour in front of her she ought not to be in charge of a car at all, Willow drove with all the slow, terrified care of a learner until she was half-way round Trafalgar Square. There all the usual frustration with other drivers changing lanes without signalling, jumping red traffic lights, stopping abruptly for no obvious reason and hooting fruitlessly forced her back into her usual decisiveness and she drove across the top of the square and out into the Charing Cross Road without the slightest hestitation.

Almost as though taking control again had prejudiced the fates in her favour, she found a free parking meter right outside the door of Weston & Brown and discovered that she had enough of the right coins to give herself two hours' peace of mind.

The receptionist smiled at her with recognition and said that Ann was expecting her.

'Yes, I know. And I'm a bit late, but I wanted to ask you first whether you had any dealings with Gloria Grainger.'

The young woman rolled her eyes and dragged down the corners of her mouth like a sad-faced clown.

'All too often. She used to accuse me of not answering the phone quickly enough and losing calls and generally being useless and awful. I once got Mrs Slinter to beat her up for me – verbally, I mean.'

'How sensible!' said Willow. 'Can you remember the last time she rang here?'

'Oh yes. It was a couple of days before she died. She wanted Vicky Taffle and although I tried to head her off she insisted. It was after half-past five and I was on my way out but I saw the light flashing on the switchboard and so I answered. I wish I hadn't.'

'Oh?' Willow smiled encouragingly. 'Why was that?'

'She only wanted to pour the usual diatribe over poor Vicky. I listened a bit and I did wonder if I ought to just cut them off. I sometimes did that, you know, to give Vicky a break.'

Willow laughed.

'You're obviously a good friend to her. What was the diatribe about?'

'Vicky had recently sent her a list of editorial changes she wanted to the first six chapters that Gloria's secretary had sent us. Gloria said she thought the changes were ludicrous, rude, unnecessary – all the usual stuff. When I heard that Vicky was managing all right, I stopped listening, switched the system on to the night lines and scarpered.'

'I see. Thanks. I'll have a word with Vicky about it. I want to gauge Gloria's mood in her last few days.'

'Horrible!' said the receptionist, grimacing. 'But it always was. Ann's waiting for you, you know.'

'So she is. I'd better go up. Thanks.'

Ann, who was looking more fashionable than usual in a long, tight skirt, a very waisted jacket and laced ankle boots, welcomed her author with a clear smile and an outstretched hand. When Willow took it, she was surprised to see Ann inclining her face. Obedient, but wary, Willow pushed hers forward until their cheeks met briefly.

'I'm sorry I was so abrupt yesterday,' said Ann as they each straightened up again. 'I had the money men here and it was all rather grim. They can't understand that books aren't like shoes or brands of baked beans. You simply cannot do precise market research and know how many "units" you're going to sell a year ahead of publication. You can guess all right, but no more than that. Books are too different from each other. They're not "product" and they

205

don't work like it. I . . . Still, you don't want to hear it all. It's not your problem.'

'Perhaps not at this moment,' said Willow, 'but I am interested – very interested – in the economics of publishing and how you can target the right audience for a novel and all that sort of thing.'

'We must have a good session one day when there's time. Now: to the Gloria memoir. I'm beginning to get the impression that you're not as interested in it as you once were and, as it's not one of my top priorities either, I do wonder whether we ought not simply to cut our losses and drop the whole idea. It'll save you time you badly need for your own book, and the more I think about it the less saleable I think it would be.'

The sharpness of her disappointment surprised Willow and she started shaking her head even before Ann had finished speaking.

'Oh no, you can't drop it now,' Willow said. 'At least I hope you won't. Um. I'm not really quite sure how to put this, but there is an aspect to it that will, I suspect, make it much easier for you to sell than you'd originally thought.'

'Is there?' Ann's face brightened. 'Perhaps I'd better have Vicky in after all. She asked whether she could edit the memoir and I originally said yes, subject to your approval.'

'Fine,' said Willow. 'She can keep a confidence, can't she? Nothing I'm going to tell you should be repeated outside this room.'

'Oh, good Lord yes, she's safe as houses. Pretty secretive actually.' Ann picked up the telephone receiver by her elbow and dialled two numbers. 'Vicky? Good. I've got Willow here. It looks as though the memoir may be going ahead after all, and so we'll need you. Could you come straight away?' Ann replaced the receiver without even waiting for an answer.

'All right,' she said, looking back at her author, 'so tell me.'

'Look,' Willow began, having second thoughts about publicising her new discovery, 'I don't think anyone except you should know this for a bit, but Gloria was murdered.'

'What?' Ann seemed to grow paler as Willow watched her.

'Yes,' said Willow. 'And when the news breaks there's going to be a lot more publicity about her than you could have expected. From the crudest commercial point of view the memoir is going to be a good bet for you after all. Do let me go on with it. Please.'

'God Almighty! Who did it?'

'I don't know yet. But the police must be dealing with it now. There'll probably be some news before the funeral.'

'But that's tomorrow. Vicky and I are going.'

'To what?' asked Vicky from the doorway.

'Gloria's funeral,' said Willow, when she saw that Ann was still too dazed to speak normally. 'I'll see you both there. Look, Ann, I'm sorry that I haven't got the synopsis printed out for you yet, but I am almost there, I promise.'

'Oh, that's all right,' said Ann, sounding strained. Vicky looked at her in obvious astonishment.

'I've got a bit of a headache,' said Ann, noticing her subordinate's expression. 'Could you bear to make some tea, Vicky? Willow, would you like some?'

'D'you know, I'd love some,' she said, wanting to finish her private conversation with Ann.

Looking angry, Vicky left the office.

'Willow, are you certain?'

'Yes, I'm afraid so. It's been looking into it all that has distracted me from finishing your synopsis.'

'I'm not surprised you've been distracted. But how did you . . . ? What made you . . . ? Damn! How do you know?'

'Honestly, I think I'd better not go into it all, Ann. If you don't mind. I'd never have said anything yet if you hadn't thrown me by saying you wanted to cancel the whole idea. You see, I really do want Gloria to have a decent memorial. I know that sounds sentimental. And I know that she behaved vilely to a lot of people, but I've come to realise that she was quite a tragic figure, too, and I'd like to put it on record.'

Vicky returned then with three thick mugs of tea.

'Willow's just been telling me that Gloria is a figure of tragedy,' said Ann, speaking in a high voice quite unlike her usual measured drawl. 'Does that make sense to you?'

Vicky handed each of them their tea and frowned.

'It's not something I can immediately relate to. What makes you think it, Willow?'

Willow shrugged and drank some tea as she tried to organise her thoughts.

'Chiefly that her books and the way she arranged her life were the result of a flight from truly horrible childhood experiences. The tragedy is that she got it all so wrong and made people hate her. If she could just have been more honest about herself and her circumstances, she might have found a much better escape and learned to live with people on a level instead of apart . . . above, whatever. Do you see what I mean?'

'No, I don't think I do,' Vicky admitted. 'What have you found out about her childhood? And how? She always kept it pretty dark.'

'Ah, well, Gerald Plimpton gave me a few clues.'

Ann smiled and looked more at ease. 'Dear Gerry. He is one of the sweetest men I've ever known, although I do sometimes wonder whether he's cloaking rather a lot of unsweet stuff beneath the charm.'

'He can certainly be ferocious when he's crossed.'

Willow looked at Victoria, thinking that she seemed a great deal more confident than she had only a few days earlier. Despite having been sent out to make tea as though she were the office junior, she was making a real effort not to let herself be sidelined in the discussion. Congratulating herself for having sown a seed that was sprouting so quickly, Willow smiled and added what she hoped would be a little fertiliser.

'Ann's looking very surprised and it's a new idea to me. Tell us what you meant, Vicky.'

'Don't you know what I mean, Ann?' said Vicky almost patronisingly. 'You must remember that time when Gerald completely lost his temper with one of the cleaners. She'd assumed that the manuscript he'd left balanced across the top of the wastepaper basket was meant to be thrown away. It was years ago, but I'll never forget his volcano of rage. And there have been other times like it. There was one just before the staff outing in the last year before he retired, when he . . .'

Willow was laughing, but Ann snapped at her subordinate.

'Dirty linen, Vicky. Not to be washed in public,' she said, before turning to Willow. 'It was understandable. He was under great pressure. Losing his temper with stupid staff wasn't at all what I meant.'

'It doesn't matter anyway,' said Willow. 'Your dirty linen is quite safe with me. After all, I'm writing about Gloria, not the history of the firm.'

'Fine,' said Ann with more of her usual briskness. 'So, Gloria Grainger, figure of tragedy. Well, it's an interesting line. Presumably you'll have to delve quite deeply into her psyche.'

'I suppose I shall. Perhaps I ought to have the manuscript vetted by a shrink when I've finished, just to make certain that my assumptions about her make sense.'

'Good idea,' said Vicky firmly before Ann could say anything. 'Now, can you give us any idea when you might finish? The synopsis is taking quite a long time.'

'Really, Vicky,' said Ann sharply. 'How can Willow possibly know that yet? You're exceeding your editorial authority.'

'But it matters, Ann. As you know, I'll be getting that huge saga from the States to translate into English English in about two months' time, which is pretty much when you said we were expecting the memoir. The Americans have said their author is completing the final draft now and they should be able to airfreight it to us just about then. Once it's here, I'm going to be tied up for ages, and it's the lead title for next year. At the same time you want the memoir rushed through, crashing all the production schedules. I'm not sure it's going to be possible unless we can stagger the two projects.'

'Excellent,' said Willow. 'Vicky, I'm proud of your firmness. How long will your translation and everything take?'

'Oh, three weeks minimum,' she said, looking faintly surprised by the praise. 'It's going to be at least a thousand pages.'

'That's not a problem then, Ann, is it? Speed isn't quite as essential as we once thought. Why don't I aim to get the memoir finished in three months? Ann, isn't that all right?'

The managing director came out of her reverie, looking startled.

'What? Yes, yes, all right. That sounds fine. Willow, you and I need to talk. Um, when . . . ?'

'I'll see you tomorrow at the funeral,' said Willow, 'we can fix something then. There's someone else I really have to see this evening. I can't let it go any longer,' she added, badly wanting to have re-examined and eliminated most of her first suspects before Tom spoke to her again. 'Could I use your telephone to fix it?'

Ann got off the sofa and pulled the telephone on her desk towards Willow, saying:

'Just dial nine and you'll get an outside line. Vicky and I will be outside. Come along.'

Willow dialled the number of Posy Hacket's flat as the other two left the office, shutting the door behind them.

'Posy,' she said when her call was answered.

'Yes?' came the cautious reply.

'Willow King here. I wondered if I could come and talk to you again.'

'What about?' There was enough abruptness in her voice to make Willow emphasise the more innocuous of the two things she wanted to ask Posy.

'I have a theory about one of the ways in which Gloria's childhood experiences might have affected her behaviour, but I may be barking up quite the wrong tree. Could I come and see you so that I can explain myself and see what your reaction is? You're a kind of expert, you see, and I can't think of anyone else who'd be more help.'

There was a pause before the journalist said harshly:

'You'd probably do better with a psychiatrist or someone who runs one of the battered wives' refuges. My views are too personal.'

'I'd rather talk to you. It's an emotional reaction I want rather than a theoretical one. Please?'

'Oh all right,' said Posy ungraciously. 'But it'll have to be this afternoon. I'm busy all tomorrow.'

'This afternoon would be fine.' Willow saw that it was nearly five o'clock.

'Fine. I've got to go out just after six.'

'Right. I'll hurry,' said Willow, putting down the receiver and going out into the passage.

She found Ann there, straightening the laminated jackets that had been pinned up on a display board. Vicky Taffle was talking to a young man in jeans at the far end of the corridor. He was holding an immense typescript in his arms as though it were a baby.

'Ann, I've got to go,' said Willow. 'You don't want anything more from me now, do you?'

'No, I don't think so. Not here anyway, but I've a lot I want to ask you when we can talk. You will take care, won't you? It all seems appallingly melodramatic and dangerous, but . . .'

'I'll be fine,' said Willow. 'Don't worry. But I must rush now.'

They kissed again and Willow walked a little way down the passage to call out:

'Vicky, I'm off, but it was good to see you – and looking so well too.'

The editor came running down the passage to shake hands.

'And you. I did so much enjoy that dinner we had.'

'So did I,' said Willow, congratulating herself again on having managed to trigger something in Vicky that had made her stand up to the world a bit better. 'Thank you for your letter. There was really no need to write.'

'Oh, I had to,' said Vicky, smiling. 'You took so much trouble and you really made me understand something important. Thank you.'

'It is good to see you so cheerful. I must run. I'll see you tomorrow. 'Bye.'

211

Twenty minutes later Willow had only just eased her car round Russell Square and was wishing that she had left it at the parking meter outside Weston & Brown and taken the tube up to Islington. It took her another twenty minutes to get to Posy's flat and park the car once more.

Willow was breathless by the time she rang the bell and gasped her name into the intercom. It seemed to have been repaired for Posy's command to 'come upstairs' was followed by the conventional buzzing sound. Willow pushed open the door and hurried up the stairs.

Posy was waiting for her, clearly dressed to go out in a calf-length black dress and a long cardigan jacket that sparkled with beads and black sequins. She looked startlingly good and her complexion seemed to glow with health. Willow looked more closely and saw that some of the radiance was cosmetic.

'Sorry to hold you up,' said Willow. 'The traffic was simply awful. I see you're about to go out. You do look marvellous.'

She looked away and slyly examined the old hats to check her memory of the pins that attached them to the wigstands. There they were: immense blobs of jet, amber, coral or pearl pushed into each of the hats. Willow wished she could pull them out to examine the long steel pins that must be attached to them.

'Thanks,' said Posy, who did not seem to have noticed Willow's preoccupation with the hat collection. 'There's no time for tea, but would you like a very quick drink?'

Willow looked at the tray to which Posy was gesturing and then shook her head.

'No thanks, but can we sit down? I don't think I can talk to you while you're standing there like the "Stern daughter of the voice of God".'

Posy made herself smile.

'Sorry. I didn't mean to seem unwelcoming. It's just that time's a bit short this evening and I'm rather nervous. Now what is it that's so urgent?'

Willow collected her thoughts, trying to cram everything she wanted to know into a single sentence and failing.

'Would it make sense to you that, after experiencing all that violence in her childhood,' she said, 'Gloria could let herself become affectionate only towards men with serious disabilities?'

'Physical or mental? I'm virtually certain she would avoid mental instability.'

'I meant physical. Wheelchair, blind, something like that.'

'Absolutely. He'd be no threat and she could allow herself to spill all the pent-up love over him and . . . ' Posy's voice wobbled but she controlled it in order to add: 'Even to trust him.'

'That's what I thought,' said Willow. 'Say she became fond of a man – a younger man – with such a disability, do you think her feelings could extend to the possibility of leaving him a fortune in her will?'

'I'd have thought it extremely likely. After all, she'd pretty well cut herself off from the family, hadn't she?'

'Yes, and she'd no children, no spouse, apparently no particularly close friends. And then,' said Willow mainly to herself, 'if she discovered that he'd been shamming . . . '

'She'd be devastated,' said Posy quietly.

Willow saw that she was kneading her hands together as though there was a ball of particularly recalcitrant dough between them. 'All her terror of trusting anyone would return, and with it the most terrible anger.'

'Partly at herself, perhaps, for having pulled down her defences.'

Posy looked at her watch and stood up again.

'You're not suggesting she killed herself, are you?' she asked, looking at Willow with real suspicion in her dark eyes.

Belatedly remembering that she was supposed to be researching Gloria's life for a memoir rather than her death in pursuit of a murderer, Willow achieved a laugh.

'Good heavens no! I'm just on the track of a failed romance of hers and I wanted to find some rationale for the failure. I think you've helped there.'

Posy looked once more at her watch and then swore.

'I wish I could stay and hear about it, but I really do have to leave. I'm due to collect an award this evening and speak, and so I can't be late.'

'Congratulations.'

'Thanks, but it means I'll have to throw you out.'

'I'm on my way,' said Willow, picking up her bag and wishing that she had simply asked Posy the questions over the telephone instead of wasting so much time in traffic jams. 'D'you want a lift anywhere? You're not likely to pick up a taxi here.'

'Would you drive me? A mini-cab was supposed to be here ten minutes ago, but I can't wait for it now. A lift would really help. If you drop me at King's Cross I can get a taxi without taking you too far out of your way.'

'Okay, if you'd rather. But I could take you all the way to wherever it is and save you risking the glad rags on the street. I'm parked up here.'

The late rush-hour traffic was even heavier than it had been earlier and after fifteen minutes Posy decided that it would be quicker for her to take the tube than to sit in Willow's car and then wait for a taxi. She asked to be dropped at Camden Town station. Just before they got there, Willow said casually:

'You dropped in to see her, didn't you, just before she died?'

'What?'

'Someone suggested to me,' said Willow, improvising madly, 'that Gloria had told her that the case would probably be settled after all. That made me think you must have been to see her and sorted something out with her at the last minute. Everyone's told me that she didn't leave the house at all in the last week of her life, so I thought you must have been to see her.'

'I told you,' said Posy through clenched teeth, 'that I would rather have died than settled that libel case and apologised in open court, which is what she was demanding. I don't know where you got this stupid story from, but it has nothing to do with me. I wouldn't have gone near her for anything in the world. I went to her house once to interview her and that is the only time we ever met.'

'Oh, I see. Perhaps it was your lawyer then. Or perhaps someone else advised her to drop the case. I know that at least one of her influential friends thought she was mad to be suing you at all.'

'Oh,' said Posy, sitting back and breathing more calmly again. 'Perhaps that was it. Sorry I shouted at you. I'm still not quite sane on the subject of Gloria Bloody Grainger, despite your various bombshells. Look I must go, but don't let's lose touch. I'll ring you some time when things are less harassing. Okay?'

'Fine,' said Willow, pulling up outside the tube station. She was almost convinced by Posy's violent outburst, but not quite.

Alone in her car again, Willow let her mind play around the other suspicious figures who had circled around Gloria. Pictures of the candlelit dinners Marilyn had had to serve to her own boyfriend and her tyrannical aunt filled Willow's mind as did memories of Peter's charming smile and lovely deep voice. He must have cut a highly romantic figure in his wheelchair as he sat at the beautiful mahogany table Willow had been shown in the panelled dining room between Gloria's private study and the garden.

'And how Marilyn must have hated watching them lord it over her!' Willow said aloud as she eased her foot off the brake again to drift a yard or two further down the congested road. 'But was that all that Marilyn felt? She let me see that she was angry about it, but what else was there that she hasn't let me see?'

The emotions swirling around the Kew Green house must have been horrible, Willow thought once more, and it ought not to have surprised anyone that they had got out of hand. But who was it who had finally lost control?

The suspects processed through her mind like the ghostly kings that tormented and excited Macbeth after he had first seen the weird sisters. Posy, Marilyn and the doctor, Peter Farrfield, the powerful Sue Robinson, who was so obviously her weaker friend's champion, and indeed Patty herself.

Weak people had killed before, Willow reminded herself, only just managing not to push her hand hard down on the horn as the car in front of her stopped unnecessarily at a traffic light that had barely turned orange. And Patty had a key to the basement. Surely she could have let herself in on the night before Gloria died, assuming that her so-called illness would be enough of an alibi?

At that point Willow stopped thinking about anything but the road ahead. Rain splashed heavily down on to her windscreen, making it almost impossible to see the rare gaps in the traffic. Pushing her wipers on to the fastest speed, she concentrated on her driving.

She did not see any clear road in front of her car until she had inched round Trafalgar Square and under Admiralty Arch. There, as the traffic thinned out into the wider road, she breathed a sigh of relief and put her foot down, knowing there could be no obstruction until the traffic lights half-way along. Even the rain cleared as suddenly as it had begun.

Willow was admiring the perspective of the narrowing red road, the muddled lines of the fountain and the cold discipline of the floodlit palace behind it, when two women stepped off the pavement into the road about two feet in front of her car. Stamping on the brakes and cursing loudly, she heard a squeaking sound and a hoarse human scream, but she just managed to stop without touching either of the women.

Pulling up the handbrake and putting the gears into neutral Willow wiped the sweat off her face and leaned across to open the nearside window.

'What the hell do you think you were doing?' she demanded furiously.

In a strong foreign accent one of the women said:

'It is sorry. We are not understanding the traffic.'

Willow cursed again, using a word that shocked even herself, wound up the window and, as soon as she could, set off once more.

*

Later that evening she ate another spectacularly good casserole, which Mrs Rusham had left in the bottom oven of the Aga with a baking potato so perfectly crisp that it must have been cooked for at least two hours, and drank half a bottle of Saint Emilion.

When she had finished Willow wrote up her notes, trying to work out the 'who?' and 'how?' and 'with what?' of Gloria's murder. She wished that she could talk to Tom, checked once more that there was no message from him on the answering machine, and dictated yet another request on to his.

That done, she went back to her notebook and started to list all the questions she still had to answer.

Eventually one question that affected almost all the others forced her to telephone Marilyn.

'Hello. It's Willow here,' she said. 'I was just ringing to find out how you are.'

'I'm fine. The bruises are fading already into a disgusting yellow colour. How about yours?'

'Much the same. I still ache if I move too quickly, and the effects of the shock seem to play odd tricks with my mind – nightmares and so on – but otherwise I'm all right.'

'Good. I have a vague memory of behaving rather badly when you were here,' said Marilyn tentatively. 'I think I swore at you.'

'It wasn't me you swore at,' said Willow, laughing. 'And so there's nothing to worry about.'

'Oh, good. I was a bit shaken up – in both senses of the word. Is there something I can do to help?'

'There is actually.'

'What?' Marilyn actually sounded eager. Willow crossed her fingers like a superstitious child.

'You weren't really waiting alone all that time in the kitchen on the night your aunt died, were you?'

'Why do you say that?' Marilyn's voice was sharp, suspicious.

'Well, there was something about the way you described that evening originally that doesn't square with other things you've said and the way you've said them.' Willow thought she would not add that Mrs Guy had said Marilyn often skived off and left her aunt alone. 'I can't help thinking that if you were cross enough with her you might have gone to your cottage and hoped she'd be ringing her bell in frustration.'

There was silence for a while before Marilyn said:

'You must be a witch.'

'No, a novelist,' said Willow, hiding her satisfaction. 'It's my job to work out how people would behave in any given situation, even if the characters in my particular sort of book don't generally behave much like real people. Perhaps that's why it's taken me so long to work out what you were doing.'

Marilyn laughed, too, and said in a confiding rush:

'Well, you see, you're right. I'd hardly seen Sarah at all that day. She'd had to put herself to bed already and I wanted to see her before she went to sleep. And bloody Aunt Ethel had behaved even worse than usual. Something had annoyed her terribly and she was very breathless all day. Oh, God! Doctor Trenor has said it's not my fault and that even if she did have a heart attack because she was so cross when she rang the bell and I didn't answer it, it doesn't count as my fault. I feel awful now that she's left me such a lot and I've had such horrible feelings about her.'

Could anyone who had deliberately killed an elderly relative be that ingenuous? Willow asked herself. Aloud she said:

'Whatever your feelings now, they can change neither the awful way she behaved to you nor the facts of her life and death. Clearly the doctor is right and you couldn't be held responsible. How long were you away?'

'I'm not sure, but it might have been an hour, perhaps even a little longer. Well, yes, in fact it must have been longer. I left her with her dinner at seven-thirty and I didn't actually go back to check until well after nine-thirty.'

'I see. Thank you for being so frank. I'll see you tomorrow. Good bye.'

Willow put down the telephone. So, she thought, there

had been quite some time when Gloria Grainger had been alone in her house. Despite what Andrew Salcott had told Willow about the length of time it might take for blood leaking into the pericardium to stop a heart, it seemed much more likely that the stabbing had taken place that night. Otherwise, Willow could not see why Gloria had kept quiet about her assailant. Presumably if the spike had been held for long enough the tear would be big enough to let out as much blood as necessary to stop the heart there and then.

'But how,' said Willow loudly, 'did the killer keep Gloria still – and quiet – while that was going on?'

Willow paced about her flat, considering one suspect after another and thinking back over everything they had said and done in her presence.

'Surely,' she said aloud, 'it has to have been either Peter or Marilyn, unless the two of them were in it together?'

16

THE NEXT MORNING MRS RUSHAM woke Willow at seven thirty, saying:

'I'll have your breakfast ready in ten minutes.'

'Why so early?' asked Willow, who had been heavily asleep and in the middle of a disturbing nightmare, the details of which had already gone from her mind, leaving only a weight of anxiety and a worrying sense of responsibility. There had been something that only she could prevent and she had failed.

'You changed your appointment with the governor of Great Garden Prison to nine o'clock so that you could be sure to be back in time for Miss Grainger's funeral.' Mrs Rusham's voice was as calm and severe as usual.

Memory began to seep back into Willow's mind, displacing some of the distress left by her dream.

'I think you've far more time than you could possibly need since the funeral is not until three-thirty, but you did ask me to wake you when I arrived.'

'So I did. Thanks.' Willow noticed that Mrs Rusham was not wearing her white overall. She had obviously only just arrived in the flat. Once more Willow blessed the existence and conscientiousness of her housekeeper. Dismissing the anxiety, Willow pushed back the duvet, and got out of bed.

'I may be a little more than ten minutes,' she said as she opened the doors of her big wardrobe to select a suit. It took a minute or two to decide against black or grey. Prisons looked miserable enough without visitors adding to the prevailing greyness. She reached for an emerald green suit with large brass buttons on the jacket.

After a quick bath, she dressed and made up her face, trying not to think of the undertakers performing the same task for Gloria Grainger. As Willow brushed her hair, she noticed that it was time she had it cut. The bluntness of the line had gone, which was always a sign that she had let it grow too long. She suddenly felt as though she had been letting all sorts of things go unchecked. If she did not deal with them quickly something irrevocable was going to happen.

Mrs Rusham had provided kedgeree for breakfast and Willow ate most of it before clearing the fishy taste away with a tangerine and then two cups of cappuccino.

'No toast, thank you,' she said when Mrs Rusham offered to make her some. 'I'd better get off.'

She cleaned her teeth again, reapplied her lipstick, checked that she had both notebook and tape-recorder in her quilted bag before saying goodbye to Mrs Rusham.

'If Tom Worth telephones, would you tell him that I must speak to him, preferably before half-past one today? If he rings before, say, half-past ten, get him to telephone me in the governor's office at the prison. After that find out exactly where he'll be when and I'll ring him back.'

'Very well. I hope you have a good journey. The roads were very icy as I came here this morning.'

'Thank you, Mrs Rusham,' said Willow, recognising in the apparently disinterested statement a tactful translation of: 'drive carefully'.

The roads were indeed icy and Willow felt the tyres sliding whenever she had to break suddenly or swerve. She drove more and more slowly, relieved that the bulk of the traffic was coming from the opposite direction.

It seemed a pity that she could not have spent the previous night at the mill, which was only a twenty-minute drive from the prison, but its solitary charms would have to wait until Gloria Grainger's murderer was safely in police custody. Once that was achieved, Willow thought that she would be able to return to the mill for a few days at least to concentrate on her own work.

'Or perhaps,' she said aloud, 'on Tom.'

The ice on the road was beginning to melt by the time she reached the Hammersmith flyover and she let herself drive faster, hating it when a passing lorry flung up fans of muddy spray that covered her windscreen. Apart from the lorries there was very little traffic until she saw in the distance, somewhere between junctions nine and ten, a trail of red brake lights. At the same time she saw the first flashing signs in the central reservation warning her that the right-hand lane was being closed ahead.

Checking in her mirror that there were no cars in her way, Willow put her foot down on the brake pedal and switched on her left indicator. That responded as efficiently as ever, but after the first slight slowing down there was a horrible tearing sound under the bonnet, and the car immediately leaped forward. Pushing down harder on the pedal, Willow remembered her emergency stop the previous day, and assumed it must have somehow damaged the brake cable.

There was no response to her increasingly terrified stamping on the pedal and the trail of almost stationary cars ahead was coming horribly close.

Having seen on the television news what happens if a handbrake is applied to a car driving at high speeds, Willow knew she would have to rely on her gears. Pulling back from fifth to fourth, she was jolted by the sound of the grinding engine. Mercifully the car was slowing down, but the gap between her and the traffic jam was closing far too fast.

Her mind was not working properly and it was only as she had begun in desperation to pull up the handbrake, little by little, that she thought to put on her hazard warning lights. They at least should alert other drivers that she was not fully in control. Edging the car towards the left-hand lane, pulling up the handbrake infinitesimally, second by second, she brought the speed down towards 40mph.

There was a Rolls Royce at the back of the queue, beside a tiny, very dirty orange Deux Chevaux. Willow did not want to crash into the back of either. Pulling up the handbrake more sharply, she felt the wheels spin and lurch and let it go again, instead changing down to third.

Once more the car jerked and growled as the needle on the speedometer crept down past 30mph. There was a child in the back of the Deux Chevaux and it was waving to Willow. She could see the glee on its face and the blondeness of its curls and even, in her mind's eye, the blood of its broken body after she hit the car. With her tongue gripped firmly between her teeth and the sweat making her hands dangerously slippery, she pulled the handbrake up again, switched her left hand to the gear lever and changed down to second. With both hands on the juddering steering wheel, she got the car on to the hard shoulder just as she saw ahead of her, instead of welcoming space, the yellow bulk of a huge steam roller surrounded by traffic cones.

Pressing the heel of her right hand on the horn and then whisking it back to the steering wheel so that she could once more change down and pull on the handbrake, she had brought the car down to about 10mph when it struck the steam roller.

She heard and felt an immense bang as a big white bag inflated in front of her, saving her from being crushed against the steering wheel, and she shut her eyes. Shouts sounded and car horns and something in her brain crackled and groaned. Heat and cold mixed and a wave of something rolled over her as she fell into heavenly unconsciousness.

Rough hands were pulling at her and voices, deep male voices, asked her questions that made no sense.

'Careful,' said one. 'She may be injured.'

'Doubt it. She's got one of them bag things.'

'Could be bleeding inside. What the hell's she doing

careering along the hard shoulder like that? Bloody maniac! Can't have been in that much of a hurry.'

'Must have been. But it hasn't done her any good, has it?'

Willow was aware of the voices but could not make out how many different ones there were.

'Can I help at all?' A more authoritative male voice broke into the others. 'I'm a doctor. Is she all right?'

The great tiredness that had overwhelmed Willow as she fainted seemed to prevent her from forming words, but sound of sort issued from her throat.

'What's that?' The commanding voice asked her quite kindly.

Willow managed to lift her eyelids against the weights that seemed to be holding them down. A pain in her mouth took all her attention until she realised that her tongue was still gripped between her teeth. Deliberately she relaxed and pushed her bitten tongue between her lips, tasting blood. One of her hands seemed to work and she felt about with it, discovering something wet and harsh. She squinted down and realised that she had been laid down on the ground behind her car.

'Brakes,' she mumbled, trying to focus on the faces that were hanging over her.

'Trouble with them?'

'Not working. Is the child . . . okay?'

'Child?' demanded the doctor. 'Good Lord! Check the car at once.'

One man ran off before Willow could find the right words.

'Not mine. In a de . . . de . . . '

'De?' said the doctor gently. 'Can you tell me?'

'Deux Chevaux,' said Willow with an enormous effort.

'It'll be fine in that case. You only hit the steam roller. I want to have a look at you. All right?'

Willow pushed herself into a sitting position and nodded.

'Careful,' said the doctor. 'We don't know what you've broken.'

'Nothing. Must get on. Must talk to Tom.'

'You're not going anywhere except hospital, young lady,'

said the doctor with a manly chuckle. Willow pulled herself to her feet, gasping as she felt the new injuries on top of her old bruises, and looked the doctor in the eye, suddenly feeling much stronger, but still finding it hard to articulate distinctly.

'There's nothing wrong except my mouth. And shock,' she muttered, staggering and finding it necessary to lean against the stalwart support of one of the road menders. 'Nine o'clock appointment. Must go.'

'Calm down,' said the doctor. 'I've a mobile in my car. I can ring up anyone you need. But I'm getting you to the nearest hospital for a check. You've been astonishingly lucky not to be injured – or trapped in the car – but shock is dangerous in itself, as you must know,' he added in deference to her increasingly obvious intelligence. 'Besides, you may have internal damage. An X-ray is absolutely essential.'

She started back towards her smashed car without trying to say anything.

'What is it?' said the doctor, holding her back.

'My bag.'

While one workman went to fetch it, the other held her upright, and the doctor walked back to his dark-blue Mercedes, which he had parked ten yards behind Willow's crumpled car. The first man extricated her handbag from the car and brought it back to her. She opened it with fingers almost as clumsy as they had been in the undertakers' chapel. Everything she needed was still there, undamaged.

'Here's the phone,' said the doctor. 'What's the number?'

'Hold on,' she said with difficulty. 'Address book.' She took it out of the bag, which she hung over her painful left shoulder, and found the number and the name of the governor. The doctor insisted on making the call and spoke to the governor himself, before handing the mobile telephone to Willow.

'Mr Alkerton. Willow King, here. I'm sorry. I can't get to you. I've had a crash. They're making me go to a hospital.'

'It doesn't matter at all, Miss King, provided you're all right.'

'Yes. Shaken and sore.'

'I'll see you at the committee next week then, and when you feel like facing the motorway again, we can make another date.'

'Thanks.' She handed the telephone back to the doctor, before saying: 'Oh, can I have it back?'

'Just let me ring an ambulance for you, and . . . '

'No ambulance.'

'I'm afraid you must have one. I can't spare the time to take you into wherever the nearest hospital is myself and these men can hardly take you on their steam roller.'

'Sorry,' said Willow, remembering something that the doctor appeared to have forgotten. No telephone calls are allowed to be made on motorways, even on the hard shoulder, even after an accident. She congratulated herself on her returning wits and wished only that the power of easy speech had returned with them.

'It's all right. I'll also ring the AA for you. They can tow away the car.'

'No,' said Willow, determined to break the law in order to get hold of Tom. 'Please let me call someone. It's important.'

The doctor raised his eyebrows, telephoned 999 and explained to the ambulance service what had happened and exactly where on the motorway they were all standing.

'Yes,' he said into the telephone. 'I'll wait till your chaps get here and hand her over. Yes. We'll wait in the car. Come along, Miss King,' he said, making Willow jump. 'We must sit in the car.'

'How do you know my name?'

'You used it when you spoke to the governor of that prison,' he reminded her gently. 'You see, you do need help.'

'I'm not losing my marbles,' she said angrily, seizing the telephone from him and dialling the number of Tom Worth's office.

'DCI Worth, please,' she said indistinctly when the call was answered. There was a pause and a variety of clicks before the voice said:

'DCI Worth is not available.'

SCI Sales Corporation, Inc.
6501 Legacy Drive
Plano TX 75024-3698

Tax Group: TX / TX Weekly Plus Associates
Pay Begin Date: 01/10/2016
Pay End Date: 01/23/2016

Check #: 000107
Advice #: 00000000776712
Check Date: 01/29/2016

Cynthia Louise Watson
252 MAIN ST
HOPKINTON NH 03229

Employee ID:	00006744301
Department:	001201-Nbhd
Location:	02416-Concord, NH
Job Title:	Customer Service Specialist
Pay Rate:	$11.250000 Hourly

TAX DATA:

	Federal	NH State
Marital Status:	Single	n/a
Allowances:	0	0
Addl. Percent:		
Addl. Amount:		

HOURS AND EARNINGS

Description	Rate	Current Hrs/Units	Earnings	YTD Earnings
Regular	11.250000	73.90	831.38	1,569.38
Credit App InPay $2	2.000000	13.00	26.00	44.00
Holiday Pd-Not Work			0.00	83.25
TOTAL:		**86.90**	**857.38**	**1,696.63**

TAXES

Description	Current	YTD
Fed Withholdng	81.24	159.18
Fed MED/EE	11.12	21.97
Fed OASDI/EE	47.53	93.93
TOTAL:	**139.89**	**275.08**

BEFORE-TAX DEDUCTIONS

Description	Current	YTD
401k Savings Plan	34.30	67.87
HRA1000	83.50	167.00
Dental Pretax	7.32	14.64

AFTER-TAX DEDUCTIONS

Description	Current	YTD
Charitable Donation	2.00	4.00

Description	Current	YTD
Total Gross	857.38	1,696.63
Fed Taxable Gross	732.26	1,447.12
Total Taxes	139.89	275.08
Total Deductions	127.12	253.51
Net Pay	590.37	1,168.04

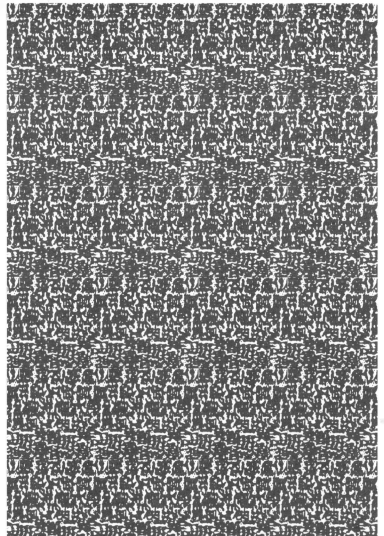

'Hell!' she said, tears of shock, frustration and anger flooding into her eyes. 'I must speak to him.'

The doctor took the telephone out of her hands.

'I am a doctor. Miss King has just been involved in a serious car accident. It is imperative that she speaks to this man. Is he merely unavailable or not in the building?'

The confidence – or perhaps the maleness – of his voice had an immediate effect and two seconds later he was talking to Tom. Willow heard only the doctor's side of their brief conversation before he gave her back the telephone.

'Will, is it true?' His voice was urgently distressed in a way that warmed her. She wished that she were alone so that she could tell him so.

'Yes. Brake failure. Tom, listen. Did you get the photographs?'

'Are you all right?'

'No. Tell me: did you get the prints?'

'Yes,' he said with some impatience. 'I've got a forensic colleague looking at them. Why?'

'Whoever did it, sabotaged my brakes. I'm sure. Will you get someone to look at the car? The doctor wants to call the AA, but he mustn't.' Her voice was rising in her anxiety to make Tom understand. 'They'll mess up the fingerprints.'

'All right, Willow. Don't worry about that. But tell me how you are.'

Willow became aware of the two workmen staring at her with a mixture of fascination and fear, as though she were a rottweiler on the rampage, and the doctor as though she were a tedious, hypochondriacal patient.

'Tom, swear you'll do it?' She could not be certain that his gentle voice and apparent obedience might not be designed merely to stop her making a fuss in front of other people.

'Yes, all right,' he said again. 'Calm down, Will. Is that doctor still there?'

'Yes.'

'Okay, put him on. I'll deal with it. Don't worry about the AA.'

A siren sounded in the distance.

'Here's the ambulance, Tom. Promise you'll get it looked at?'

'I promise.' He seemed to understand her fear for he added: 'I've a mate I was at Hendon with who's quite near you now; he'll see to it. Don't worry. When you get to the hospital ring me again.'

Willow handed the telephone back to the doctor, saying:

'Sorry and thanks. He wants to talk to you.' She dug into her wallet while the doctor was talking to Tom and, when they had finished, she held out a five-pound note. 'Here. Take it.'

'You seem to me to be a most dangerous young woman,' the doctor said, completely ignoring the money, which Willow eventually put back in her bag. 'I'm inclined to come with you and make sure you do actually stay in that ambulance.'

'I can't do anything else,' said Willow, gesturing to the wreckage of her car.

He smiled, looking more natural than he had done until that moment, and nodded at her.

'True. I wish I could hear the whole story, but . . .'

'But you can't wait,' said Willow, silently adding: Thank heavens.

The ambulance pulled up then and a uniformed woman sprang out and came running towards them. The doctor started to explain what had happened, while Willow spoke painfully to the workman who was still standing beside her, holding her up whenever her legs threatened to tremble uncontrollably.

'I must look under the bonnet,' she said, not convinced that Tom would be able to get his friend to the scene before the local police had the car removed, even if he had taken her seriously. That she would not be able to find the fingerprints without equipment was horribly frustrating. She did not have enough skills to deal with what was happening to her once-frivolous investigation and she felt too weak to cope with the consequences.

'Okay, love, but it's all squashed up in there.' He led her

carefully towards the wreckage of her car.

'Now, now,' said the ambulance service paramedic from behind them. 'You can't go wandering about on a motorway. You're in shock and it's dangerous.'

'Don't stop me. You don't know.'

'Come on, love. What's your name?'

'King,' said Willow, desperate. 'I must look.'

Strong hands took her camera from her, shut the lens cap and put the camera back in her shoulder bag. A firm arm surrounded her back and she was urged towards the ambulance. At the back double doors were opened and some metal steps let down.

'Miss King,' said the doctor, holding out a small rectangular card, 'do let me know how you get on at least.'

Willow took it, unable to resist any of them any longer and let herself be strapped into one of the bunks inside the ambulance. The paramedic in her green boiler suit sat at Willow's side, holding her hand and talking gently to her.

Two hours later Willow had been X-rayed and examined, and had explained as fully as she could about the injuries she had received when she fell down the spiral staircase at Kew. The doctor listened in silence and then started to test Willow's reflexes. When everything responded as it ought, Willow was given some painkillers for her increasingly painful mouth and head. The young casualty doctor in her long, white coat, stood in front of the bed on which Willow was lying in a crackling paper gown.

'Well, you don't seem to have damaged anything except your tongue. There's no sign of any internal injury and everything seems to be working fine.'

'I told them everything was all right,' said Willow, still furious at the time she had had to waste and desperately worried about what might have happened to her car and its crucial evidence.

'No doubt, but you could have been wrong. Now, how are you going to get back to London?'

'No idea.' Anger and helplessness chased each other

through her mind until her brain began to work again. 'The obvious is to hire a car. Is there anywhere near here that I can do that?'

'Do you really feel up to driving? Wouldn't a taxi to the station be better? There are London trains very frequently, probably about every half hour.'

'I suppose it would be quicker,' said Willow ungraciously, but feeling relieved that it was easier to talk. Then she smiled. 'I have caused you just as much trouble as the accident caused me. Sorry to be rude. Thank you for checking my wounds.'

'That's all right,' said the doctor. 'Now, don't forget you've had a severe shock. Don't drink any alcohol. Repeat the painkillers in four hours' time if you've still got the headache, and go and see your own GP in a few days if you're at all worried or if anything still hurts badly. All right?'

'Yes, thank you,' said Willow again.

'Good, then if you'd just give the receptionist the details of your doctor, we can let you go.'

Willow had to sit on an uncomfortable, plastic-covered chair for another fifteen minutes until her mini-cab arrived, but there was a London train waiting on the station platform when she emerged from the ticket office.

She found an empty first-class carriage and sat down in the forward-facing window seat and admitted to herself that she felt dreadful. The bruises from her fall down the spiral staircase at Kew all seemed to have been reactivated by the car crash, her headache was getting worse, her tongue felt as though it had been through a blunted mincing machine, but worst of all was the terrible weakness that seemed to have overtaken both her body and her mind.

Whenever she shut her eyes she saw pictures of what might have happened on the motorway: her own and other people's bodies laid out on the damp tarmac, petrol tanks on fire, one of the huge articulated lorries ploughing into the line of bodies. Each picture was more horrifying than the one before and it took an immense effort of will to remind herself that none of them was real. The bonnet of her car had been crushed, and she had been bruised and shaken, but nothing had happened to anyone else.

17

TWENTY MINUTES LATER THE TRAIN drew in to Paddington. Willow looked at her watch and decided that it must have stopped. But the second hand was bouncing merrily around and, when she looked out of the train door, she saw that the station clock confirmed that it was still only ten minutes to one.

Gloria's funeral was not due to take place until half-past three. Willow realised that she still had enough time to get to it and that if she were there she might be able to surprise whoever had damaged her brakes into giving him- or herself away. She hurried, wincing, to the taxi rank and asked the first available driver to take her as quickly as possible to Chesham Place.

He got her there only fifteen minutes later and she tipped him lavishly before climbing the steep stairs up to her flat.

'Good heavens! Miss King, what happened?' asked Mrs Rusham by way of a greeting.

Willow managed a small laugh. 'I crashed the car,' she said, and then had a moment's sickening, wholly unrealistic suspicion of Mrs Rusham. Willow shook her tousled red head just as her housekeeper said:

'Was it a skid? The roads looked very slippery.'

'No. My brakes failed,' said Willow, watching with considerable relief the expression of surprise and shock on Mrs Rusham's face.

'Have you seen a doctor?'

Willow nodded.

'Good. Then you ought to get straight to bed. I can heat some soup in no time at all.'

'I can't, Mrs Rusham; I have to go to the funeral. Have you pressed my new black suit? The one with the longer skirt.'

'This is the first time you've mentioned it. Sit down in the dining room and I'll bring you some soup and bread. While you're eating it, I'll deal with the suit.'

Too tired and battered to care what she ate, Willow did as she was told and soon found herself spooning up mildly curried parsnip soup, much hungrier than she had imagined. It was only when she had finished it that she recognised – and appreciated – Mrs Rusham's mixture of concern, censure and obedience. What more, Willow asked herself, could any woman want?

On cue the telephone rang. Knowing that her housekeeper was busy with the iron, Willow went into the kitchen to pick up the receiver.

'Hello Tom,' she said when he asked furiously why she had not rung him from the hospital.

'I forgot. But there's nothing to worry about. I'm back and all in one piece. And it's a bit rich for you to criticise my silence. I've been trying to speak to you for days. You've been deliberately obstructive.'

'I've been in the middle of a hell of a case, Will. I'm sorry,' he said peaceably. Then his voice sharpened again. 'But sometimes you drive me completely insane with worry. What makes you think that someone deliberately sabotaged the car? What on earth have you been up to since you took the photographs at the undertakers?'

'Trying to tie up the loose ends,' she said blandly. 'As I told you I would. I'm glad that you believe me at last.'

'Who do you think damaged your car?' he asked, making no comment on her last statement.

'I don't know for certain, although I suspect it must have been Peter Farrfield. I know it's sexist, but I just can't see Marilyn being capable of finding a brake cable in an engine. She didn't even know what one had to do to claim on a motor policy. She said she'd never driven a car. The only difficulty is that I've no idea where Farrfield could be – or even if that's his real name. Probably not, now I come to think of it. It sounds like an invented name.'

'How . . . ?' Tom was beginning when he sighed. 'No. We can't do this on the telephone. Stay there and wait for me. Will you do that? And not let anyone else into the flat? Promise?'

'Yes. I'll do that if you come straight away, but I'll have to leave by half-past two at the very latest.'

He put down his receiver without any valediction and Willow made a face at hers before turning to switch on the kettle. Hearing a sound behind her she turned to see Mrs Rusham looking extremely cold.

'I have pressed your suit,' she said. 'Is it coffee that you want?'

'Please,' said Willow, seeing that she had offended by infringing her housekeeper's territory. 'I'll change now, so if you could bring it to my bedroom . . . '

'Certainly.' Still frowning, Mrs Rusham held open the door that led from the kitchen to the hall. Willow walked through it, trying not to feel like a schoolchild on detention.

That and the amusement it produced helped her to relax as she undressed and washed off the effects of her car crash. By the time Mrs Rusham brought her coffee, Willow was dressed in clean underclothes and tights and was repainting her face.

'Thank you,' she said, smiling. Mrs Rusham's rigid face did not relax and she withdrew without saying anything at all. Willow shrugged, drank some coffee and finished making up her eyes.

She dressed in the collarless black suit Mrs Rusham had pressed, black tights and plain black leather shoes. There was a cossack-style hat she had bought a couple of years earlier, but she decided to go bare headed to the funeral.

When Tom Worth arrived, breathless from his run up the stairs to her flat, she was sitting in the drawing room, going over her notes.

'My God,' he said when Mrs Rusham had admitted him, 'you look as though nothing whatever had happened.'

Willow lifted her head and smiled at him, feeling the damage inside her mouth as the muscles stretched.

'To tell you the truth, I feel bloody awful.' She stuck out her tongue to show him how badly she had bitten it. 'But there's no serious damage and I hate lying in bed when there's work to be done.'

Tom stood staring at her as though he had not actually seen her for a long time. Willow raised her eyebrows.

'Did you get a vehicle examiner to deal with the car?'

'My chum has had it towed away and will deal with it. No results are expected for some hours. Do you seriously think your brakes were maliciously damaged?'

'They were certainly not generously damaged,' she said, laughing at him.

'Oh Christ! Willow, I wish you'd be serious. And I wish you wouldn't do stupid things. One day you're going to get killed. You've . . . No,' he said in answer to the expression on her face. 'If it's true about the brakes, then I admit it's partly my fault for not taking your intuitions seriously. I ought to have had the sense to lock you up days ago.'

'Well, then it's a good thing you didn't or a murderer would have got away with it.' She looked at her watch, not even noticing how casually she had taken what he said. 'And I'm damned if I'll let you lock me up now. I'm off to the funeral in ten minutes.'

'I'm coming with you. But we've got time to go through precisely what you think has happened.'

'All right. Go and ask Mrs R. to make you some coffee or a sandwich or whatever you want and then come back here.'

'I don't want anything,' said Tom.

'Fine,' she said and proceeded to explain to him once more exactly what Andrew Salcott had told her and what she had seen in the chapel of rest, why she had taken the photographs and what she had said and thought since then.

'Willow.' Tom sounded wary. 'You haven't noticed the crucial flaw yet, have you? What's happened to your mind?'

She stiffened at once. Her mind had never been available for criticism. There might have been changes to her emotions but some things were still sacrosanct.

'Don't look at me like that,' he went on. 'Just think. If someone stabbed Gloria Grainger twenty-four hours before she died, or even twelve, four or thirty-six, don't you think she would have mentioned it to someone? However little apparent damage it might have done at the time, she would have known that someone had stabbed her – or at least hit her. Even the Empress of Austria knew she'd been hit.'

'I know that.' Willow sounded desperately tired but there was anger in her voice, too. 'There must have been something that prevented Gloria from knowing what had happened. She was asleep or drunk or something. I'm sure I saw sleeping pills on her bedside table: it could have been them. There was no post-mortem and so she could easily have had too many barbiturates or alcohol. Tom, take it seriously. I know that someone killed her – and tried to kill me.'

'Will, I know that you've been badly shaken up by the crash and by your fall at Kew, and I'm not surprised that you think someone was involved in what happened to the car. But there are all kinds of other reasons why your brakes might have failed. I heard the other day about someone backing his car out of its parking space and discovering that the brakes didn't work at all. It turned out that the entire cable had been removed some time in the night, not deliberately to cause an accident, it was decided, but simply because another driver needed a new cable for his own car.'

'That certainly didn't happen to me,' said Willow, showing more impatience than fragility or stress. 'My brakes worked perfectly well between here and the motorway. It was only when I tried to stop at great speed that the cable snapped. I know it was attempted murder. I'm going to call a taxi to get to Kew. Are you really coming?'

'Yes. I'm worried that . . . I want to see all these suspects of yours.'

Wary of his apparent capitulation, but glad enough to have his company, Willow got out of her chair, with some pain, and ordered a taxi. The controller told her that there was one two minutes' drive from her front door. Willow decided to fetch her hat after all in case there were any press photographers at the church, who might produce useful publicity for her books. She returned to the drawing room pulling on her gloves.

'Ready?' she said. Tom nodded and they left the flat together.

The taxi drove out through Kensington to Hammersmith, and was forced to wait in a traffic jam outside Olympia for ten minutes. Even so, they reached Kew with half an hour to spare. Willow allowed Tom to help her down from the high step of the cab, paid the driver and then set off for the church. She noticed that round the outside of the apse at the East end had been carved:

WHAT MAN IS HE THAT LIVETH AND SHALL NOT SEE DEATH

Tom followed her and watched her reading the inscription, a small smile on his lips.

They were shown into a pew on the right-hand side about half-way up the well-lit church. As she sat down, Willow felt his hand on her knee.

'Who are they all?' he whispered.

She looked around, identifying as many people as she could. In the front pew on the left was Marilyn Posselthwate, wearing what Willow at least recognised as an exceedingly expensive black coat. Her hair had been well cut, too, and there were fat pearls in her ears and round her neck. But the most telling difference in her circumstances was the way in which she held herself. Once more Willow acknowledged what a lot money could do for a woman's confidence.

There was a man beside her, who turned his head as

though he could feel the strength of Willow's interest. She saw that he was in his sixties or seventies, grizzled and lined. He looked not only tired but also defeated.

'That must be her father,' she whispered to Tom. 'Gloria's brother. He doesn't get anything from the will as far as I know.'

'And the smooth man in the front pew on our side?'

Willow switched her attention away from Gloria's relatives and saw Gerald Plimpton leading the friends' pews. Dressed with old-fashioned formality in black morning coat and striped trousers, he bowed to an elderly woman in dark-grey silk and an enormous feathered hat, who was being assisted into the front pew by one of the young ushers. Willow saw him take a black top hat from the seat to his left and get it out of her way.

'I don't know who she is,' said Willow, 'but in the pew behind the Posselthwates are the two secretaries and Mrs Guy. She's the one in the black Persian lamb. They're all beneficiaries. Presumably that's why they're over there – and to disguise the fact that there are so few relations.'

'What about your chief suspect, Farrfield?'

Willow looked round as discreetly as she could and then shook her head.

'No sign of him, but presumably it would be too embarrassing to appear with his legs working and even worse to be back in a wheelchair. Besides, if he really did damage my brakes he's probably keeping out of the way deliberately.'

A rush of new arrivals diverted her attention from Tom and she watched them being distributed among the pews. She began to recognise various luminaries of the book world. Among them were one or two literary editors of national newspapers, which surprised her; the secretary general of the Society of Authors; a very famous libel lawyer and his wife; a member of parliament who had recently been knighted either for his many years' service on the back benches or for his few highly acclaimed literary novels. There was also Samantha Hooper, just as Marilyn had promised, looking the acme of glamour and not at all sad.

Willow pointed her out to Tom, who claimed never to have read any of her books.

'Too loyal?' Willow said, rather touched.

'I just don't like that sort of thing,' he said, too honest to pander to her vanity.

She leaned against him for a moment in acknowledgment and pleasure, and then straightened up to look back at the new arrivals.

Almost everyone was wearing black, although there were one or two excursions into grey for the men, dark blue or violet for the women, but there were very few hats. Willow began to think that both she and the woman beside Gerald Plimpton were overdressed.

Feeling a push beside her, she looked round and saw Evangeline Greville.

'Move up a bit, Willow. Is that your policeman?'

'Yes. I'm surprised Samantha Hooper has actually come here; aren't you?'

'Presumably she came out of curiosity. Or a desire to make sure Gloria's really dead. Or perhaps even a smattering of gratitude. It undoubtedly helped her to get an agent to be able to say she was once Gloria's secretary. How are the fallen mighty, eh? Publishing's wheel of fortune is particularly instructive to watch.'

There was a movement at the back of the church and almost every head swivelled round. The vicar emerged from the porch in full black vestments richly adorned with silver embroidery. The congregation stopped chattering in their sibilantly low voices and stood to watch him process slowly up the aisle followed by the coffin, draped in embroidered and heavily fringed black velvet, carried on the shoulders of six stalwart, black-uniformed men of military bearing.

A huge suck of air presaged the first notes of the organ as it began to play the 'Dead March' from *Saul*. The vicar bowed to the black-veiled, flowerless altar and turned. The coffin was laid on velvet-covered trestles at the foot of the chancel steps. The last sonorous notes of the organ faded into heavy silence. In a remarkably beautiful voice the vicar began to recite the words of the 1664 funeral service.

Willow felt her skin shiver as all memory of Gloria's actual death was subsumed into a recognition of the power carried by the ancient traditions of the English Church. She felt absorbed into it, disbelieving still but full of admiration and a certain envy for the glory of its language.

Later only small things stood out from the rest: a fair, sturdy boy singing *Pie Jesu*; a young woman with an icily precise soprano singing a short and wholly unexpected song about 'cold, cold despair'; a magnificent *Libera Me*; Gerald Plimpton ascending the pulpit to talk with generous diplomacy of his dead author; and the sudden, unexpected, sound of tears from someone in the pews ahead of hers.

'No wonder the funeral took so long to arrange,' hissed Eve in Willow's direction. 'Collecting all these singers in itself is a coup. Who fixed it?'

'Plimpton, I understand,' said Willow, aware once again of Gloria's tragedy.

The thought of her planning such an elaborate funeral while ensuring that no one could have any kind of equal and affectionate relationship with her seemed heartbreaking in its utter perversity. Presumably she had wanted to make sure that she impressed the world in death as she had always tried to do in life. No wonder she had surrounded herself with the weak, the miserable and those who could be relied upon to behave like courtiers. No wonder Peter Farrfield's chattering of Gloriana had pleased her so. No wonder someone had lost control and killed her.

Willow's attention sharpened as the vicar stood at the head of the coffin, saying:

'Go forth, oh Christian soul.'

'Are you going on to the cemetery, Willow?' asked Eve as they were politely waiting for the family and most important supporters to leave their pews. Ann Slinter swept past wrapped in a huge black cashmere serape with Victoria Taffle in a grey coat and an extraordinary woollen bonnet hurrying along beside her and not looking at anyone.

'No. That's private. But we're all supposed to go for tea at the house until Marilyn and co. are back. Coming, Eve?'

'It seems a bit hypocritical.'

'Hardly more than coming to the service. Besides, some-one will have to entertain Tom here while I talk to Gloria's friends and relations.'

Eve reached round Willow's tall figure to shake hands with Tom.

'We haven't met, but I'm her agent. Eve Greville,' she said.

'Tom Worth.' He shook her hand briefly. 'Hadn't we better get going? We do seem to be almost the last. Willow, are you sure you're up to standing about with a teacup in your hand?'

'Certainly,' she said. 'Come on.'

They emerged into the light and cold and saw the black procession crossing the Green to Marilyn's house.

'Hurry up.' Eve was pulling on her gloves. 'It's too cold to hang about. I need some tea. I hate funerals.'

'Do you?' said Willow. 'I thought it was magnificent.'

'The chill factor was certainly high,' said Tom.

Willow looked at him and suddenly recognised something in him that she had never understood before. Her eyes met his and after a moment he nodded.

'We do, you know.'

'I know.'

'Do what?' said Eve, who had not noticed their express-ions. 'Come on, hurry up.'

Tom said nothing, leaving Willow to laugh with assumed lightness.

'Share the odd idea,' she said casually and felt his hand gripping hers before he set it free again.

Four icy minutes later they were inside the house being offered thin white china cups of tea and plates of sandwiches by uniformed waitresses. Willow saw that the two secretaries were in charge and slipped away from Tom and Eve to talk to Susan.

'Hello,' she said. 'You're doing wonders.'

'It's easy enough,' answered Susan. 'Patty and I have often organised things together. And without Gloria to criticise her every move and word, Patty is enormously capable. You know, I don't think I shall ever be able to forgive Gloria for what she did to Patty. She took a perfectly intelligent, reasonably happy woman and systematically reduced her to a terrified, incompetent wreck.'

Willow looked at her critically. 'You really hated her, didn't you?'

'Oh yes,' said Susan without any hesitation at all.

'You're very frank.'

'Why not – now? You can't libel the dead.'

'Slander,' said Willow automatically. 'Libel's written, you know. Tell me, Susan, what did you do before you started to temp?'

'I was a skeboo nurse until the deaths became more than I could bear and I decided to learn to type.'

'What on earth is a skeboo?'

'Sorry. One forgets that the familiar acronyms of everyday can be quite foreign to other people. SCBU. Special Care Baby Unit.'

'That must have been heartbreaking, but I understand now why you're so protective of Patty Smithe.'

'I don't quite see the connection unless you mean that I'm used to looking after helpless, desperate beings. Patty's tougher than that. She just lets herself be bullied. Good Lord!'

'What?' asked Willow, looking behind her. She saw Peter Farrfield standing in the doorway, a shy, delightful smile on his good-looking face. She put out a hand so that she could lean on a chairback for support.

'I'd better get him out of here before Marilyn gets back. She'd go absolutely ape,' said Susan. 'I'll be back.'

Willow watched as the tall, broad-shouldered young woman moved across the crowded room. She was almost exactly the same height as Peter Farrfield. She spoke to him. He shook his head, smiled again and reached out to the tray of a passing waitress to take a cup of tea. He said something that Willow did not catch and Susan glared at him.

'The little tick!' she said when she reached Willow's side

again. 'He told me Gloria always said she wanted him at her funeral and he felt obliged to obey her wishes, despite the embarrassment it causes him. I can't think of any way of removing him. I hope there won't be a scene.'

Willow knew that she ought to talk to Peter, to test his reaction to her presence and trick him into an admission of guilt, but she felt too weak and stupid to get it right. Feeling feeble, she looked round for Tom, but could not see him.

'Are you all right?' asked Susan, looking at her carefully. 'You're very pale.'

Willow made herself smile. 'Yes, I just feel a little faint. I was in a car accident this morning. Can you see the man I came with anywhere? He's called Tom Worth. Tall and a broken nose.'

'No,' said Susan after a moment, 'but I think you ought to sit down while I try to find him. Come on through to the study. You can be quiet there and recover.'

Willow allowed herself to be led out of the crowded room and across the hall to Gloria's study. There she found the elegant, elderly woman who had sat beside Gerald Plimpton in the church.

'Hello,' she said in a deep voice as Susan pulled forward one of the wing chairs for Willow. 'I'm Serena Marker.'

'Susan Robinson. I worked for Gloria Grainger. And this is Willow King. She's not feeling well.'

'I'll take care of her if you want to go back to the crowd.' Serena Marker smiled at Willow and explained that she had been the editor of one of the women's magazines that had regularly serialised Gloria's novels in her heyday.

'I had to sit down, too,' she added. 'Arthritis, you know.'

Willow, who was feeling better, explained herself and the reason for her own infuriating weakness. A little later she asked what the other woman had thought of Gloria and her books.

They were soon deep in a discussion of changing tastes in popular fiction when they were interrupted by the sound of Marilyn's voice, angry and shrill, coming through the wall:

'How dare you come here?'

'Gloria always said she wanted me here,' came Peter Farrfield's cocky answer. 'She cared for me, even though you clearly never did.'

'She didn't in the end,' said Marilyn spitefully. 'I used to despise her for her lack of perception sometimes, but I was misled. She was clever enough to see through you, you utter . . . toad.'

'She hasn't got her aunt's facility with words,' said Serena Marker, smiling at Willow. 'I used to think it a pity that Gloria used her talents so much more effectively in furious letters than in her books. Do you think we ought to warn Marilyn that she can be heard?'

'No,' said Willow at once, far too interested to mind compromising Marilyn's reputation.

'What do you mean?' Peter did not even sound worried.

'You didn't believe me, did you? But, like I told you, she changed her will. Isn't that why you really came? Because you knew the beneficiaries were to be told what they'd inherited after this wholly enchanting party and you didn't believe you were getting nothing? Well, it's true. Like I said, she cut you right out. All those months of sycophancy and pretence were for nothing. You'll just have to work for your living now, or prey on some other stupid cow like me.'

There was the sound of a hand smacking into flesh.

'I think perhaps you really should intervene now,' said Serena, holding out a hand like a twisted claw. 'Whichever of them it is hitting the other it ought to be stopped.'

Willow hesitated.

'Go on! I can't get there in time and it's not just embarrassment Marilyn's risking. Go on.'

Reluctantly Willow opened the communicating door into the panelled dining room at the back of the house to see Peter Farrfield with a reddening mark on his cheek. He stood bunching his hands into fists at his sides. At the sound of the opening door he turned to face her. She took a step back at the sight of the rage in his eyes.

'Who the hell are you?' he demanded, apparently not recognising her from their brief encounter in the cottage.

'Control yourself, Farrfield,' came a commanding voice from the other door into the room. Gerald Plimpton stood there.

'Are you all right?' he asked Willow. She nodded.

'Good. Now, please calm down, both of you. You can be heard all over the house.'

'You're the executor, aren't you?' said Peter, his mouth distorted into a sneer. 'You're very like your photograph.'

'And what were you ever doing in my aunt's bedroom?' Marilyn spat out the words. 'The only photograph of Gerald is by her bed.'

The young man flipped his head round to face her again.

'None of your fucking business. Is what she said true, Plimpton? I get nothing?'

'Nothing at all, I'm afraid, out of the last will.' Gerald stopped for a moment, as though measuring their respective capacities for bad news and then added: 'And you were never among the major beneficiaries at all, although it is true that her previous will left you a little.'

'Bitch! She strung me along.' His once-handsome face was so contorted that he looked both ugly and pathetic. 'And you're just as bad, Marilyn. If I . . . '

He strode across to where Gerald Plimpton was standing, pushed him out of the way and flung himself out of the house, slamming the front door behind him.

The other three were still standing in silence, looking at each other, when Susan Robinson appeared with Tom at her elbow.

'Will, are you all right?' he asked.

'Yes,' she said, taking him out of the dining room and into the hall. She explained what had happened as quickly as possible. Tom listened calmly, saying nothing until she had finished.

'And do you still think it was he who did it?' he asked.

'It must have been,' Willow said, suddenly discouraged and feeling each one of her bruises and scrapes. 'But you're right: there's no evidence. And he genuinely seemed not to know who I was, so perhaps I'm wrong about it all and he never went near the car after all. Perhaps no one did. Perhaps I really am losing my marbles.'

'That's absurd,' said Tom comfortingly. 'But I think we'd better go, don't you, before you pass out. You look frightful. Come on, Will.'

Tom looked hard at Willow as he spoke and she realised that there were several interested people listening to them.

'I must still be suffering from shock,' she said, longing to be flat on her back in bed and completely forgetting that she had meant to talk to Marilyn's father about his childhood with Gloria Grainger.

18

THE NEXT MORNING WILLOW WOKE alone, feeling far more confident than she had when Tom brought her home from the funeral and put her to bed. Despite the bruises all over her battered body, she had slept almost uninterrupted for twelve hours. Her brain felt as though it had been cleared of a lot of extraneous ideas and fears.

Lying against the soft linen-covered pillows, she set herself to work out once and for all what the information she had collected about Gloria and her death really meant.

It seemed sensible to work backwards from the car crash, which Willow was once again certain could not have been an accident. The car was less than a year old and had shown no earlier signs of brake failure. The emergency stop she had had to make in the Mall had been impeccable and modern brake cables do not suddenly snap for no reason. Someone must have damaged them during the night before her journey down the motorway. Since she had no personal enemies, it could only have been done by someone who wanted to stop her asking questions about Gloria's death.

The only people who knew for certain that that was what Willow had been doing were Ann Slinter and Tom. He was obviously not a suspect, and Willow had never considered that Ann might be guilty. However much she had disliked being persuaded to publish Gloria's books, she was quite powerful enough to stop them coming out without killing their author.

The scent of grilling kidneys reached Willow before she had even listed the evidence for and against her suspects, and she let her head twist sideways on the pillows so that she could look at the clock. She saw that it was already nine o'clock. Pushing away the duvet, she got out of bed, groaning as the movement stretched all her damaged muscles. There were plenty of painkillers in the bathroom and she got herself there laboriously, leaning on pieces of furniture as she went.

She took two powerful pills and did not even attempt to dress. Barefoot and with only a soft dressing gown around her nakedness, she walked painfully into the dining room, where Mrs Rusham was laying her breakfast table.

'Good morning. Did you sleep well?'

'Thank you, yes,' said Willow, pushing her hair out of her eyes. 'The kidneys smell wonderful.'

'Shall I bring them now?' asked the housekeeper, pouring orange juice into a heavy tumbler.

'Please.' Willow laid a napkin across her aching knees and picked up the glass.

As she drank, she thought about Marilyn Posselthwate. Whether or not she had deliberately pushed Willow down the spiral stairs, she was still the likeliest suspect in the murder investigation and could have sabotaged Willow's car quite easily. Marilyn had pretended to know nothing about cars, but that could well have been a piece of deliberate misinformation.

She had seen Willow's car often enough to be able to identify it, and she could have found out where it would be parked at night. Willow's address was not in the telephone book, or in any of the writers' directories, but too many people had it for it to be considered at all secret, and she always kept the car in the street outside.

Posy Hacket had had the same opportunities as Marilyn,

but Willow could not help thinking that Posy would have been both more subtle and more efficient if she had decided to kill someone. Damaged brake cables might kill the driver – and any passengers – of a car travelling at high speed, but they might just as easily have caused a tiresome but not fatal accident in the middle of a town.

Attempting to silence someone like that had been silly, Willow thought, and ill-considered. Someone must have been thrown into a panic by something she had said or done.

Peter Farrfield might have done it, but if so, he would have needed Marilyn's help. Even if he had guessed during his short encounter with Willow what she was really doing in Kew, he would have found it hard to track her down. He did not even know her name and had never even seen the car.

'One way or another, it has to have been Marilyn,' said Willow, wondering why she was still not convinced.

She smiled at Mrs Rusham, who brought her a heated plate of grilled kidneys and tomatoes. When she had gone again, Willow picked up her knife and fork and cut one of the kidneys in half. Thin blood oozed out of the cut and spread out over the flowered porcelain. Willow laid down her knife, unable to eat after all.

As she stared at the blood, trying not to feel sick and thinking about the tiny wound in Gloria's chest, Willow's doubts about Marilyn began to grow.

It would have been so much easier for her simply to smother her aunt as she slept than to stab her. Everyone knew that it was possible to kill by suffocation, but comparatively few people would be likely to know about the effects of a small tear in the heart wall. Marilyn had had access to her aunt's house at any hour of the day or night. Why would she have fiddled about with a spike of some kind when a pillow would have done the job for her just as well, more quickly and with less chance of discovery?

Surely only someone who could not reach Gloria's bedroom while she was asleep would have risked stabbing her.

'Damn!' said Willow as she reached that conclusion. She

was back with the same problem that had always made nonsense of her deductions. Why had Gloria said nothing about her assailant?

Having put the question directly to herself, Willow was determined to find an answer. She searched her memory of the things she had been told during the past week.

At one of their meetings, Marilyn had said that Gloria had complained of a terrible headache on the day she died. It had felt 'as though she had been hit on the head with a hammer'.

'Are you ready for some coffee now?' Mrs Rusham's voice disturbed Willow as she was trying to decide whether a sharp blow to the head might have made Gloria not only lose consciousness but also forget what she had been doing just before she was struck.

'Is there something wrong, Miss King? You're not eating.'

'What? No, I'm sorry, Mrs Rusham. The accident seems to have taken away my appetite. I'm not hungry, but some coffee would be lovely. Thank you.'

The housekeeper took away the rejected offal and returned a moment later with a big cup of cappuccino, which Willow accepted with a quick smile. She was still trying to assemble relevant facts from the welter of half-remembered conversations. Concentrating hard, she tried to recreate them all. Marilyn's plaintiveness, Vicky's pessimism, Ann's impatience, Susan's practicality, and the Weston & Brown receptionist's sympathy were carried back to Willow as she ran through the things they had said to her.

'Susan said she'd been typing a whole chapter herself the day before yesterday.'

'I thought it might toughen her up . . . She's dealt with the old bag for years now but it hasn't made any difference.'

'I suppose someone might have come after I'd gone back to Patty in the flat, but Marilyn never mentioned anyone.'

'She'd had a terrible headache the day before. She said it felt as though she'd been hit on the head with a hammer.'

'She's had one of those burdened, virtuous lives: looked after an elderly parent.'

'Most non-fiction editors have to tackle everything from self-help to . . . oh anything.'
'I think she'd had a very minor stroke, too, about a year ago.'
'She's safe as houses. Pretty secretive actually.'
'It was a couple of days before she died. She wanted Vicky Taffle.'

'Gloria wanted Vicky Taffle,' said Willow aloud. 'Could it be?'

She tried to remember exactly what Vicky had said to her as they parted in the dark outside the restaurant. They had been talking about muggers, and Vicky had said something like: 'No one's ever molested me yet and I do have one of those shrieky alarms and . . .'

'And what?' Willow said, staring down at her coffee. 'Was she going to say, "and I've never had to use it yet"? Or could it have been "one of those shrieky alarms and a hatpin to defend myself with"?'

Willow wondered why she had never even considered something that seemed appallingly obvious. She felt as she occasionally did when completing a crossword puzzle: a clue would make no sense at all, even though she had at least half of the necessary letters; she would stare at them, trying to work out what the cryptic clue could possibly mean, testing it for hidden puns or anagrams; and then suddenly the whole word would appear in her brain, making the clue seem easy after all.

She had been concentrating on who might have gained money or other practical benefits from Gloria's death, ignoring all the latest statistics that suggested that up to ninety per cent of murders are unpremeditated. Perhaps Tom had been right all along: motive was indeed the least important part of any murder investigation.

'She'd been nagging me and so I hit her,' the illiterate murderer had written in the letter Elsie Trouville had shown Willow in the Home Office. Surely that was also the likeliest reason for killing an elderly woman with a weak heart who might have died at any time?

'Vicky Taffle,' Willow said again as she tried to think of something that would blow her new theory away.

There was nothing. Even Tom's description of the chief suspect in his murder case seemed to reinforce Willow's conviction that Vicky must be guilty. He had described the suspect as pretending to be miserable, but being unable to suppress completely a smile of secret satisfaction. Willow thought of the moment when she had watched Vicky sitting at her desk, unaware that she was not alone. There had been a smile then, Willow remembered, unlike any that Vicky had shown other people.

The front door bell rang before Willow had decided how best to proceed. Looking down at her dressing gown and thinking of her face, pale and undefended without any makeup, she listened warily to Mrs Rusham as she walked to the front door and opened it.

'Is she up yet?' Willow heard Tom say out in the hall. She relaxed at once.

'Yes. She's at breakfast.' Mrs Rusham sounded as though she thought that he ought to wait. Willow could not suppress a smile at the very different welcome Richard Crescent would have received.

'Tom?' she called. 'I'm in here. Come on in.'

'Will?' He appeared in the doorway 'How are you? Any better?'

'Aching all over,' she said, 'but, yes, much better. D'you like kidneys?'

'Love them. Why?'

He put a hand lightly on her wrenched shoulder and kissed her. Willow noticed that the painkillers had started to work and kissed him back.

'Mrs R. produced them for my breakfast but I found I couldn't face them. If you'd like them, get her to hot them up for you in the microwave. I think I could just about manage some more coffee while I watch you eat.'

He looked at her, obviously worried by her loss of appetite, but he did as she asked. Five minutes later they were sitting opposite each other at the round mahogany table in the dining room.

'You still don't look yourself,' said Tom when he had

finished the kidneys, 'even if you're not quite as white as you were yesterday.'

'That's just lack of makeup. Without mascara my eyes have always looked like gooseberries veiled in raw eggwhite.'

'Nonsense.' He laughed. 'I've seen you first thing in the morning often enough to know. And it's not just the car crash either. You look shocked about something. Can't you tell me about it, whatever it is?'

She wrinkled up her nose and shook her head.

'I suppose I'm just a bit disgusted with myself about something.'

'What?'

'You're very inquisitive today, Tom,' she said and then shrugged, deciding to tell him part of it, if only to stop him asking any more questions she was not ready to answer. 'Oh well, all right. I had been congratulating myself for effecting a useful revolution in someone I thought I quite liked, and . . . ' She stopped and frowned.

'And?'

'And I now realise that I had been completely misreading both the unrevolutionised state and the reasons for the revolution. They were nothing whatever to do with my kindly intervention. I feel a fool: an arrogant, almost danger-ous, fool.'

'That's all extremely cryptic, Will, and I'm not really in the mood for codes this morning. There isn't time.' He ate the last piece of kidney. 'You're presumably talking about the Grainger murder.'

'Aha,' she said, producing a smile with difficulty. 'Can it be that my arguments have at last managed to convince the most sceptical man in the Met after all?'

'Partly,' he admitted. 'But I have to confess that it's more the fingerprints on your car's engine than your arguments that have convinced me. I don't suppose you've ever had the car serviced by a woman, have you? The prints are definitely the size of an adult female.'

'No,' said Willow. 'As far as I know, they're all men at the garage. So, I was right about the brakes after all.'

The thought of what might have happened to her as she drove down the motorway filled her with cold, implacable anger and a determination to wring an admission of guilt out of Victoria Taffle before the end of the day.

'I've sent a woman police constable to Kew to invite Marilyn Posselthwate to come to the station for a chat,' said Tom. 'I'm on my way there now, but I wanted to see you first. What's the matter?'

'I don't think you'll find that Marilyn's fingerprints match the ones on the engine,' said Willow. 'Sorry and all that.'

Tom looked at her across the breakfast table. There was a hint of a smile in his dark eyes.

'All right,' he said at last, 'tell me about the latest brilliant deduction.'

'I'm not sure I can yet,' said Willow, suddenly very glad that it was Tom who was trying to build a shared life with her. 'I sometimes think,' she went on, 'that my amazingly brilliant powers of observation have occasionally let me down and that therefore some of the deductions may have been wrong.'

'Willow, I know I started it, but this is too serious for jokes,' said Tom. 'What more have you found out since we last talked?'

'Nothing. I mean, no more facts. But I am inclining towards a different interpretation of the ones I've been telling you about for the past seven days,' she said. 'I'm still not absolutely sure about it and I need a few more bits of information. Why don't you go and talk to Marilyn and come back for lunch? I ought to have sorted out my ideas by then.'

'No,' said Tom. 'I'm not prepared to stand by and let you do something else stupid or dangerous.'

All her old resistance to him resurfaced for a moment, even though she recognised the fundamental benevolence of his insult and his determination to protect her.

'Don't bully me, Tom,' she said, and then she laughed. 'I'm so stiff I can hardly move. I couldn't even leave the flat, let alone get into a fight with anyone. Be back here at one o'clock and I'll have everything you need.'

'I don't trust you, you know.'

'You should, Tom. After all, I trust you.'

'No, you don't,' he said casually as he looked down at his watch. 'I'll have to go, but I'll be back as soon as I can. Don't take any more risks. It half kills me when you get hurt.'

He did not wait for her to say anything, which was lucky because she could not think of a suitable comment. Her old instincts told her to make a joke, but her newly peeled emotions would not let her.

When Tom had gone, Willow pushed herself up from her chair and went to dress in her loosest, most comfortable trousers and sweater. Then, lying back on her neatly made bed, she telephoned the flat shared by Gloria's secretaries.

Her call was answered by Susan Robinson.

'It's Willow King here,' she said briskly. 'There are a couple of questions I quite forgot to ask you and Patty when we last met.'

'Oh yes? And what are they?'

Willow appreciated the automatic defensiveness of her superficially polite question.

'One of you, presumably it was you, Susan, told Marilyn that Gloria had been typing the day before she died. Can that be right? How did you know it was she who had done the actual typing?'

Susan laughed and the relief sounded clearly in her voice.

'It can't have been anyone else. Marilyn never took any part in the books. I don't think she can type even as well as Gloria could. When I came into the office the morning before she died, I saw at once that she'd been down there. Everything on the desk was arranged differently and the chapter in my basket was not the one I had typed, even though it had yet more arrows and handwritten alterations. She must have worked down in our office for at least two hours after Marilyn had left her for the evening.'

'Did she often work on her books after you had left?'

'Oh yes. One would imagine one had seen the last of the idiotic Miss Whatsit's pursuit of the wicked Earl of

Wherever, and then there it would be next morning, all to be done again. Drove you mad sometimes.'

'I'll bet. So what was her typing like?'

'Not up to professional secretarial standards, but it was always perfectly clear.'

'And that day, are you sure the typing was hers?'

'You mean you think someone else did it, don't you?' The defensiveness was back. 'No. I didn't talk to her about it, but I am sure it was hers. It was unprofessional. Not the work of a trained secretary.'

'It's all right, Susan,' said Willow at once. 'I'm not accusing you or Patty of anything.'

There was a short pause, followed by an artificial laugh, and then Susan said:

'I'm glad to hear it. Then what is it that you are asking me?'

'Simply whether Gloria and no one else could have done the typing that evening?'

'I suppose I can't categorically answer "yes". Work produced on electric typewriters doesn't have any distinguishing marks to show precisely whose fingers pressed the keys.'

'I see. Thank you. Now I need to talk to her editor about this last chapter she was working on. I know Gloria had Vicky Taffle's home telephone number. Have you by any chance got it there?'

Susan dictated it and then said: 'I'm afraid I must go. There's someone at the door. Good bye.'

There was one other piece of information Willow needed. She rang Andrew Salcott and discussed people with headaches that felt as though they had been hit on the head with a hammer. Having got the information she needed, she said good bye to him and lay, staring up at the ceiling, with the buzzing receiver in her hand. She wanted to make certain that she could control her voice before she spoke to Vicky. At last she rang the number Susan had just given her.

'Hello, Vicky,' she said when the telephone was

answered. 'It's Willow King here. I was wondering whether I could persuade you to come and have some lunch with me today. I'm at a loose end and I so enjoyed our dinner together.'

'That's very kind,' said Vicky, sounding half asleep and puzzled.

'Did I wake you?' Willow looked at her watch and saw that it was nearly eleven o'clock. 'I am sorry.'

'No, it's all right. I always sleep late on Saturdays and then work on Sunday. It's easier that way.'

'What a shame that I've disturbed you. But how about it? Lunch today?'

Willow half-expected her to decline, and was trying to invent another way of engineering a meeting.

'But how kind,' said Vicky after a moment. 'I was just thinking how bleak the house is on this awful day. What time should I come and where?'

'Come here to the flat.' Willow gave both address and directions. 'And come at about half-past twelve if you can manage it. Then we'll have plenty of time to drink before my housekeeper gets lunch. Is there any sort of food you're allergic to?'

'Only brains.' There was a laugh that was half a snuffle.

'Don't worry about that,' said Willow briskly. 'I don't take risks with things like Mad Cow Disease. I'll see you later.'

'You're kinder to me than anyone else has been in years,' said Vicky, making Willow cringe. 'I'll see you as near to half-past twelve as I can then.'

In fact it was nearly ten to one by the time she arrived. Willow had gone into the kitchen five minutes earlier to ask Mrs Rusham to keep the quails hot in their madeira sauce for a late start.

Mrs Rusham brought the guest into Willow's drawing room and said she would fetch the champagne.

'How luxurious!' said Vicky. Willow was not sure whether it was her creamy-yellow room or the prospect of champagne that excited the comment.

'Good,' she said meaninglessly, detesting the other

257

woman. 'A friend of mine is going to join us a bit later. I hope you don't mind.'

Vicky looked taken aback and Willow wondered whether she could have been planning another assault with her hatpin. Willow almost hoped that she might be faced with it. She felt an unprecedented urge to hit, scratch and throttle.

'Not at all,' said Vicky. 'But are you sure I won't be in the way?'

'Quite sure. Ah, thank you, Mrs Rusham. Champagne, Vicky?'

'Lovely. Are we celebrating something?' Vicky asked so sweetly that Willow had a moment's sickening doubt.

'In a way. I had a brush with death yesterday when my brakes failed on the motorway. Having survived makes me feel pretty wonderful in spite of my aches and pains.'

Vicky looked quite pale and sat, silent, for a full minute. 'How dreadful!' she said at last. 'Do they know why?'

'Why I survived or why the brakes failed?'

'The latter.' Vicky's voice sounded almost normal, but there was enough obvious wariness in her face to calm Willow's doubts.

Watching Vicky, she began to understand that the pleasure she had always imagined her heroines taking in their revenge was nothing like the real thing. She had assumed that there would be satisfaction, but she felt none. Instead she felt a certain tingling excitement, but there was also real tooth-grinding anger, and a kind of disgust. Suppressing as much of it all as she could, Willow made herself smile.

'No. The car's with a mechanic at the moment. While you're here, can I ask you one or two more questions about Gloria?'

'All right,' said Vicky, looking surprised, 'although I do rather long for the day when I never have to think of her again.'

'I bet you do,' said Willow, hoping she did not sound as tart as she felt. 'It was actually your last editorial meeting with her that I wanted to discuss.'

'But we haven't had one for months.'

'Perhaps it didn't count as a meeting,' answered Willow casually. 'I meant when you went out to Kew the evening before she died.'

'It wasn't that day,' said Vicky quickly. 'I didn't see her that day at all. It was the one before.'

'So it was,' said Willow casually. 'Silly me. Was she very difficult?'

'Not especially.' Vicky moved her feet closer to the bag she had left on the floor. Thinking of the hatpin, Willow was determined to remove the bag out of Vicky's reach as soon as she could. 'She was always tiresome. I told you that before.'

'She made you retype a whole chapter for her, didn't she?'

'Yes.' Vicky seemed happy enough to answer. 'But how on earth do you know? There was no one else there with us. Marilyn had gone to the cottage as soon as she'd served Gloria's dinner. I didn't see her at all that evening.'

'Susan – the temp – told me.'

'How very odd. Gloria must have told her the next day.'

'Why . . . ?' Willow was beginning when she heard the front door bell.

A moment later Tom appeared in the drawing room, saying: 'You were right, Will. They didn't match. Now you must . . .'

'Hello, Tom,' said Willow, with a distinct warning tone in her voice. 'This is Victoria Taffle, who visited Gloria before she died. We were just talking about their last meeting.'

'Oh,' he said, his eyebrows snapping together. 'Any champagne left for me, by any chance?'

'Plenty, and Mrs Rusham has cooked enough quails for us all. We'll eat in a minute or two. Vicky's just telling me what Gloria said that night.'

'There was nothing very unusual,' she said, half turning to examine Tom. 'She did her best to humiliate me and make me lose my temper, but she always did that.'

'I didn't know you had a quick temper.' Willow smiled encouragingly. 'You seem enviably placid to me.'

Vicky laughed with a high, disagreeable sound. 'She could always find ways of pressing my buttons.'

'From all I've heard, she sounds a thoroughly unpleasant old woman,' said Tom, walking round the back of the sofa and sitting at the other end of it from Vicky. He looked at Willow and then back at Vicky. 'You must have had a dreadful time of it.'

Victoria simply nodded and then, dismissing him, smiled at Willow again and raised her eyebrows.

'So, you retyped the chapter for her,' said Willow, picking up the thread of her interrogation. 'Did she sit and watch while you did it?'

'Yes.'

'In her bedroom?' asked Tom, puzzled.

'No, of course not. Why should it be? I've never been in her bedroom. We were in the secretary's room in the basement where the typewriter is.'

'What time are we talking about here?' asked Willow, frowning at Tom to stop him asking stupid questions.

'After dinner. About ten I should think. She'd rung me at the office and told me to come straight round. I . . . I was pissed off with her and very busy and so I told her I couldn't come until at least half-past nine and that she'd have to pay for a taxi to take me home.'

'And did she?' asked Tom.

Willow glared at him again.

'Oh yes. She gave me thirty pounds out of her handbag. I got back home at about midnight.'

'It was quite a long session then?' said Willow.

'Yes. I've never been a typist and it took me ages and then she started scribbling all over what I'd just typed.'

'Goodness how irritating! Didn't you protest?' Willow tried to make herself sound sympathetic.

'Certainly. It was the most ludicrous waste of my time. I told her so.'

'Did that get you any kind of apology?' asked Tom.

Vicky laughed again, for once sounding thoroughly amused.

'You must be joking. She told me, in that revoltingly syrupy voice she could put on, that she really sympathised with me for being so unattractive in character as well as appearance. She said she did hope I was behaving better with my other authors because, if not, Ann would have to sack me and no one else would be charitable enough to give me a job.'

Tom laughed and the two women both looked at him in surprise.

'Come on,' he said, 'people just don't talk to each other like that.'

'Oh yes they do. That wasn't the worst by any means. You should have heard her sometimes.'

Willow was silent as she tried to think how best to force Vicky into a confession. Slowly Willow became aware that both the others were staring at her. Abandoning all idea of finesse, she said abruptly:

'And was it then that Gloria had her stroke?'

Tom's head jerked upwards and Willow could see him controlling himself with difficulty.

'I don't know what you mean,' said Vicky shrilly. 'She didn't have a stroke. She died of a heart attack at least twenty-four hours later.'

'Oh come on, Victoria. Of course she had a stroke. Just a small one. Stertorous breathing, blankness, loss of speech and consciousness. That was when you stuck the hatpin in her.'

Willow saw Tom standing up and moving behind Victoria, who said nothing.

'You nursed your own parents, didn't you? And one of them had had a series of strokes,' said Willow, leaning forwards to scoop up the handbag Vicky had left at her feet. 'That was how you knew what was happening to Gloria. When she lost consciousness you saw your chance to stop her tormenting you for ever and stabbed her.'

Willow opened the shabby black-leather handbag. Pushing aside the muddle of cheque book, receipts and paper hand-kerchiefs, she found the 'shrieky alarm' with its red-plastic cap and right at the bottom of the bag a ten-inch carbon steel hatpin with a large elaborately jewelled knob at one end.

'With this.'

Victoria sat unmoving, her face grey and her eyes staring at nothing. Tom looked over her head at Willow and held out a hand. She took the hatpin to him and returned to her chair.

'Wasn't that what happened, Vicky?' said Willow sharply.

Victoria flinched, looked at her interrogator, and then shook her head.

'There's no point pretending any more, Vicky. It won't be difficult to prove it all now that we've got this far. Even if you've washed the hatpin in surgical spirit, they'll probably be able to find traces of blood on it somewhere; or on the lining of your bag. I am right, aren't I?'

There was a long silence. Vicky rubbed both hands across her face and through her hair.

'She stopped talking,' she said at last in a calm, vague voice as though she were remembering something from long ago. 'And fell forward on to the desk as I was typing her rubbish. I knew at once what was happening because my father had had a series of those little strokes before the big one that killed him. Some made him lose consciousness, some didn't. Hers did. And I thought how wonderful it would be if she would only die. Then, you see, I had to make sure that she would. Not all strokes kill. I knew I'd have to help it along a bit.'

She looked up. Neither Willow nor Tom spoke.

'Anyway, I knew how the Empress of Austria had been killed and I thought that a hatpin might do as well as a stiletto. I got mine out of my bag, lifted her up and stuck it in between her ribs up into the heart.'

She stopped talking and Willow risked a prompt.

'And then?'

'Well then I thought it was such a thin little spike that it might not do enough damage, so I kind of waggled it about until I heard something outside and thought Marilyn must be on the prowl.' Once again Victoria smiled. There was no lunacy in her expression just a kind of satisfaction that made Willow feel cold.

'So I pulled it out and put it back in my bag. There was a

little blood on it, but hardly any on her. I shoved a hanky up under her clothes to wipe up what there was. Then I tidied up the desk and let myself out of the house. I couldn't believe it the next day when I rang up and discovered that she wasn't dead at all. Apparently she'd even slept in her own bed. She must have come round after the stroke and remembered nothing. I couldn't believe it. It was as though I'd dreamed the whole thing. I didn't sleep at all that night, thinking that I was going to have to face her again.'

'Have you been able to sleep since?' Once more it was Tom who asked the question.

'Oh yes. It's been heaven really. Do you know that bit at the end of "Porphyria's Lover"?'

'I can't say I do,' said Tom, trying hard not to look as astonished as he felt.

'It's when he's strangled her with her own hair,' said Victoria dreamily, 'and he says something about how they've sat there all night and God hasn't said a word. It's been like that, you see. There hasn't been a thunderbolt or the horrors or a nightmare or anything, just peace.'

She laughed and added: 'The only difficulty has been pretending to be as miserable as I always used to be. I managed it for a day or two, but I couldn't go on. People were beginning to notice. Even you, Willow. And then you started asking all those questions. And saying things to Ann Slinter.'

'Was that why you tried to dispose of me?'

'What?' The happy smile was gone from Victoria's face and the fading, peaceful voice had sharpened considerably.

'We know that my brakes were sabotaged. Tom's people have found fingerprints on the engine. Yours I presume.'

Victoria folded her fingers into the palms of her hands.

'It won't be hard to match them.' Tom's voice was quiet, but it was implacable too. 'Come along, Ms Taffle, we'd better get you down to the station so that things can be properly sorted out. Will, would you ring this number and tell them I've asked for a squad car?' He scribbled a telephone number on an old envelope from his pocket and moved a little closer to the other end of the sofa.

As she punched in the number, Willow heard him reading Victoria her rights. A few moments later Willow asked for the car and heard Victoria laugh, before she said:

'But you can't expect me to repeat any of that now you've cautioned me, can you? I'm not that stupid.'

19

'BUT WHAT I DON'T UNDERSTAND,' said Ann Slinter, 'is why Vicky Taffle was carrying a hatpin in her handbag in the first place.'

'Don't be frivolous, Ann.' Gerald Plimpton sounded angry, but Willow answered the question as though it had been seriously asked.

'For protection, I think. When I asked her whether she was frightened of walking alone in the dark she told me that she wasn't afraid of either two- or four-legged predators any longer because she carried a personal alarm and . . . Then she stopped and I was fool enough not to press her to tell me what she meant.'

'It's such an incredibly Victorian idea,' said Ann with a pitying smile. 'But I suppose in some ways she was rather Victorian – the despised, unhappy, impoverished, governessy kind of Victorian.'

'I should've thought it was quite a dangerous idea, too,' said Willow, trying to find a light enough tone to keep her from thinking too much about the actual killing. 'I'd have thought that, unless she were actually to wear it in her hat, it would constitute an offensive weapon. I must ask Tom.'

'Can't you two concentrate on the fact that this young

woman actually murdered Gloria? Don't you find it completely horrifying? We've known her for years, Ann, and had no idea she was capable of something like that.'

The three of them were sitting in Ann's office. An open bottle of claret stood on the table and the pleasant chaos of publishing was all around the room. The sun had already gone, although it was barely half-past three, and a peaceful, lavender-coloured twilight filled the room.

They had met to decide on the propriety or otherwise of publishing anything at all about their once-star author who had been murdered by their least starry editor. Eve Greville was expected at any moment to discuss how much Willow should be paid for the work she had already done, and until she came they were filling in the gaps of each other's knowledge of what had happened at the house on Kew Green.

'Of course it's horrifying,' said Ann, pouring more wine into Gerald's glass. 'But we must face the fact that Gloria would have been going to die quite soon, and that she was not particularly happy in her life.'

'How can you possibly judge that, Ann?' Gerald's voice was stern.

'It's not a question of having to judge. No one who could behave so badly to the people around her, who could be such a bully and so misuse her power, could possibly be happy.'

'I think that's rather sentimental,' said Willow, idly turning her wine glass round and round between her long fingers. 'Lots of horrible people have positively enjoyed being beastly. Gerald?'

'Hm?'

'Will you tell me what was in the first will?'

He uncrossed his legs, smoothed the fabric of his wonderfully cut suit, and then brushed his silver hair back over his ears.

'After all, it can't harm anyone now,' said Willow with a quick smile at Ann.

'I suppose not.' He frowned in irritation. 'You know, if

you had come to me honestly when we first spoke and told me what you suspected, things would have been very much easier. And this ghastly business of an exhumation at dawn tomorrow would never have been necessary.'

'I doubt if you'd have believed me. In any case, I was still only exploring the possibility when we spoke. Now, tell me: the first will.'

'All right.' He clasped his hands lightly on his knees. 'The house was always going to Marilyn with the bulk of the money, although fifty-five thousand was to have been left to Peter Farrfield.'

'Ah.' Willow's green eyes sparkled. 'Which means that you lied to him.'

'I suppose by implication I did. It seemed the only way to defuse that explosive atmosphere and prevent a worse scene.'

'But if Marilyn was always going to get that much, why on earth did Gloria make such a point of telling her to expect nothing?' asked Ann.

'Can't you guess?' The irritation had gone from Gerald's face, to be replaced with a sadness that made him very attractive.

Ann shook her head.

'I suspect that she wanted to make quite sure she was not surrounded by hypocritical love,' he said. 'She always found it immensely hard to trust anyone's affection. Provided Marilyn expected nothing from the will, Gloria would never need to question the way Marilyn behaved to her.'

'Good heavens!' Ann was laughing again. 'With the way Gloria carried on, she need never have worried about any sort of affection, hypocritical or otherwise.'

She was tossing her gleaming hair back as she spoke and so she did not see Gerald's expression. Willow did. He looked as though he was in physical pain and she realised that some of her assumptions about Gloria's feelings might not have been wide of the mark after all.

'It's terribly sad,' Willow said. 'If only Gloria could have been a bit more open with Marilyn, they might have given each other what they both wanted so badly. Posy Hacket, too, could have been a friend – even a supporter – if Gloria hadn't spent her entire life hiding what she really was and felt.'

Ann looked from Gerald to Willow and back again. 'What actually made Gloria change her will before Vicky . . . before Vicky's intervention? Come on, you two. Stop exchanging meaningful glances and tell me what's going on. I feel left out of this.'

'Hasn't Willow told you about Peter Farrfield and his little charade of disability?' asked Gerald.

'She's explained the charade. But how did Gloria discover it?'

'Marilyn told her just before Christmas,' said Gerald casually, clearly rather enjoying the expressions on the faces of both women. It was Ann who spoke first.

'Are you telling me that she knew he wasn't a cripple?'

'Oh yes, I think so, don't you, Willow? Somehow she managed to convince Gloria that she'd only just found out herself.'

'I hope that Doctor Trenor never discovers it,' said Willow, realising at last what had made Gerald so angry during his final lunch with Gloria. 'He adores Marilyn and thinks of her as the saintly put-upon little woman who suffers and serves.'

'From the little Gloria told me about her doctor, I imagine he'll pretty soon work it out. He sounded quite intelligent, if bluff and rather hidebound. D'you know how much he knew of Farrfield?'

'Not a lot,' said Willow slowly as she ran through her mind the things Marilyn and the doctor had told her. 'Farrfield wasn't his patient. Everything the doctor knew must have come from Marilyn, and she'd have done all she could to foster the idea of dissension between them to avoid any suspicion that they were conspiring to fleece Gloria of her fortune.'

'But what a risk Farrfield was taking,' said Ann. 'He must have known that Marilyn might do the dirty on him.'

'He could hardly have carried it off so effectively and for so long without her help,' said Gerald. 'I wonder when she decided that she could do without him?'

'If she did,' said Willow. 'We still don't know whether that very public quarrel at the funeral was genuine or not.'

'I know,' said Gerald, his face showing real anger. 'And we probably never will. It's not as though either of them's going to have to answer for what they've done in court – unfortunately. I'd like to see the pair of them behind bars, instead of living off Gloria's money. Marilyn will probably put the house up for sale as soon as probate's been granted.'

'Well, this is all very cosy.'

The overhead light was switched on and a harsh glare made them all blink. The three of them had turned at the sound of the hard voice and they saw Eve Greville standing in the doorway, looking as neat and controlled as ever in one of her crisply tailored dark suits. She was wearing a thick, ochre-coloured silk shirt under the black jacket and long, elaborately set amber earrings.

Her half smile expressed all the ambivalence of the agent who wants her author to be on good terms with her publisher and yet not so cosy as to become too dependent on the publisher's judgement. There might come a time when Eve had to argue with Ann about one of Willow's contracts or threaten to sell her books elsewhere if Ann did not offer a big enough advance. If that happened and there was even the slightest possibilty that Willow might take Ann's advice instead of her agent's, Eve's job would be impossible.

'Hello, Eve,' said Willow warmly, looking at her with real affection. 'We've been having a post-mortem. Oh, dear. Well, you know what I mean.'

'Yes, I know,' Eve said, coming to join them and accepting a glass of claret from Ann. 'The whole episode sounds as though it's been very melodramatic. Have you recovered from your various accidents?'

'Nearly. Most of the bruises are fading.'

'Bruises?' asked Gerald.

'Marilyn pushed me down the spiral stairs in the palm

house at Kew,' she said. 'I still have no idea whether it was deliberate or whether she merely slipped. I noticed that she did have metal edges to the heels on her boots and most of the steps are worn in the centre, so a slip isn't wholly out of the question, even though it is unlikely. But could there possibly have been two murderous young woman in the same small circle of people?'

Eve took out a cigarette and lit it.

'Well, they all sound pretty revolting and selfish.'

'Aren't most people?' said Ann cheerfully. With the entrance of a fourth person she was no longer feeling like an outsider to the other two's conspiracy. 'We've pretty much decided, Eve, that we ought to drop the idea of a memoir of Gloria, despite all the useful publicity of Vicky's trial.'

'I can see why you might want to play down the Weston & Brown part as much as possible,' said Eve with a smile. 'Willow, what do you think?'

'I'm prepared to drop it now,' said Willow, who had belatedly come to the conclusion that submerging herself in other people's lives had been even more dangerous and uncomfortable than living her own.

'As you say, they were a pretty unpleasant bunch of people. Talking to them all has been instructive, one way and another, but I'd be glad if I never had to think of any of them again.' Willow stood up and looked at her watch.

'I'm going to have to leave you to your negotiations,' she said. 'I have an appointment elsewhere.'

Eve squinted up at her through the cigarette smoke, her mouth twisting in amusement and irony.

'Any thoughts on the new book? It's beginning to look rather urgent, isn't it, Ann? Particularly if you're not going to write the memoir.'

'Lots of thoughts,' said Willow without waiting for her publisher's comments. She smiled. 'I haven't even started to write a synopsis yet, but I've just this minute decided to concoct a novel around a group of people, each one of whom is kind, trustworthy, interesting and attractive.'

'Oh God!' said Eve in a sepulchral voice. 'That would be a

270

disaster – and boring too.'

Even as she spoke, Gerald Plimpton was looking worried and shaking his elegant head and Ann Slinter had raised her eyes to heaven.

'Honestly, Willow,' she said, sounding as tactful as any publisher having to criticise a bestselling author, 'I really don't think that would be a very good idea.'

'I suspect she's teasing you,' said Gerald, who had been looking at Willow's reaction to their protests.

She laughed and left them for a meeting with her solicitor who had drawn up a deed of gift that would hand a half share in her mill over to Tom Worth. When it was signed, she thanked the lawyer and put the document in her quilted leather shoulder bag. Her next stop was at a locksmith's, who was cutting a duplicate set of all her keys. As she paid for it, she felt bathed in benevolence and rather enjoyed the sensation.

Then she drove back to her flat for tea alone in front of the drawing room fire. Tea over, she had a long bath, reading an excellently funny novel that had been waiting in the pile beside the bath since before Christmas. Warm, comfortable, amused and at ease, she dressed in a pair of jeans she had just bought and the same thick, smooth violet cashmere sweater that clashed so interestingly both with her hair and the copper cushions in the drawing room.

'Old habits die hard,' she murmured as she felt the silkiness and the warmth of the expensive wool. She grinned at her reflection in the long looking glass inside her wardrobe door. Behind her she could see the pile of psychoanalytical text books she had bought.

Pushing open the kitchen door a few minutes later, she said:

'Mrs Rusham, didn't you say you were collecting jumble for a bazaar?'

'Yes, I did. Have you got some after all?'

'Yes, if these will do for the bookstall. Can you carry them all?'

'I expect I'll manage. May I say how well you're looking?'

'Thank you,' said Willow, surprised by the compliment. Before she could say anything else, Mrs Rusham had turned back to the large pan she had just put on the Aga. Dismissed, Willow left the room.

Tom came soon after that, looking wary.

'I got your message,' he said. 'What is it that you want to give me so urgently? A formal warning of dismissal?'

She shook her head, unsmiling, and took the document and the spare keys from her bag.

'These,' she said abruptly, thrusting them at him and looking over his left shoulder so that she did not have to meet his eyes. 'There's not the remotest obligation, but if you'd like them, I'd quite like you to have them.'

He looked at what she had given him for a long time and then up at her face. She looked rather tired, but as though something in her had been freed.

'By gum!' Tom said unexpectedly, like a 1920s schoolboy. 'That's pretty dangerous, isn't it?'

'Possibly,' said Willow coolly. 'But not half as dangerous as what I have been doing.'

'Oh, and what's that?' He was smiling as he watched her think about how to phrase whatever she wanted to tell him.

'Becoming more and more of a slapper every day – emotionally speaking that is,' she said at last, her green eyes gleaming as she smiled.

'Well, well,' he said, taking her hand. 'And you're prepared to say that, not to speak of giving me this magnificent present of half the mill, even before I've abased myself for not listening when you first said that La Grainger had been murdered, are you?'

Willow nodded. Tom looked down at the deed of gift again and then said slowly:

'Come to think of it, this looks as though you're offering to make an honest man of me. Or am I jumping the gun?'

Willow's face put on, if not the light of children praised, at least unshadowed happiness.

'Actually,' she said, 'that was rather the idea. Will you?'

'Ah, Will,' he said, hugging her. 'Who's like you?

Absolutely no one in the world. Yes, please.'

'Good,' said Willow decisively.

Tom stood looking at her, a smile licking around the corners of his eyes and lips.

'It looks as though you must quite like me after all,' he said.

'D'you know,' she said with wholly artificial earnestness just before she bit his earlobe, 'I think I must.'